SMALL
WORLD

ALSO BY LAURA ZIGMAN

Separation Anxiety
Piece of Work
Her
Dating Big Bird
Animal Husbandry

SMALL WORLD

A NOVEL

LAURA ZIGMAN

ecco
An Imprint of HarperCollins*Publishers*

SMALL WORLD. Copyright © 2023 by Laura Zigman. All rights reserved. Printed in the United States of America. No part of this book may be used or reproduced in any manner whatsoever without written permission except in the case of brief quotations embodied in critical articles and reviews. For information, address HarperCollins Publishers, 195 Broadway, New York, NY 10007.

HarperCollins books may be purchased for educational, business, or sales promotional use. For information, please email the Special Markets Department at SPsales@harpercollins.com.

Ecco® and HarperCollins® are trademarks of HarperCollins Publishers.

FIRST EDITION

Designed by Angela Boutin

Library of Congress Cataloging-in-Publication Data has been applied for.

ISBN 978-0-06-308828-3

22 23 24 25 26 LBC 5 4 3 2 1

I came to explore the wreck.

—*Adrienne Rich*

No one is really alone; those who live no more
echo still within our thoughts and words, and what
they did is part of what we have become.

—*"The Blessing of Memory," Meditations before Kaddish*

SMALL
WORLD

There's a photo, an old snapshot—black-and-white, with the date going up the border in typewriter font—*1969*. Women in Peter Pan–collared blouses and teased hair and men with white shirts and skinny ties, straight from work, are in the living room, smiling at the camera from behind their cigarettes. Your mother is in the center, holding Eleanor in her lap. She's smiling, and so is Eleanor, but Eleanor always looks like she's smiling. Born with cerebral palsy, complicated by a severe seizure disorder, she doesn't walk or talk, her head tilts back, and her mouth hangs open as if she's hungry for air. Back then the blanket term for children born like Eleanor was *retarded*—and that's what you and Lydia say when you're asked about your family. *We have a sister who's retarded.* Later, when you're asked where she lives during that one year she doesn't live at home anymore, you'll say: *At Fernald.* Which is short for the Walter E. Fernald State School, once known as the Massachusetts School for the Feeble-Minded, the institution outside Boston where the children of the people in the picture live, too.

There's another photo: a faded Kodachrome color snapshot—
1973. The furniture is different but almost all the adults in it
are the same, only now with bigger hair and thick sideburns, in
short skirts and turtlenecks and bell-bottoms, sitting on low-slung
couches and on the floor around the kidney-shaped coffee table
covered with ashtrays and Styrofoam coffee cups. Your mother—
Louise Mellishman—who didn't graduate from college and barely
knows how to boil an egg but never takes no for an answer—
will eventually become one of the leaders of the national parents'
movement fighting for the rights of people with developmental
disabilities. But here, before she starts lobbying Congress, before
all the pictures of her with governors and senators and families
from all over the country, she's just part of a local parents' support
and advocacy group, focused on the rights of their children—the
ones who are institutionalized, and the ones still living at home—
talking about methods of toilet training; about the merits of
swimming-pool therapy; about how the less significantly impaired
students at Fernald earn tokens for candy and watching *Sesame
Street* and listening to records by learning simple skills in the class-
room or by sweeping and emptying wastebaskets and straightening
up the outdated and mismatched collection of donated toys in
the playroom at the end of every day.

In this picture, Eleanor, then six and in a wheelchair, is in the
center. When you look closely you find yourself next, and then you
find Lydia. You're on one side of the living room, and she's on the
other. *Typical.* You're always separate; always there but not there;
always on the periphery of the action that swirls around you but
doesn't include you. You're four; Lydia is eight; the painful irony of
your mother fighting for inclusion that doesn't include you is still
decades away. You've been called down from the top of the stairs where
you were playing quietly together—Chutes and Ladders or Sorry! or

some other board game—to grab a brownie or a Toll House cookie or whatever else someone has baked and brought to the meeting, before saying good night to everyone and going to bed. Like you're the guests. When you appear, a few people smile and wave and give both of you little half hugs, but because you're physically able and don't need help, they quickly go back to their cigarettes and purple mimeographed agendas about upcoming fundraisers and raffles. They have work to do.

For years there will be parents in your living room talking about their sons and daughters—some toddlers; some already in their late teens and early twenties—eternal children, they're called then. The Fernald families focus on vocational training, trips into the community, Christmas parties, Easter egg hunts. The other families, like yours, are concerned with community support, inclusion, and raising awareness. There is always something to plan, something to fundraise for, something to look forward to. Other times the conversation turns darker when parents ask, in whispers or in full-throated wails, what will become of their children after they die, who will look after them when they're gone. The idea of leaving them alone in the world, at the mercy of a state institution without them there to check in on things, or to be looked after by older siblings or distant relatives, is unthinkable, and Louise is always the one to steer the discussion away from that grim abyss of a question when the lack of an easy and comforting answer is too much to bear.

Small world, big deal, she says like a chant, or a mantra, keeping the focus on the immediate changes they're fighting for: health services, education, and employment opportunities for the disabled; improving the quality of life of children who sleep in wards of metal beds and are bathed and fed and changed by strangers; making administrators and people in power care about families other than their own.

Later, when Louise reluctantly agrees to send Eleanor to Fernald, too, you'll come to understand that she's also thinking about the parents like herself, who were told by doctors that they had no choice but to put their children there, and the guilt they feel for having sentenced them to small lives of containment and confinement and exclusion. Though she won't ever talk about it, not even when you're grown, you will always know that she never forgives herself. You will also know, in some fundamental way that you are unable to articulate but that feels as natural and as constant as breathing, that whatever you and Lydia do or say or accomplish or become in life will never feel like it matters quite as much.

PART ONE

Small World

Only Idiots Smile All the Time

I start turning posts on Small World, the neighborhood site for people in search of local goods and services, into prose poems before Lydia moves in. The fact that I once wanted to be a writer is only part of why I develop this secret habit of making pretend poetry. The bigger part is a childlike desire for comfort. Little problems getting solved all day long—strangers in need, getting answers from strangers in the know—gives me hope. I grew up feeling like there was no one looking out for me when I felt lost or sad, so this allows me to believe otherwise. Helpers are out there. All I have to do is look for them.

Both of us are divorced and childless when she finally comes back to Boston from LA after almost thirty years. I say *finally* when I tell friends because, really, it was time already, wasn't it? Lydia had moved away as soon as she graduated from college, leaving me alone with Louise and our sad family past, and a tiny part of me had been waiting for her to come back and make it up to me ever since. Not that I'd ever admit that to anyone. It's such an infantile and entitled thing to say that I can't even believe I said it right now. Sometimes I wonder if I'll ever stop thinking that my sister should apologize for leaving me behind.

Especially since Lydia's not even the one who owes me anything—she got as little as I did in terms of emotional support. If anyone owes both of us something, it's our parents, but they're both dead now, so it's too late, and even if I allowed myself that equation—of being owed—it doesn't seem fair to hold them accountable for payment. It never has. No one could blame them—two good people who had cared for a disabled child for almost ten years at home, then institutionalized her, then grieved when she died only a year later of the flu, of all things—for not giving us their full attention. How could they have? I never really expected Lydia to come back, because there was nothing much for her to come back for. Plus, she's always done her own thing. Until now, that has never included me.

WHEN I FIRST JOINED THE SMALL WORLD SITE—THE SMALL WORLD "community"—I needed advice on recycling and parking permits and handymen and car mechanics. That was a year after Tom left and a year before Lydia moved in. He had taken care of those kinds of things, as well as almost all the cooking, when he was still around, but once he was gone, I had to figure all that out for myself. Which was fine. I was single again now, and while a part of me was deeply ashamed and devastated—it was Tom who left me, not the other way around—I was game to start over. Because when you start over you get another chance to make things right. Because what feels like the end is often the beginning. Isn't that what all the stupid divorce books and social media affirmation posts promised? With Lydia here, I have different needs: her needs. Museums, art supply stores, barre and yoga classes, and lots of takeout choices, since she is as uncomfortable and uninterested in the kitchen as I am. Small

World is another world, an endless rabbit hole to disappear into and get lost in where no one can find me. It's the perfect hiding place, even from myself. Especially from myself.

But I never post questions of my own on Small World. Letting my neighbors know my business—my odd jobs in need of doing, my dietary cravings, my sister issues—would be too revealing. Instead, I lurk, stealing answers from other, similar posts. It feels like cheating, because it is, but eavesdropping on the site is better than getting involved online or in person. I grew up with people constantly in our house, in our living room—crying and sad and desperate for comfort. Now that I'm in charge of my life, I prefer to keep to myself.

SOMETIMES I LOOK FOR APARTMENTS ON SMALL WORLD FOR LYDIA. Not for now, since we're having such a great time together getting to know each other as adults, but for later, down the road. Just in case. There aren't many rental leads on the site, which is surprising, and dumb: finding apartments seems like a big problem that it should prioritize solving. But, like so many things in life, that's the way it is. I'm not desperate for her to go. In fact, the constant challenge of trying to get my sister to pay attention to me so that we can finally be close gives my life purpose and focus in this strange postdivorce phase, and I'd be lying if I said having someone to share expenses with again hasn't been a relief. So it's nothing like that. I'm thinking ahead, planning for our futures, which are now, finally, connected.

Maybe someday I'll write to the developers of Small World, suggest they ramp up their local real estate listings—neighbors seem more reliable than those online rental sites when it comes to hearing about available apartments and places for sale. They could provide a valuable service to people like me trying to help friends and relatives move out and transition from dependent houseguest or codependent roommate to independent renter or homeowner. Until then, I'll keep looking. There are a few listings here and there—mostly short-term sublets, in-law suites, rooms in basements or third-floor attics, the occasional decent studio or one- or two-bedroom—nothing great, nothing that would appeal to Lydia and rise to her high design expectations, even temporarily, I'm certain of that. But you never know. It doesn't hurt to check.

At some point during all that scrolling, a totally unrelated post catches my eye:

ANYONE KNOW IF THIS CAT HAS A HOME?
A stray cat sneaks into our backyard all the time now, eating the birdseed that falls from the bird feeder hanging on the tree. He/she is obviously hungry. I'm worried that he/she will get into the neighbor's rat-mitigation bait—that curiosity (and hunger) will actually kill the cat. The city has a stray rehoming program, but I wanted to first see if this is anyone's beloved missing kitty.
(see photo)

I don't usually read lost-cat posts. I'm not a cat person, and there are so many lost cats in the neighborhood I can't keep them straight (I hate to judge, though of course I do: *Why can't these people manage to keep their cats inside?*), but I think it's funny that I've come across a post about the "stray rehoming" process of cats when I'm thinking about the future "rehoming" process of Lydia. Mostly I'm intrigued because the post seems more concerned with misgendering the lost cat than with finding its owner. I'm mildly annoyed, too, to be totally honest, since there was recently a whole thing about pronouns at work with a colleague (he/him) who manages to work the subject into almost every meeting about every project the company (they/them) is working on. And I'm someone (she/her) who couldn't possibly be more pro-pronouns! Maybe that's the unlikely spark that causes this strange new habit to form—the habit that makes me cut and paste and reformat and retitle Small World posts into poems on my computer:

Pronouns
A stray cat
sneaks into our backyard
all the time now,
eating the birdseed that falls from
the bird feeder hanging on the tree.
He/she is obviously hungry.
I'm worried that
he/she will get into the neighbor's
rat-mitigation bait
—that curiosity (and hunger)
will actually kill the cat.
The city has a stray rehoming program,
but I wanted to first see
if this is anyone's
beloved missing kitty.
(see photo)

I love my new little prose poem. It's so cute I can hardly stand it. In my job, the one I'm supposed to be doing when I'm wasting time on Small World—as an archivist for EverMore, a local company that digitizes photos and documents for families and institutions (that's the short version)—I'm always trying to figure out the value of various pictures, papers, and film clips that arrive on my desk in boxes: what to include in whatever family legacy project I'm working on, and what to leave out. It's the perfect job for me. I seriously can't believe I get paid to indulge my extreme curiosity about other people's families, who they are and where they come from, how their parts—their parents and all their siblings and all their siblings' spouses and children—fit together, or don't.

But it's stressful sometimes, too. How do I know if I'm getting another family's narrative right? Who am I to determine what's important to people I've never met and know only through their photos and videos? I'm not exactly an expert in this field, given my tiny family of origin. Which is why making my little poems feels like such an escape, especially when I craft this first one. It reads like a super-short story, full of tension and action and pathos—in only a few lines. All I want is more, so I reformat one of the replies and make another poem out of it, too:

Their People
I'm an ornithologist at Harvard
and, in case you haven't heard,
birds are dying
in record numbers
and stray cats—
unhomed, unhoused, uncontrolled—
are to blame.
Animal Control suggests spraying them
with a garden hose
which I sometimes do out of desperation
(my partner is allergic so we can't risk feline allergens
seeping in through open doors and window screens),
but I'm not a believer in

injuring cats
even if they're loose
and causing trouble.
First, I try to figure out who owns them
so that I can return them
to their people
even if their people don't deserve them
since they've failed to keep them safe inside.

AT SOME POINT AFTER LYDIA ARRIVES AND ONCE I REALIZE SHE doesn't seem to be going anywhere and might never leave—this is now the time period around which I frame everything—I begin copying my Small World "poems" into notebooks. It calms me. I copy them with my favorite black pens, the ones I use for work and the ones I used to use for my own work, a long time ago when I still wanted to be a writer. Bad teenage poetry and then some short stories in high school and college. Not to brag, but I showed promise. When I told my mother about my ambitions back then she said: *I hope you're going to tell important stories.* Which was her way of saying, *I hope you're going to tell other people's stories.* Louise was an advocate, a solver of problems, a fighter for the rights of others. But I wasn't that kind of person, and I wasn't interested in becoming that kind of writer. I was too shy to knock on people's doors and ask them questions they didn't want to answer. And besides: I had my own problems. Someone had to advocate for me.

Making my Small World poems has become a kind of therapy, a form of silent meditation. Obviously I don't show them to Lydia: in fact, I hide my habit from her, being careful to put my current notebook under another notebook in the drawer full of notebooks even though the notebooks are full of other people's words, not my own, and don't actually need to be hidden like my own writing would, if I even did it. Maybe my behavior is less about what I'm hiding and more about wanting to keep things hidden. Secrecy feels like power. And safety.

Writing these mini-stories down, collecting them in notebooks— these little problems in search of solutions—is a way to contain the anxiety of the people who originally wrote them. And my own. Because at a time when I thought my life would be settled—I'm a year away from turning fifty—I'm single again and engaged in a complicated and somewhat demanding rebound relationship: with my sister of all people. She's not easy, and neither am I, but what I once wished for—reconnection with her, a do-over life with her in it, the friendship I hoped would develop if only we'd lived in the same place—is actually happening. Sort of. Sisterhood, like marriage, takes hard work. And, like marriage, both sisters have to really want to be in the relationship to stay together.

EVERY NOW AND THEN, AMONG THE *BABY BLUE JAY INJURED, SEEKING Free Prom Dress, Are These Your Goats?, Flying Squirrels?!* headlines, I find a post that transcends the genre:

Egyptian Man, Looking to Make Friends
I ride the bus for work every day
I smile and wave and say Hello
to people I pass
but almost no one answers.
I still don't know anyone
after ten years.

I wish someone would say something.
I am lonely.

And a response that transcends most second chapters:

Response to Egyptian Man
I'm a foreigner too
and had the same experience as you.
It is still a mystery to me
as I have lived other places
all over the world
where people are pleasant
and kind,
if only just on the surface—
a smile at the bank or
supermarket—small gestures.
I have one friend now
and have stopped trying
for more.
I am happy alone.
My advice to you is:
Don't try too hard.
Don't be too friendly.
Don't smile too much.
I was told once, years ago,
that "only idiots smile all the time"
We may be lonely foreigners
but we are not idiots.

"Egyptian Man" and "Response to Egyptian Man" are the sad-
dest things I've ever read on Small World. Sometimes I think they're

the saddest things I've read anywhere. Does it get more tragic than wanting to connect but being told that people who try too hard are idiots? Maybe I'm meant to read this right now. Maybe I'm meant to understand that I shouldn't risk looking like an idiot with Lydia. That decades of long-distance living can't be bridged in only a few months' time. That closeness will come, or it won't, but forcing it might be worse than not trying at all.

Malocclusion

Your father, Lenny, is an orthodontist. Posters of teeth dressed up like people and plaster models of jaws on shelves that look like little silent screams are all over his office. He and his twin brother, your uncle Murray, have a successful practice in the 1970s, not far from where you and Lydia live now. Two big-nosed Mellishman brothers, both snappy dressers—one married with children, the other single and swinging—telling corny jokes to everyone's kids after school as they tighten wires and glue on brackets before sending them back out to the waiting room, where their mothers quietly tear out articles and recipes from back issues of *Better Homes & Gardens* and *Good Housekeeping* and *Bon Appétit*.

After Eleanor goes to Fernald when she's nine, and after she dies there a year later from a sudden and virulent flu her body can't fight off fast enough, everything changes, though you at eight and Lydia at twelve don't completely understand how and why. First, Lenny has trouble getting to work on time, or staying a full day, or remembering whose mouth is whose. Then, Uncle Murray gets into some kind of trouble—something to do with money or taxes or the government or all of those things; you are too young to ask all the questions you'd ask now—and disappears for a while. You can't remember if it happens slowly or all at once, but their practice eventually dissolves. So does your family. Lydia, who'd gotten her braces on early, has to go elsewhere to finish her orthodontia. Two sets of plaster impressions, which you still have somewhere, in a box or in a drawer, and which were made on a Sunday afternoon, when the office was closed to patients but not yet abandoned, are the sum total of your experience with your father's expertise. Your parents eventually divorce, Lenny's pill-taking goes off the rails, and years later, Uncle Murray will tell everyone at the funeral that his brother's death was an accidental overdose, even though no one knows for sure. Before you've even graduated from college, you've lost both a sister and your father.

There's a term for crooked teeth, Lenny once tells you, for bites that are off: *malocclusion*. To correct them, brackets are attached, and wires are tightened in paced increments to move them at the right speed and with the right amount of force. *Move a tooth too slowly and it will never arrive at its corrected position. Pull it too fast or too hard and you risk loosening it, and losing it, in the process.* You don't realize that what he's telling you is a metaphor, but you sense, even then, that he's not just talking about teeth.

"With braces, patience is everything. But in life, health is everything." He says this when he's still Lenny, still your dad: when he's still living at home, still going to work, still telling corny jokes— still saying *good morning* and *good night* and lighting the Hanukkah candles and leading the Passover seders and raking leaves and shoveling snow.

"*Luck* is everything," Louise would correct.

Orthodontia as metaphor: You are born into malocclusion. Into an unlucky family with a disabled child, then a dead child. The hole caused by her absence will eventually cause everything and everyone to shift, and drift, the same way teeth do, after an extraction.

YOU COME FROM A FAMILY OF CATASTROPHIZERS. LENNY'S PARENTS, both from Poland, have Old Country phobias: fear of doctors; fear of fire from candles; fear of eating less than extremely well-done meat. Louise's parents, from Russia, round out the list: fear of sledding; fear of being too thin; fear of bringing shame to their families. Born with first-generation optimism, they plan to raise you without superstitions and fears, and if things had been different, they might have succeeded. But life has other plans for all of you. Catastrophizers aren't born; they're made.

By elementary school you have your own growing list of phobias: fear of winter (and summer) (and team) sports; fear of being called on in class to read out loud; fear of making Louise mad for not doing enough to help or support or honor Eleanor. By high school, then college, your list grows: fear of never leaving Boston; fear of never knowing what really happened to Lenny after he left; fear of never doing anything Louise-worthy. The latter is really an off-shoot of a larger umbrella-like one—the fear of not knowing what will become of you—which appears during your teenage years, when you realize that you will likely end up being unemployed after college, since you're Only Good at English.

That's Mellishman Luck for you, Louise says, referring to what you think is the deeply ironic fact that in the age of computers neither you nor Lydia (who is Only Good at Art) can do math or science well enough to break into this new field and get a job with medical benefits.

Later you will come to understand that Mellishman Luck refers to something much bigger than whether you will ever find a job in technology or not. Mellishman Luck is bad luck. It is Louise's way of saying that you, as a family—physically, genetically, emotionally— are doomed.

YOU STAY NEARBY FOR COLLEGE, THEN WORK. YOU'RE THE PLEASER, the glue, the one who tries to keep what's left of the family together. Lenny is gone by then, and Louise is constantly traveling, but you want to be around, in case he reappears, which he doesn't, or she needs anything. For years, she's wholly self-sufficient—work, advocacy, and travel with friends—until she isn't: she has a stroke at seventy, and one day she's gone, just like that.

"At least she lived to see us both get married off," Lydia says when you call her on the phone with the terrible and unexpected news. You don't disagree. Despite Louise's ferocious independence, her relentless activism, she was, at heart, a product of the fifties. She never quite got over the failure of her own marriage, the intense shame of being left by a husband she never seemed that connected to, before, and especially after, Eleanor's death. You wonder what she would think of her daughters now: both of you left by your husbands, too, and living under the same roof like spinster sisters— failures, essentially, in her terms, and proof of Mellishman Luck—as if you'd never been married at all.

LYDIA DOES THINGS DIFFERENTLY. A FEW DAYS AFTER GRADUATING from art school, she and her boyfriend pack a minivan and drive west to Los Angeles. She is twenty-two when she leaves, waving goodbye to you on the burnt slope of the lawn on a humid June morning. She wears sandals and a halter top, her shoulders bony and tan, paint still under her fingernails, tendrils of hair falling from a loose bun. There is no illusion of incremental movement, of proximity, of availability. Of staying in case Louise eventually needs anything. Or if you do. She will drive until the highway stops and she gets to the other ocean.

I can't wait to be away from this, she says. In your memory, she's looking at the house, at Louise wrestling with the garden hose to water the shrubs and flower beds on a rare weekend home, at you in your IHOP uniform already late for your shift, when she says that. *I can't wait to matter.*

You do matter. You struggle to whisper the words out. *You matter to me.*

Eleanor is the only one who ever mattered. Eleanor is the only one who will ever matter. That's never going to change. So maybe you should leave, too, and have a life. Your own life.

You shield your eyes from the sun, and then, as they fill with tears, from Lydia. You think about Eleanor in the living room, on the little scooter she sits on and pushes with her legs that Lenny made with wood and wheels and safety straps in the basement, like a retainer he fashioned at his office for a patient. Or on the rug with Louise and an ad hoc "therapeutic playgroup" of other children with disabilities and their parents. You remember the monthly evening meetings, the poster making, the raffle ticket selling, the bowls of salted mixed nuts from vacuum-sealed cans, and the industrial-sized coffee urn in the kitchen with its red light on, always on, next to the stacks of Styrofoam cups and bowls of sugar and powdered Coffee Mate. Lydia wants to be free of feeling in perpetual service to a cause, of feeling invisible when Eleanor is there, and even when she isn't anymore; free of the burden of a situation that you both have always been silent bystanders to. You don't think she will ever come back. Now, when people ask about your family, you say: *I have a sister who lives in California.*

But she does come back. Orthodontists have a term for this, too: *root memory*. When teeth drift back to their original positions, even after they've been corrected.

WHEN YOU THINK ABOUT HOME ALL THOSE YEARS AGO, A GOPRO'S view of your little white Colonial plays like a silent movie. You float past the '70s splendor of the decor—wall-to-wall gold carpeting in the draped living room and dining room; colorful mod floral wallpaper everywhere; pink-and-red shag rug and black leather recliner in the wood-paneled den. On the rare occasions when the house is quiet, Louise reads through a pile of newspapers in one room; Lenny watches the evening news in another; Lydia is in her room drawing with pastels, charcoal, crayons, Magic Markers. On your way upstairs you see the three gray wood frames, the five black-and-white department-store studio baby pictures in each: Eleanor, Lydia, and you, all in a row. *One of these things is not like the others. One of these things just doesn't belong.* That's what you always hear—the *Sesame Street* song—when you pass them. *Three of these things belong together. Three of these things are kind of the same.*

Sometimes Louise forgets to make dinner; other times she cooks all weekend and puts everything—soups, casseroles, chicken breasts stuffed with Uncle Ben's wild rice—in plastic containers for the week ahead or into the freezer so she doesn't have to think about it. Food is always a necessity; never a comfort, or a pleasure. When you're home together, she almost never asks you or Lydia how you are, how school is going, what your friends are doing. It's not that she doesn't care, or that she doesn't love you—you know she does— it's that somehow those things don't seem relevant. *You're fine.* She can see that. You two can walk and talk and dress yourselves. You don't need to be lifted and moved and fed and cleaned.

When Eleanor lives with you, there is always an aide, a student, a physical therapist who knows exactly what she wants and loves—a stuffed elephant on her lap; the sound of running water and the feel of it on her hands from the kitchen and bathroom sink faucets; "happy" music on the record player that makes her rock in her chair and flap her hands. They come in shifts, arranged on a schedule—a big paper calendar that Louise keeps in pencil on the back of the cellar door, the names and times in each little square constantly erased and rewritten because everything is always in flux. But even after Eleanor is at Fernald, Louise is consumed by her. First by her absence, then by anger and guilt at having reluctantly agreed to put her somewhere that failed to take care of her. Then by grief. The house is either full of people talking and smoking, or utterly quiet when it's only the four of you. You don't remember there ever being an in-between.

At your friends' houses, everything is different. You have sleepovers in blanket tents in living rooms, use finger paints in bedrooms, play badminton and hide-and-seek and jump on furniture. You learn to do somersaults, do handstands, climb trees. You ride in the backs of tiny Volkswagens and giant station wagons with other people's parents and siblings. For a few hours in the afternoon or an overnight stay, you feel part of something, but always apart from it. You do not belong there. You are a guest. A visitor to another world.

Back home, you stand in the kitchen, near the little light from over the stove, and think about your friends and their families: all their brothers and sisters, all the sneakers and skates and hockey sticks and guitars and cellos in the hallways and on the stairs going up to cluttered rooms, all the dogs and cats and unmade beds and clothes on the floors. You envy them—the giant Victorian houses and sprawling modern ones, rooms connected to other rooms, big enough to hide in and get lost in. You envy the rice paper ceiling globes, the frayed Persian rugs, the long low modern sofas, the expensive stereo systems, the huge potted floor palms. You envy their canoes and kayaks and hiking boots and ski boots, their mudrooms full of parkas and baseball caps and cleats. You envy their laughter over dinner, and in the morning, what funny thing the dog did, how the cats are absolutely incorrigible.

Mostly you envy their stairwells: Christmas photos and beach photos and trips to Paris and Rome and Maine and Cape Cod hang on the walls. Not a disabled, then dead, child. You don't remember a time when you don't wish you came from somewhere else.

———

A Cat Killed Our Baby Bunny
We loved the baby bunny
who played in our yard
for weeks.
So imagine our horror
and sadness then
when our little bunny-friend was killed recently,
attacked and mauled and dragged away
by a devil cat.
So much beauty and horror
in nature.
What a loss.
Sometimes small things like this
have such big effects.

Which Came First

When Lydia texts to tell me that she wants to move back to Boston, I'm too excited to believe it's true: My sister, my first friend, my childhood-validator-in-chief, is moving home! The fantasy, the one of my life with her in it—where the two of us will be close now that a continent isn't separating us any longer, cooking together, taking walks, binge-watching and hate-watching television shows—plays in an endless loop in my head and floods my brain with happiness hormones. Images of the past appear, like the start of one of the digitized family albums or mini-documentaries I work on at EverMore, with the title card CHILDHOOD: That's the two of us baking tiny cakes with our old turquoise plastic Easy-Bake Oven! The two of us in our shared bedroom with twin beds close enough to hold hands in the dark before falling asleep! The two of us walking the beach in the morning and again in the late afternoon in the summer, searching for sea glass, right before Lydia gets mad and turns around and goes home ahead of me because I found more sea glass than she did and it's not fair.

Okay, so maybe I won't use that last memory in my private montage next time. Still, I'm hopeful.

"But you hate it here," I say, when I call her, which I almost never do because, like me, she hates to talk on the phone. One of the few things we have in common.

"I do. It reminds me of our childhood."

"Then why are you coming back?"

She pauses, then sighs. "The divorce is final. I'm selling the house. Maybe I'll go back to school or look into teaching. Or maybe it's just time to come home already."

"Where will you live?"

"I don't know yet. I haven't thought that far ahead."

Lydia never thinks that far ahead. Which I secretly envy. Her spontaneity has always been something I admire but am far too uptight to emulate.

"Well, then, by all means, move in with me and complain about it until you find a place of your own!" Without thinking, I have offered her the spare bedroom, my office, in my Cambridge apartment. The movie fantasy continues in my head—the one with hot chocolate and microwave popcorn and wine (the dairy-grain-gluten-sugar-alcohol-free kinds, because Lydia is super careful about everything she eats)—a perpetual slumber party, what we never did as teenagers, or adults. We have so much catching up to do.

"I'd love to."

"I was hoping you'd say that!"

"You were?"

"Of course! It'll be fun!"

"Uhm, Joyce?"

I laugh loudly, then stop abruptly, drowning in shame. Maybe someday I'll be able to project coolness instead of desperation when it comes to forging our bond.

"We don't know if it'll be fun. It might not be. We've never lived together as actual people."

I nod, collecting myself. "Not since we were teenagers."

"And 'fun' isn't exactly our word."

She's right. *Fun* has never been what either of us associates with our family or our childhood. "Then I'll consider it an early birthday present."

"You just had your birthday."

"I know. But the next one is a milestone. The big *Five-Oh*." The minute the cheesy abbreviation for the number has left my mouth, I regret it.

"Say the number, Joyce. It's just a number. I've been that number for four years now, and it's really no big deal."

———

Create Your Own World of Make-Believe
We're giving away
this cardboard and curtained
puppet theater
which entertained us
and all our friends
for years.
Take this miniature stage home
and create your own world
of make-believe, too!
Note: This is merely the framework
and scaffolding.
You bring the puppets + your imagination.

———

A week before she arrives, I clean and organize. Lydia hates clutter. Her house, the one she'd shared with Brad until recently, was white and modern and full of built-ins. A place for everything, hidden away. One time, when I was out there, visiting them, I went from room to room, trying to figure out what was missing from all the counters and shelves. When she asked me what I was looking for, I said, *Your stuff.* Specifically: photos. Photos of the two of them together, with friends, with family. Except for one picture of Brad's parents in a thick clear crystal frame on his desk that made them look like they were floating in midair, there were none.

Once I finish Phase One, I turn my office into the guest room. Her room. With Tom gone, I'm free to put my desk in my bedroom and work from there. Or any other space that he no longer shares with me. No one cares how I configure my apartment; no one cares if I have piles of work clutter where there should only be nonwork clutter or no clutter at all. Including me. I failed my marriage, it failed me, and none of the small stuff feels like it matters anymore. So what if I go through a client's family photos and letters and recipes and documents from bed? So what if I spend more time than I should scrolling through my neighbors' online posts on my phone, waiting for their little problems to be solved, their little questions to be answered? So what if I'm in my own world of Small World because it's easier than being in the real world?

———

Minimalists
Who wants to
declutter their homes
and live a minimalist lifestyle?
Is that you, too?

I've made some progress
but my house is still
a mess.
I believe getting together
with like-minded people
to exchange tips and methods
for straightening,
organizing,
and donating
would help.
We could even be accountability-partners
for specific decluttering projects
like tackling a basement or attic or spare room.
I am not a hoarder
but minimalism will never come naturally to me.
I like my things.
I find comfort—too much probably—in possessions,
in their meaning and memories.
But I'm trying hard
to change that.

———

It's a gray January afternoon when I pick Lydia up from the airport, the kind of day that always reminds me of how hard it is to live here, on the East Coast, in New England. When, in the cold wet shock of air in the open parking garage, she says about the weather, "Great. I've really missed this," I resist the urge to apologize for it, even though it still feels like my fault, this freezing-cold welcome home, a bracing slap across the face. Which, I can't help but think, she kind of deserves for leaving me alone here for so long.

She has two bags, a carry-on and a large silver metal case that she'd checked, and when I put them in the trunk, I compliment her on her light packing job.

"Everything else is in storage," she says, pulling a thin bright orange puffer jacket out of her carry-on for the ride home. "Brad was kind enough to offer to ship it once I get settled."

"That was nice of Brad."

"Wasn't it? But then, Brad's always been a nice person. Much nicer than me."

It occurs to me then that Brad was my brother-in-law for almost twenty years, and yet I have no idea how true that statement is. *Who is Brad? Who is Lydia?* Living so far away from each other made it almost impossible to know. And now, it doesn't even matter. Divorce makes the past irrelevant. He's gone, and she's here, and now, for the first time in years—probably since Louise's funeral five years ago—we're both in the same car, heading home.

I take the scenic route back from the airport, making sure to go Storrow Drive and then Memorial Drive so that Lydia can see what she's missed all these years: the sexy curve of the Charles River; the runners snaking alongside it, despite the cold; the indigo sky a color and texture only Van Gogh or Turner could mix. I park on the street in front of my apartment, on the first floor of a midnight-blue Victorian on a leafy street not far from Harvard Square, and on the way into the house she stops, resting her bag on the brick sidewalk. She stares up at the sky and takes in a long, deep, cold breath, then exhales it in a big gray cloud. All the trees are bare, and the tiny bit of light that guided us home from the airport is fading fast.

"Winter," she says softly, reverentially, looking at me over her shoulder with an unusually sweet smile. Somewhere nearby, someone's fireplace is lit, and we both can smell it. "I've kind of missed it."

For a second, I step outside myself: my sister, who has not lived here in decades, is finally back, on her way into my apartment, where the two of us are about to be roommates for a while. Suddenly—too late—I'm terrified. This could be a disaster. It likely *will* be a disaster. All the old wounds, of childhood and beyond, will definitely resurface. And then we'll fight. And then we'll be stuck together in the same house for who knows how long. And then she'll leave, and it will end badly, really badly, so badly that we might never talk to each other again after that. Whose idea was this?

"I don't believe you."

"I said I *kind of* missed it, not that I *really* missed it." She pulls on her bag and follows me up the walk and inside the vestibule. As I lead the way, I think I hear her say, *I'm so excited to see your place again*, but part of me is certain I imagined it.

INSIDE, SHE WALKS SLOWLY THROUGH MY APARTMENT, COZY IN THE late-afternoon gloaming, looking at everything. Her fingers trace an invisible line on the walls of the foyer, then the living room, dining room, and kitchen, and on the furniture, too—the backs of chairs, the arm of the couch—as she passes. I do the same thing to ground myself when I'm nervous and distracted and worried. Like now.

"It's nice to be in an old house again and not some fake-stucco prefab box built in the fifties. I know it's a cliché to say *I love what you've done with the place*, but I love what you've done with the place."

"It was better before Tom left. There was more furniture. It looked really good."

"It looks good now."

Compliments from Lydia are so rare that I assume she's being sarcastic, even though, this time, she probably isn't. After art school—or after Brad, really, since they met there—she became hypersensitive to bad design. Allergic almost. I still tease her about the time the two of them stayed at the house while Louise was traveling and repositioned the furniture in almost every room on the first floor, even replacing the shiny chrome pulls on all the kitchen cabinets with white-painted knobs.

They were just so ugly, Brad had said to me in the backyard, where we both had gone to escape Louise's rage when she saw the big reveal. She'd demanded that the pulls be replaced and that every piece of furniture be returned to its original position, something she and Lydia were arguing about in the kitchen. Their voices drifted out to the patio through the window screens over the sink while Brad picked at the weeds between the flagstones with quiet disdain. He and Lydia had been dating for over a year, and it was the first time he and Louise had met. Now that he'd finished weeding, he turned his attention to the outdoor chairs and table—dated glass and wrought iron—which he clearly didn't like either. He'd grown up in a sprawling modern house in New Canaan, the only child of two architects, Lydia told me once. Who could blame him for reacting so strongly to our painfully unstylish Colonial?

I sided with them that day, of course. I was still in high school and trying to imagine what it was like to be in college, to have a boyfriend, to walk around in slim paint-stained chinos and white Fruit of the Loom T-shirts like you knew everything about everything. When he'd said our house was ugly, it felt like he was doing all of us a great favor, saving us from our bad taste, our sad lives lived in ignorance, in bad design. I was so grateful. Someone was looking out for me.

Like, why are all the doorways so wide? he asked me out in the yard, bringing up yet another ugly thing that was still bothering him. *And why aren't there any doors downstairs? Old houses are supposed to have doors.*

Louise was suddenly on the patio. *I'm glad you asked, Bradley. We had the doorways widened and the doors removed so that Eleanor's wheelchair could fit. Haven't you ever heard of "accessibility design"?*

Lydia was on the patio now, too. Brad reddened and looked at her, and then at me, for help. *I'm sorry*, he said, *but who's Eleanor?*

THAT COLD JANUARY DAY IN MY DINING ROOM, LYDIA POINTS TO A large framed photograph on the wall. She looks at me like I stole it from her.

"You gave it to me," I say defensively. "Don't you remember?"

"I do remember. I'm just shocked that you still have it."

It's a blowup of a black-and-white print of the two of us when we were little. We're at the beach, standing in front of a small gray-shingled cottage that our family used to rent every summer on the south shore of Massachusetts. It's one of the few pictures from that time that Eleanor isn't in, even though she was there, too. Is that why Lydia used it in her senior thesis—the one where she enlarged a group of negatives of family photos, then applied layers of tinted oil paints to them? Is that why I hung it? When she'd moved west after graduation, those giant photos ended up in Louise's basement. Eventually I found this one and took it with me. Louise couldn't have been happier. She loved when we ridded her of our old possessions, of anything from the past.

I move closer to the photo, like I'm seeing it for the first time. In a way, I am: I've never looked at it with Lydia before. Lydia the creator and Lydia the subject. I remember those bathing suits, the matching pink one-pieces, their odd combination of terry cloth on the top and stretchy nylon on the bottom. How I always felt chubby next to her and how I still do.

"Look. Your sneaker is untied," she says, pointing to one of my little white Keds in the photograph. I hadn't ever noticed it, but there it is and now I see it. Then she closes her eyes. "I can practically hear our flip-flops slapping against our feet as we walked down the street to the beach, or to the post office, or to Cumberland Farms for ice cream."

"Me too." I remember how, years after that photo, when Eleanor was at Fernald and then after she'd died, we still went to the beach for part of the summer. We raced toward the sand in the morning to see who was already there on big towels and blankets, who'd beat us to the sea glass, the waves, the shovels for tunnel digging and pails for castle building. Louise was always behind us with her scalloped head scarf covering her hair, carrying a full-sized folding chair, a book to read, and peanut butter sandwiches and grapes and a thermos of lemonade for lunch so she didn't have to leave the beach to feed us all before dusk. She was there, but not there; chatting with the other mothers, but not really. Later she would joke that all they talked about was recipes and sex. *I had nothing to add on either topic. I'd just lost a child, and no one wanted to talk about that. The minute I had my nose in a book, they left me alone. I never read so much in my life.*

I show Lydia to what used to be my office. "Your room is back here." My desk, my double monitors, my professional-grade flat-bed scanner and color printer, are in my bedroom now, with all my work files in boxes on the floor underneath it. I made up the guest bed, which I used to read and nap on during work breaks, with all-new bedding, and brought up her old desk from the basement, another rescue from Louise's house that I'd kept after selling it. I'm pretty impressed with myself. I'd live in this guest room forever.

She touches the Marimekko quilt, the big pink florid flowers themselves a nostalgic reminder of our teenage years; all the matching pillows; the bedside table; the lamp. I put a lot of time and effort into making up her room. I want her to be comfortable, to feel welcome, to feel like she belongs. That this room and this apartment, for however long she wants it or needs it, is home.

"Someone's been watching a lot of HGTV."

I let her snide remark hang in the air for a second or two before answering it with a tight smile. "You're welcome."

"I meant: Thank you. I also meant: You didn't have to go to this much trouble. I'm not staying forever."

"No one said you were. And no one wants you to." We both laugh. The couples' counselor, the one Tom and I went to after he said he wanted to leave but before he moved out—the one tasked with the impossible job of trying to save our marriage after it was already long gone—explained to both of us that we could use humor to defuse tension. We'd looked at each other, and then at her, like she was insane. Nothing about our situation or our feelings was the least bit funny. But now I see that such a thing is possible.

"Also," I say, "I was trying to be the anti-Louise. Sorry if I went a little overboard in trying to make you *too* comfortable."

She rolls her eyes, as I do, at the memory of all the weekend trips and vacations and holidays in the years after college: how the beds were never made up and how we'd both have to move the piles of books and papers she'd covered them with—extra makeshift desk space for all the work she was doing on disability rights legislation—onto the floor before finding fresh sheets and extra blankets, and, in the winter, turning the valves on the radiators so the rooms would be heated.

"But what about your office?" she says.

"I'll work out of my bedroom, which is fine for what I do. I'm not exactly making art in there, like you are."

"Being the creative director for an online travel site is hardly making art. Not that I'm complaining. I'm lucky they're letting me work remotely."

She walks past me and pokes her head into my room, then comes back out. She looks around, then toward the front door, then suggests we put my desk in the foyer, right in front of the window. "It's the perfect place for a desk."

I stare at the patch of floor and wall that I've never really noticed before—wasted airspace where I take my jacket or sweater off and turn around to hang it on the coat tree.

"I'll measure it later, but I'm sure it'll fit."

I can't really picture it—how she will transform nothing into something—but I remember Lydia's place in LA, the miraculous things she and Brad had done with small vertical spots in their canyon house. I know she'll make it happen.

"Plus, if you hate it, it'll be temporary. Like I said before, I'm not staying forever."

ONE NIGHT, SHORTLY AFTER SHE MOVES IN, I TEXT HER BEFORE BED to say good night. When she doesn't answer, I knock on her door and she opens it and waves me in. She has a large collage in progress on her desk. Her old pine drafting table is tilted almost flat and covered with photographs and pages torn from journals; X-ACTO knives and scissors and different kinds of glue and tubes of paint are at the edges of the canvas. I know she doesn't like people to see her work until it's done—or, at least, she didn't like that when we were younger, when I'd go into her room to borrow a shirt or a jacket and she'd cover up whatever she was working on before I could catch a glimpse of it—sort of the way I hide my Small World poetry notebooks. It seems to be a family habit, keeping what's ours away from everyone else. But tonight, she doesn't seem to mind. She even moves to make space for me at her desk so I can see without having to be sneaky.

"That looks like your old backyard." I'm trying to place a faded color picture of a lush garden, one that looks like it was run through a 1970s retro filter.

"It is. That was our version of late fall, almost winter."

"I think I only visited you in the spring or summer."

"Such a missed opportunity," she says. "You should have come out when it was cold and grim here. To get away. A respite."

"I know." I stare at the layers of photos and glue and paint that look like they're still wet. "Do you miss it?"

She sits back, sighs. "I miss the flowers and the lemon trees and the orange trees. I miss how you can be outside all year round without losing four months to cold and darkness. But I don't miss who I was there."

I scan the room to see if she's put out any photos since she moved in. But there is still only the one: a small black-and-white picture of her and Brad, from college, taken at their favorite bar in Providence. "Who were you there?"

"Oh, you know," she says, stretching and yawning. "Just some industry asshole's wife."

"Was Brad an asshole?" Except for their wedding, and a few visits before and after it, I know very little about him and their relationship, except that he had something to do with visual effects in films. It's the closest I've come to asking her anything about her divorce, and I wonder if even that question goes too far.

"No, actually, he wasn't at all," she says softly. "I was the asshole."

"I doubt that."

"You'd be surprised. Or maybe you wouldn't be surprised." She smiles, nudges me with her elbow. "I'm not sure if you know this, but I can be a little difficult sometimes." She snorts at the understatement, then looks back down at her collage.

If we were different—the kind of sisters who had grown up living in each other's rooms in pajamas and slippers, doing homework together and sharing late-night snacks and school gossip—we would have sat down on her bed and talked until dawn to make up for all the years of living three thousand miles apart. But we've never been those kind of sisters.

"I'll let you get back to work," I say, even though I'm going back to work, too, for a little while to help me sleep. We wave goodbye to each other with our fingers, the way children do when they're doing the part in "The Itsy-Bitsy Spider" where the rain comes down.

—

On nights when there are no parent-support-group meetings, and when Eleanor goes to sleep easily and isn't sick or struggling with one of her many chronic pain issues, Louise puts the two of you to bed in the room you share. She shuts off the television set in the living room, brings you upstairs, and turns the light on in your room while you change into your pajamas. When you finish brushing your teeth and washing your faces, you get under the covers and watch her turn on the musical circus lamp that used to be Eleanor's but is now on the night table between your beds since her room downstairs has too much equipment in it. Then she shuts off the big light.

Louise always sits down on your bed first, brings the blankets up to your chin, and tells you, at your request, the story of the day you were born. Then she goes over to Lydia's bed and sits down, too.

Do you have any problems? she says, while you play with the little white pom-poms that hang from the circus-tent lampshade.

Lydia says yes. *Which came first? The ceiling or the walls?*

You don't remember what Louise answers—whether she says it's the ceiling that came first, or that the walls did—which, therefore, is more structurally independent from the other or if they are both equally dependent on each other. But you do remember turning the base of the lamp with the animals on it to make the music start and tapping the pom-poms one by one, watching the zebra and the lion and the tiger go by before you fall asleep.

———

Perambulation Withdrawal
I'm originally from San Diego,
and trails for hiking and biking
are everywhere.
It's so different here.
The parks are small,
the people in them seem kind of angry,
and half the time,
instead of walking or hiking or exploring,
I'm looking for a place
to park.
I long for my old perambulations.
I'm not expecting anything miraculous,
just places less peopley and trafficky.
If anyone has suggestions for places to park and walk
please share!

Odors Minimal
One of my favorite walks is by
the Nut Island sewage treatment plant.
It's a peninsula in Boston Harbor
with beautiful views and a landscaped park
and it has the added perk
of learning about the history of the Island
(it was used by Native Americans
and then by Colonists for grazing cows,
which I didn't know.
It's also known as Houghs Tomb
or Hoff's Thumb,
which I also didn't know.)
and about what happens to your sewage
(lots of Nut Island Pumping Station informational signage
along the way).
Ample parking.
Odors minimal.

This Isn't
This isn't San Diego

Reconfiguration

O ne morning, about a week after Lydia moves in, I'm sitting in my new "office" out in the foyer when she starts pacing the apartment. She makes two full circuits before going back into her bedroom and shutting the door.

Tom has been gone for almost two years by then, and I've finally gotten used to living alone again, or almost gotten used to it—does anyone ever completely get used to it?—so her frenetic movements distract and unnerve me. Proof: I've been staring at the same file of photos from the big project I'm working on right now, archiving several centuries of a collection of papers and photographs and artwork belonging to a prominent Maine family. The photos I'm organizing this morning, or trying to, anyway, before Lydia starts pacing, is of a small Canadian branch of the family, outliers who made their way far north and who seem to have done nothing but sail for the past seventy-five years. I click on thousands of pictures in hundreds of files and look at them on my giant monitor.

I'm struck by their smugness—how much confidence families like this one has and how they telegraph to one another and to the outside world that they're untouchable by disaster or death. Privileged, entitled clans of people of means who, for generations, have gone through life like masters of the universe, playing by a whole different set of rules than my family played with, doing insanely unsafe things without fear of consequences—and with so little fear that they pose for photos while doing them. *Watch us cheat death.* When I see something reckless, careless, dangerous, as I do in today's cache of photos—children in a motorboat who aren't wearing life preservers; a toddler playing, unattended, too close to a swimming pool or the wide-open maw of a clambake firepit or an unleashed dog; a group of skiers and snowboarders holding beer cans before one last black diamond sunset run—I think of Eleanor. How everything we did at home or every trip we took to a beach or a park or a zoo revolved around keeping her, and the rest of us, safe. It infuriates me. We were touched by adversity, through no fault of our own. We were unlucky. But these people who endlessly tempt fate never seem to get punished. Their luck never seems to run out.

The way the "adults" thoughtlessly put their children and themselves so often in harm's way always makes me anxious. And agitated. And so, when I find a photo of a particularly egregious example of this sort of carelessness—there are usually so many to pick from— I fix it. With Photoshop. Subtly. So subtly that no one ever notices. Today I add a tiny gate between the toddler and the pool; attach a leash to the dog; turn the beer cans into soda cans. It's my way of correcting the past, of making it clear that the rules apply to them, too. That they have to be careful like everyone else.

But I can't concentrate on this Canadian branch of the Maine family—where they fit in with their southern relatives, the ones in goofy sun hats and visors and windbreakers and pink pants and noses white with zinc oxide—the ones with yacht club and country club and Prouts Neck vibes. They are all aliens to me, this whole

family, and I'm feeling my way in the dark with them, like I am
with Lydia. We've never had the same energy—in fact, we're com-
plete opposites. Where I can, and do, sit still for hours, staring at
my monitors, she can barely sit still at all. Even now, when she stops
pacing, I can feel her restlessness, her edginess, beaming out through
her bedroom door and across the apartment, like invisible micro-
waves in a 1950s movie. Radiating me. She makes me nervous. She
always has. Is that so wrong to admit?

More to put myself at ease than to put her at ease, I text her:

You ok? Need anything?

No. Fine. Just antsy.

I mutter, "You're welcome!" after I read her reply. I actually say
the words, out loud, but quietly, because someone has to. I love her,
really I do, but she can be incredibly rude. And while I know that
rude isn't the right word for it—*socially awkward* or *socially chal-
lenged* are both more accurate terms—her manners are frequently
terrible. I've never understood why she can't say *please* and *thank you*
more. Is it that hard?

———

Stolen Avocados
A brown paper bag of avocados
from the local farmer's market
was stolen
from our porch
where we'd left them to ripen.
This felt like a violation

even though, of course, it's a minor one
compared to true suffering in the world.
Maybe an Amazon delivery person
took the bag
or a neighbor
or a passerby—
I hate feeling like anyone
and everyone
is a potential thief.
A loss of trust like this is so
disappointing,
much worse than the loss
of the actual avocados itself
(especially since they were probably
still unripe).

(Alternate) True Crime Theory

Maybe it was raccoons
or squirrels.

Little Paws

Not to creep you out or anything
but it was probably rats
or maybe even bats
not squirrels,
as the previous commenter said,
or people, as you suspect,
that stole and ate your stupid avocados
with their little rat- or bat-paws.

Good for them.
They're sparing the world of more avocado toast
made by people who think
everyone around them
is a criminal.

Dog Poop
I would just like to say
that when dog walkers allow their pets
to pee and poop in my yard,
they are killing my plants and flowers.
Poop is an irritant but pee
is what kills.
People should not allow
their dogs to use
their neighbors' yards
as a toilet.

Dude.
Wrong thread.

———

Later that day, when I get back from an EverMore meeting at the office in Harvard Square, I notice the minute I walk in the door that my desk is no longer in the foyer. A few more steps into the apartment, and I see that all the furniture in the living room has been rearranged. I'm like Louise returning home from that trip to find that Lydia and Brad had reconfigured the entire downstairs of the house.

I feel a hot flash coming on. The meeting was long and boring, and the walk back was freezing. I was really looking forward to relaxing, to thinking about the rest of my week and making a plan for all the work I have to get done before it's over. But now I have to deal with this. With Lydia. Why can't she be normal, like other sisters, and bake cookies or roast a chicken while I'm out?

I take my shoes off slowly. Very slowly. I'm stalling for time. So much will depend on my facial expressions and my tone of voice when I address this situation—and so much will ride on her reaction to my reaction, too. Our ridiculously interconnected emotional circuitry— sometimes referred to by each of us as the other's "hypersensitivity"— will be the death of both of us.

And yet: reacting feels involuntary. As long as we're both breath- ing, we'll probably forever misread each other's faces; second-guess and misinterpret each other's thoughts, feelings, and motives in the worst possible way. I'm never generous with Lydia when I'm dealing with her actions or behavior. The narratives I create in my head about whatever it is she has done or said are always negative. I'm sure she does exactly the same thing with me. Isn't that what sisters do? No matter how much I tried to be better about that when I'd go out to visit her or she came east for a holiday, I almost always said the wrong thing, which set off a whole cascade of bad feelings and then a period of the silent treatment—all of which would lead to a big fight. So much drama; so little compassion.

But I want today to be different. I want to change the future. This is our first real moment of tension since she's been back. Assuming I don't count my suspicion that she's been taking stock of everything in my apartment and cataloguing it as being either something given to me by Louise—and thus, something not given to *her* by Louise—or something not given to me by Louise. I'm certain that every book, plate, glass, bowl, pan, and ancient container of paprika or cinnamon, the only two spices Louise ever used, makes her think: *Is this Joyce's? Or was this Louise's and maybe something I should have gotten?* Unless I've been imagining it, which is entirely possible, but I doubt it. I'm sure she's been counting, assessing, comparing. Fairness is her calculus. She can't help it.

I have my own calculus. Like right now. I close my eyes, take a breath, and try to ignore the equation that covers the blackboard in my mind in a chalky scrawl—the one where Lydia moves away and doesn't come back to help me pack up the house after Louise dies. How she and Brad come in for the funeral and then fly back after the first night of shiva because—because, why? Because they had work? Because they could? Because they knew I was there and would take care of everything? I have never been able to solve it or resolve it and continuing to feel aggrieved serves no one. Least of all me. I know this. I order myself to let it go. All of it. The past can't be changed, and people have worse problems than their sister moving in and then moving all their stuff around without asking first, I'm sure of it.

I take my coat and scarf off next and hang them on the coat tree, which is now on the left side of the door instead of on the right. *No big deal.* Then I drop my keys and phone on the new little table—one of Lydia's nightstands—on the right side of the door that wasn't there earlier. *Also no big deal.* To be honest, it's a great place for a little table. But despite the intelligent doorway redesign, I'm still a little pissed. She's made herself so at home so quickly that she already feels like it's her apartment to rearrange. Such entitlement. I would never do that if I were staying with her.

In fact, the few times I did stay with her in LA, if I ever put something back where it didn't belong, accidentally, like a roll of tinfoil or a glass or a cereal bowl, she'd get really bent, making a big show of putting the thing back where it belonged and explaining to me why it was better where she'd had it. *It's easier to reach. There's a better flow this way. These don't match; these do.* She likes things her way. She also likes *my* things her way. She always has. She still does.

"Uhm, Lydia?" I say, loud enough for her to hear.

She flies out of her room, barely able to contain her excitement. "What do you think? Don't you love it?" Clearly she's not looking for an honest response. "It's so much better to have the couch face the windows, especially once the trees start to bud in a month or two. Why have your back to that view? Plus, you know how I am: I have to move things around."

"Yes, I know."

"It's a weird tic. A fear of complacency."

"You could call it that."

"What would you call it?"

"A need for control?" I force a smile.

"That's fair."

I'm surprised by her willingness to accept my version of her—shocked, in fact—so I sit down on the couch in its new location. Sitting feels like a concession. I'm hoping she sees it that way. That it counts for something. I'm always keeping score, and right now I feel slightly ahead as the bigger person, even though she should get some points, too, for not melting down when I didn't immediately say *I love it. I love how you moved everything around while I was out even though I didn't say you could.* It could so easily have happened that I'm truly shocked it didn't. Which means we're essentially tied now. Except for her considerable audacity, which will cost her many more points than she earned. I nod with a fake smile, waiting for the right words to come into my head—something positive but also something that makes it clear that she's used up my goodwill for any future furniture moving—and that's when I see it: where she put my desk.

"No," I say, standing up and pointing at it. "No. No. No."

She follows my finger. "Why not? It's perfect there. It's like a separate alcove."

"I don't want my desk there."

"Why not?"

I shudder. "I hate that space."

She stares at me. "What's wrong with you. It's not like someone died there."

That's exactly what it's like. "It's where Tom always sat, in the months before he left. It's where the couch used to be."

"I'm sorry. I had no idea."

"There's no way you could have known." I shrug, like I'm over it, but I'm not. I remember how he would be there all day, when he wasn't working, staring out at the street. Sometimes he wouldn't speak for hours; sometimes not for days. Then he started sleeping there. I can still see the blankets and pillows he piled up, a child's fort, to hide himself away. From me. "I'm convinced he hated me by the end," I say. "I don't think I've ever told anyone that. Is that weird?"

"Which part? That he hated you or that you've never told anyone?"

"Both."

"Every couple who splits up hates each other by the end." She sits down. "Though you and Tom always seemed like the perfect couple."

"So did you and Brad."

"We were. Until we weren't anymore."

"Us too."

"Not that I'm in any position to judge you and Tom as a couple, given how little I saw of you over the years. You guys didn't like to travel."

I glare at her. *The gall.* "Why was it up to us to come out there? You guys almost never came east."

She nods. "True. I take it back."

Another capitulation. I'm so confused.

"So what happened?" she asks.

Her question is so direct and unexpected that I don't know what to say. During the year after Tom lost his job and before he found another one, he had more time to focus on us as a couple. On what was wrong with us as a couple. And me as a person. How I never wanted children—or even a dog—like he did. How I always kept part of myself—the essential part, he said—separate from him and from everyone. All the holes were suddenly visible. *It's not your fault,* he'd always say. *I mean, look how you grew up.* Which was supposed to make me feel better about being so emotionally deficient and unnurturing in his eyes, but which only made me angry: the presumption of his assumptions; the implicit familial blame. *And what way was that?* I'd ask. *Always in the background. Always overlooked,* he'd say, as if it was obvious. Which it was by that point, but still. He wasn't there.

I shrug. "It's kind of an impossible question to answer. You know?"

"That's fair."

Again, her reasonableness feels like a trick, but maybe it's not.

"You must be tired from all the furniture moving," I say, "so I'll figure out dinner. But help me put the desk back where it was first."

———

Lost Wedding Ring
Kind neighbors, I'm desperate.
Last week,
when I was cleaning out
my drawers
in an effort to declutter
and get more organized,
I stupidly put my wedding ring
into the pocket of the pants I was wearing
and then accidently threw the pants out
with all the old clothes I was getting rid of
when I did my final purge.
Everything went into the trash
and then
the trash was picked up Friday.
I'm so upset
I can't even think of what to do next.
Suggestions welcome!

The Sorry Notes

Maybe it's some kind of unconscious desire for revenge, the secret urge to tweak Lydia the way she tweaked me by rearranging my apartment without my permission, but later that week, when I'm looking for one of my warmer coats in the hall closet, I find the envelope of old notes she wrote to Louise and Lenny when she was little.

I'd found them the first time a few years ago when I was cleaning out the house after Louise died—alone, without Lydia, as I may have already mentioned, even though I said I was going to let it go already—sifting through all the family pictures and documents she'd kept over the years. The archivist in me knew enough to save them, so I'd put them aside with all the other paperwork I wanted to bring home to eventually digitize and not shred.

The notes are still in their original manila envelope, marked LYDIA in pencil, in Louise's unmistakably perfect and authoritative cursive, and when I first took them out and read them in Louise's basement, I simply could not get over them. They're written in crayon, colored pencil, Magic Marker. Some have flowers drawn on the notes and the envelopes; some are decorated with stickers. But every single one contains a long explanation of whatever it was that had happened that day that Lydia felt the need to apologize for, officially, in writing.

Sometimes it was a tantrum she'd thrown when we were all home together as a family, or on a little day trip to the beach or an amusement park or to go back-to-school shopping. Sometimes it was a meltdown she'd had while Louise and Lenny were out, and a babysitter had stayed with us. To explain why she acted the way she did—badly, always—she'd lay out the facts of her case and then argue her own defense, in child language. *No one ever listens to me! They weren't including me! It wasn't fair!* The notes were her private courtroom; each one a tiny window into a day or evening that had made her desperate for forgiveness, justice, or, at the very least, understanding.

I call them the Sorry Notes.

Looking at them now, next to the closet, they make me sad. Lydia cried at her own birthday parties. She was shy and didn't make friends easily. She was blamed for "ruining" family outings or quiet moments at home because she'd get upset when things overwhelmed her. And things often overwhelmed her. Who could blame her? Given our home life, Lydia was always unsettled. But at the time, in those days, she was seen as the problem. Prickly, sensitive, thin-skinned. She was *a lot*. To Lenny and Louise, she was making an already difficult situation even worse. *Couldn't she just be good?*

Always, when they went out—to the movies or a dinner party or a fundraiser for Fernald—Lydia would get jealous of me: the most common perceived slight was the suspicion that the babysitter liked me more. She'd stand in the doorway while we watched TV, inside the blue light, and when we'd wave at her to come in and watch, too, she wouldn't move. A few minutes later, she'd be gone. A few minutes after that, she'd come back again, this time upset. She'd say something, which would start something—the babysitter would tell her she was misbehaving, that she was talking back—which would then make her cry and put herself to bed early. Before Lenny and Louise came home, Lydia would write a note and leave it in their bedroom, a preemptive apology, knowing they'd find out from the babysitter what she'd done and that they'd be mad. She'd put the note on Louise's bureau or Lenny's nightstand, though sometimes she'd wait for them to be asleep and then slip it silently under their door.

I'm sorry for what I did, all the notes say. And then, at the end: *I'm sorry for everything.*

I WALK ACROSS THE APARTMENT—MY RECENTLY REARRANGED apartment—maybe I forgot to mention that she moved things around in the dining room and in the kitchen, too—and knock on her door. It's late, and it's been a long day, but something propels me to show them to her tonight.

"What's this?" she says when I hand her the thick envelope.

I nod at her to look inside. She puts her hand in slowly, cautiously, like something might bite her, and pulls out a bunch of small envelopes. Looking at them, she slips a piece of paper out of one and unfolds it. It takes her a few seconds to understand what she's looking at.

"Wow," she says.

"I know, right?" I laugh first, and then she laughs, but I can tell she's shocked at seeing all the notes saved, in one place. A critical mass.

"It's not funny," Lydia says.

"I know. I'm sorry."

"I mean, I laughed, too, but it's incredibly sad. There are so many of them." She opens a few more, looks at the front and back of them, at the envelopes, then puts everything down on her drafting table. "What kid writes this many apology notes? What nine- or ten-year-old feels this responsible for the entire burden of their family's unhappiness at such a young age and never gets talked out of it?"

I shake my head. No one ever told Lydia that it wasn't her fault. That she wasn't the one who ruined everything. That sometimes life is cruel; that terrible things happen to families; that Eleanor's condition wasn't anyone's fault, especially hers. It never occurred to Lenny and Louise that the notes needed to be addressed. Eleanor affected the two of us, too. Their loss was our loss, but in a different way. They lost a child, but we lost a sister—and who they would have been as parents had Eleanor not needed so much care and had she not died. They didn't seem to understand that we were there, too.

"They really never said anything to you about the notes?"

"Like, did they ever come into my room after reading one to check on me and to try to make me feel better?" As soon as the words are out of her mouth, I realize how stupid my question was. "Seriously, Joyce." She refolds the notes she looked at, then slips everything into the big manila envelope. She hands it back to me like it's something she never wants to see again.

Now I'm the one who's sorry. "I shouldn't have shown those to you."

"Then why did you?"

I don't want to acknowledge, even to myself, the nagging desire for revenge I felt earlier, the stupid urge for score-settling that crept through my veins all evening until I saw her face fall when she looked at the notes. I did that. And now I'm the one full of regret and self-loathing. "I guess I thought that maybe, since you're here now, we should talk about stuff."

"What stuff," she says, more a statement than a question, like she doesn't really want an answer. "Because honestly, Joyce, that's not why I'm here. I'm not obsessed with the past the way you are. It's not only what you do for work, it's who you are."

"I wouldn't exactly call being interested in the past being *obsessed* with the past, but whatever. I haven't brought anything up since you've been here."

"I've been here a week. Take a bow for seven days of restraint."

"I'm not restraining myself. But you're right. I *am* much more interested in the past—our past—than you are, which isn't saying much since I still haven't digitized any of the old pictures or files I saved from Louise's house. When I saw the envelope of Sorry Notes, I didn't think about how they would make you feel. Which was stupid. I thought maybe you'd want to see them. As pieces of nostalgia. Proof of how far we've come."

"Given the fact that we're both divorced and living together in some weird state of regression, I would hardly consider where we are now as a positive thing—as proof of advancement. But good for you if you think this is progress." Before I can think of a comeback, she turns and reaches for her door to close. "I'm going to sleep now."

———

The day starts out so simply, so full of excitement. Louise comes into your room and stands between your two beds:

"Who wants to go to Paragon Park today?" she says with a sing-song lilt in her voice.

You and Lydia both sit up and push the blankets off. You're so excited that you stand up and jump on your beds, something Louise doesn't normally allow. But today even she is beaming. You all love the amusement park at Nantasket Beach, on the south shore of Boston, even though you never go on any of the fast, scary rides, including the park's main attraction—the wooden roller coaster.

"It's going to be a perfect beach day," Louise says. "Which means everyone will be down at the water, and not on the rides. We'll have the place to ourselves."

You and Lydia stop jumping. You know what's coming.

"That way Eleanor can have a good time, too."

"I thought it was just going to be us," Lydia says.

"Well, it's not. Don't be selfish, Lydia."

"Sorry."

"Doesn't Eleanor deserve to have fun, too?" Louise says.

"But she can't go on any of the rides," you say. The words come out in barely a whisper.

"And whose fault is that?"

You feel your mouth go dry and your tongue get heavy behind your teeth.

"It's not Eleanor's fault that the world isn't made to include her. Why should she be further punished by being left out of one of life's most simple pleasures: a day at an amusement park?"

When you don't answer—you don't really know how to answer—she tells you both to get dressed and brush your teeth. Then you go downstairs, where she packs a small Styrofoam cooler, filled with ice packs, cans of cold Fresca, and sandwiches wrapped in waxed paper. You always eat lunch at the park and stop for ice cream on the way home.

She asks you to check on Eleanor, so you do—she's a few feet away on the other side of the kitchen, watching *Sesame Street* on the small black-and-white television on the counter next to the stove. Eleanor loves music, loves rocking back and forth in her chair to all the songs and the rhyming words. You wipe her chin with her bib, carefully, because she's wearing her favorite elephant T-shirt, then Lydia pats her on the head and sings, in a made-up-song way, "We're going to Paragon Park and you're coming, too!" She looks at Louise, who smiles with relief. All she wants is for Eleanor to be happy. So do you. Even if sometimes you wish the focus wasn't always on her.

Lenny comes into the kitchen, wearing his usual olive-green swim trunks, a striped short-sleeve button-down shirt, and his brown sandals: his beach outfit. "One big happy family," he announces, as if saying it means it's true or will make it so.

It takes a while to leave—it always does—to get Eleanor out of the house and into the back seat, with everything she needs for an outing, most of which Louise keeps a supply of in the trunk of the station wagon: clean clothes, extra diapers, towels, and a sun hat in the summer. Once you're all finally buckled in, Lenny backs out and heads south.

You and Lydia know the drive by heart—the highway exit you take to the smaller highway to the crowded two-lane road that twists and turns until the final dramatic curve when, suddenly, the white wooden roller coaster is visible, looming like a mirage through the front windshield. Lenny pulls into the parking lot, rolls his window down, and explains to the attendant that he needs to drive closer to the park's pedestrian entrance.

"We have a wheelchair," he says.

Louise bristles. She pokes him on the arm, then leans over and lifts her sunglasses up so she can make eye contact with the attendant. "We don't *have* a wheelchair," she says sharply, before giving Lenny a look. "We have a child who *uses* a wheelchair. There's a difference."

THE SUMMER SUN IS WHITE-HOT. THE ASPHALT IN THE PARKING LOT shimmers with heat as the attendant directs Lenny where to pull up. He stops the car, takes out Eleanor's chair, and lifts her into it, while Louise grabs her bag. After Lenny parks, you all meet up again on the sidewalk and enter the park.

You and Lydia are ecstatic. You don't remember ever being as happy—as filled with pure childlike energy and glee—as you are whenever you're at Paragon Park. You hold hands and go on the teacup ride, the helicopter ride, and then, always, the haunted house ride. They're the only ones you're allowed on, because you're still not tall enough for the minimum-height requirement painted on signs at the front gate to every ride. You sit in your little ride container, gripping the bar, and then each other, as things pop out at you— ghosts, goblins, skeletons—until you're back outside, blinking in the blinding sunlight. You always want Louise to go on the rides with you—*Please? Just once? Sit between us!*—but she always stays with Eleanor no matter where you go, and today is no different. After each ride, you find her right where you left her: crouched by Eleanor's wheelchair, pointing at things for her to look at, wiping her chin, smiling at everyone who walks by.

But today Eleanor is fussy. It's hot—much warmer than Louise had anticipated—and she is uncomfortable in her chair, sitting there in the glaring sun, waiting for you and Lydia to go on each stupid ride. No matter how much Louise tries to find a patch of shade, the sun eventually moves and beats down on them. Nothing she does keeps Eleanor cool and comfortable. You and Lydia even try to block the sun with your bodies, standing behind and next to her chair, with your hands in the air, against the sky. But it doesn't help. Neither does crouching down in front of her and trying to interest her in a round of Patty Cake, which she normally loves. Instead of touching your hands, she swats at you, in the face, maybe accidentally, but you finally give up and move away.

"Well, it's time to call it a day."

"Louise," Lenny says.

"But we just got here!" Lydia says, her voice cracking. You haven't even been on the mini race-car track yet, or gotten penny candy or soft-serve cones from your favorite ice cream place on the boardwalk.

Louise takes off Eleanor's hat and blows on the back of her neck. But the tiny cool breeze she's creating doesn't help—Eleanor is writhing in her chair and making unhappy sounds.

The park is crowded now. Throngs of people—families, children, packs of teenagers—are streaming in, running from ride to ride, holding ice cream cones and hot dogs and lit cigarettes. They pass around you in swarms, in their T-shirts and bathing suit bottoms and flip-flops, staring at Eleanor as they walk by.

You and Lydia look at each other. As much as you love her at home, it's always uncomfortable to be in public with Eleanor. You are, you're ashamed to admit, even now, embarrassed by her—her yellow teeth, the drool, the sounds she makes, so loud and birdlike—the smell sometimes, when she needs to be changed. But you're also protective of her. You don't understand how the two impulses can coexist, but they do.

"Don't stare," Lydia says to someone passing by. Or maybe to no one in particular, just the air.

"That's a good sister," Louise says, then brushes Lydia's bangs away from her eyes.

She's resigned now. We're leaving. There's no changing it. "Can I push her?" she asks.

"Me too?" you say. "Can we both push her?"

You and Lydia move to grab a handle in the back of her chair—for the first time, you want to help make Eleanor's way in the world—but Louise says no. There are too many people, it's too crowded, it's easier and safer if she does it. Which makes sense. The park is packed now, and you are both too short to see much over the back of the chair and Eleanor's head to steer it without running over people's feet. Louise takes the handles and follows Lenny. You all head for the car.

Maybe it's the heat, or the stress, or all the disappointments of the day that Lydia has tried to metabolize, but Louise saying no to pushing the wheelchair is too much for her. She loses it. She starts to scream and cry.

"It's not fair!"

"Here we go," Louise says. "You're ruining the day."

"I'm not! It was already ruined! It's too hot for Eleanor! We should have come without her!"

The crying turns into a wail. People are turning and looking now—not at Eleanor anymore, but at Lydia, whose face is red and tearstained. She's in agony. Instead of calming down as you walk, she gets louder. This is what always happens. Even you wish she'd stop ruining the day.

Back at the car, with Lenny struggling in the heat to lift Eleanor into the back seat, and Louise folding up the wheelchair and sliding it into the trunk of the station wagon, Lydia's wails continue. She climbs into the back of the car, still crying, then cries louder when her bare legs hit the hot leather seat and her hand burns on the chrome seat belt buckle when she tries to fasten it. You put your finger up to your mouth to *shhhhhh* her, like they do in the library at school, but that only makes her scream louder and swat you away. You're a traitor now. Which makes you cry, too.

That's the note you find in the envelope tonight, the one Lydia wrote a million years ago after you got home and changed and ate dinner and took baths and went to bed, all in silence, all in the sad, heavy, hopeless quiet that always followed a tantrum. The one she must have gotten up in the middle of the night to write, on the floor, with a flashlight, with crayons and paper and stickers that she brought over to use so quietly you didn't wake up. The one she must have slipped under their door when everyone was asleep, exhausted from the heat and the aborted attempt at a fun family outing.

I'm sorry I ruined the day. I'm sorry for everything.

Ever Present

D on't tell me: she's still here."

Ever since Lydia moved in, this is always the first thing Erin asks me whenever we get together. Not: *Are you going to make that deadline?* Not: *Can you take on another project?* Not: *Have you tried those tiny little Trader Joe's ice cream cones? They're the perfect size, by which I mean I have four or five of them in a row and can't stop.* But this: *Is Lydia still here?*

My answer all these months is always the same: *Yes. She's still here.*

Erin and I work together at EverMore—sometimes in the Harvard Square office, and most of the time for me, from home. She's my boss, even though she's quite a bit younger, and while I used to mainly do the institutional clients—regional historical societies, law firms, nonprofits, some small private collections for local authors and artists, the occasional university project— this year she's asked for my help on many of the New England legacy projects, too, like the big Maine family history we're working on together.

I love going through decades and decades of photos, old movies, birth and death certificates, letters, maps, recipe cards, obituaries, inscriptions in old bibles and first-edition books of poetry. I'm fascinated by families who are nothing like mine—how athletic and adventurous and stupid they are—all the diving into ponds and lakes and swimming holes, the legs dangling from ski lifts and the backs of open Jeeps, the bike riding and skateboarding without helmets, the drunken nights around giant beach bonfires with sparks flying.

"Don't any of them ever get injured or die?" I asked her when I first started working on the family legacy projects.

"Joyce."

"Yes, Erin?"

"Let's not go there right now."

That's fine. I'll go there later with Photoshop and add some tiny seat belts, and other safety items.

My most favorite work thing to do is what Erin is solely responsible for—slideshows for graduations and weddings, bar/bat mitzvahs and funerals and retirements—milestone events that require a vast array of photos that progress chronologically, all tied together with the perfect song. It's like she was born to make them. Initially the company didn't even offer slideshows, but she did one once as a little bonus to a family she'd loved working with, and they were so happy with it that EverMore decided to add them to its permanent menu of services. Since then, they've become one of the most popular—and profitable—parts of the company. Everybody loves slideshows.

But nobody loves them more than me. I'm obsessed with the slideshows. They make me cry every time—even though I'm not really a crier, and even though the slideshows I watch are for strangers—people and families I've never met. It doesn't seem to matter. The minute the montage starts, and I hear those first few notes of whatever song Erin has chosen from the usual list of the best songs for slideshows that anyone can find on the internet and that all the clients love—"Time of Your Life," by Green Day; "What a Wonderful World," by Louis Armstrong; "You've Got a Friend in Me," by Randy Newman; "Because You Loved Me," by Celine Dion—my eyes fill with anticipatory emotion. I don't know exactly what the emotion is—Sadness? Jealousy? Love? All of those things? My family would never have the need for a slideshow—a slideshow requires an audience, people brought together to celebrate or mourn an occasion or an event, and really, there's only Lydia and me—but even if I created one, I'd worry that it would make people cry for the wrong reason. Because it would be grimly depressing instead of nostalgically upbeat. What a waste of a six-minute montage and all the time and work that would go into it.

So it's good that I'm usually tasked with the more formal family mini-documentaries—interviewing elderly parents and middle-aged children to "produce" a short formulaic film using a template of topics that include *How We Got Here, How We Met, How He/She Proposed, Our Home, Starting a Family, Trips We've Taken, The Next Generation.* Because watching a bar/bat mitzvah or a middle school graduation slideshow where a child goes from swaddled baby to walking toddler to prepubescent teen undoes me every time. I can never get over the transformations: the height, the teeth, the hair, the proud parents and grandparents and siblings as costars. How everyone smiles and grows and ages.

I've watched tons of slideshows that are in progress or that she's completed and is about to send off to a client—she likes to have another set of eyes on everything she does in case she's misspelled a name or a phrase or failed to catch a technical glitch. But when she emails me the link, she always makes it sound like it's a gift—like I've earned this private preview because I'm so special.

"What is it with you and the slideshows?" Erin asked me recently when I was in tears over one in her office. "They're so dumb."

"They are *so* not dumb." I tear up again, in defense of them.

"Have you ever watched one without crying?"

"Maybe. Probably." I'm lying. I definitely have never not cried while watching one or after watching one. I can honestly say I have never gotten through one of those super-manipulative slideshows without tears starting, my throat catching, then a full-on sob. Which is why I love working from home. *Privacy. I can cry in peace.*

"It's kind of cute that you like them so much."

"No, it's dumb," I say, like I'm anticipating some kind of future performance review. *Joyce cries a lot. Joyce is great but gets super emotional in an inappropriate way about the slideshows. Sometimes I worry about Joyce's emotional fragility that gets triggered when she watches them, even though it's not her job to watch them, but she somehow always manages to find a way to do so.*

"I wonder what it says about you—and about me, since I never cry. I guess I'm a stone-cold bitch."

We both laugh, and later, I'll think about the question. I'm older than Erin, by about fifteen years, which isn't that much, but it's something—fifteen extra years of life experience and disappointment—so maybe that has something to do with my emotional fragility, and my shame, too. But it's probably much simpler than that, much more obvious: seeing six minutes' worth of photographs of happy children and happy families engaging in all kinds of winter and summer sports and holiday celebrations and vacation travel makes me unbearably sad. And jealous. Why didn't I get to grow up like that?

BEFORE LYDIA MOVES IN, ERIN COMES OVER EVERY OTHER WEEK. Sometimes there's an actual work reason to get together for a drink or dinner—a new project to structure and strategize about, a problematic client that needs to be gently reined in, a slideshow or mini-documentary that is so dull we both want to die. When there isn't a reason—when one or both of us is simply bored or antsy or sick of working at home—we make one up. We brainstorm a "problem" or a "question" over the phone together that we're looking to solve, then email the topic as an official "meeting." I don't think EverMore reads our company emails or spies on our Slack channels, but you never know. Better safe than sorry.

Once we make a date, we go to the little restaurant at the Sheraton Commander Hotel. It's a few blocks away from both our apartments and Erin likes the big chairs and how the tables move easily away from the banquette if you need more room. Sometimes when she would pick me up on the way, we'd get so involved in conversation in the living room and feel so lazy that we'd end up staying in and getting takeout. But that was before Lydia's presence affected everything.

———

Typhoid Mary of the Invasive World
Evil black swallow wort!
One of the most aggressive and invasive weeds
there is!
It displaces native plants and habitats
and kills butterflies!
Crush this invasive plant
everywhere you see it

before it takes over our world!
Pull every one out by the roots
and throw into sealed trash bags!
For god's sake do not compost!
But we have to stop
clueless and selfish neighbors
from allowing it to flourish.
Someone nearby is letting it grow
in their front and backyard
and all along their fences—
a gazillion pods
full of seeds
that will soon explode
and destroy local flora and fauna.
People should be fined
for propagating and spreading it.
Such a dangerous weed—
Typhoid Mary of the invasive plant world.

End of Story
A mixture of vinegar
and boiling water
kills them without affecting other plants.
When I pour paint thinner or vinegar
straight down into the root,
they die.
End of story.

———

Erin finally meets Lydia in early spring. The weather has been bad, we've all been sick with various colds and flus, so it's March by the time she picks me up at the apartment for a "work" outing. That evening, she is on the couch, still in her puffy down coat, pouring a pre-dinner beer that I've handed her into a glass, when the door to Lydia's room suddenly opens and she comes out into the living room. She sits down on the arm of the sofa across from me in her usual uniform—old chinos and a little white T-shirt, her short hair brushed off her face like one of those androgynous models from the 1980s and '90s—and looks at us without saying anything.

I sigh. "Lydia, this is my friend Erin. We're working together on a project right now for this giant family from Maine."

"They came over on the *Mayflower*," Erin says, "so lots of super-old documents, naturally. And almost everyone is named John or Mary. Which is very confusing."

"It's a nightmare," I say, then roll my eyes. I'm getting a pathetic kick out of the absurdity of trying to make our work—archiving lots of dusty shit—sound interesting and dramatic. "They always look like they could die any minute from skiing or sailing or falling out the back of a Jeep or getting swallowed by a clambake firepit."

Erin laughs. "Usually, but not always, there's alcohol involved. Like on *The Real Housewives*. They get them drunk before taping and then it turns into a shitshow."

"You've told me about Erin," Lydia says. Like she's so bored she can hardly stand it.

I turn to Erin. "And this is my sister Lydia."

Erin shifts on the couch and waves. "Nice to meet you. I've heard a lot about you."

Lydia waves back, then stares out the window.

"It's pretty cold for March," Erin says, following Lydia's gaze out beyond the panes, before looking down at her jacket. "So I'm not really interested in taking this thing off anytime soon."

"It's not that cold," Lydia says.

"Well, I'm from Florida. It's cold for me."

"Well, I lived in California for twenty years."

"I heard."

"But I was raised here, so I guess I'm more used to it."

"Such a toughie," I say. "Didn't you complain all the way to the post office and back the other day about how cold it was? Or was that another sister of mine?"

"I don't understand why talking about the weather has to be such a thing here," Lydia says. "In California, there is no weather, so we talk about other things." *More important things*, she doesn't say, but it hangs there anyway.

"I was trying to break the ice by talking about the polar vortex," Erin says, with a sly smile at her own pun. "See what I did there?" When Lydia continues to stare at her like she's wasting her time, Erin looks over at me. "I guess this is the part where you save me from your sister."

I laugh. "Lydia, you're scaring the guest." I snap my fingers in front of her to break the weird trance she seems to be in, as if this is part of a comic routine we do when new people visit. But in reality, Lydia has been scaring the guests since we were little.

"I'm sorry," she says matter-of-factly, without either rudeness or warmth. "I'm super awkward and shy. Especially when I'm meeting someone new."

Erin seems surprised by her honesty, and relieved enough by it to settle back down on the couch. "I get it."

"Good, because I don't."

"Really? What don't you get?" She's had enough of Lydia's oppositional conversation style already and isn't going quietly.

Lydia doesn't expect the question. Usually when she's rude, or distant, or unnervingly direct, people back down or back away. Most people don't ever challenge her. Erin's pushback seems like an opportunity. "I don't get why I'm so awkward and shy even when the stakes are low, like this. I mean, you're just a friend of Joyce's and we're at home. It's not like I'm trying to get you to hire me or date me."

"Are you gay, Lydia?"

Lydia looks shocked. "No. Are you?"

"Yes."

I look at Erin. "You *are*?"

"Didn't you know that?"

"Well, no, I guess I didn't!"

Lydia laughs out loud. So does Erin.

"How could you not know!" Erin says, sitting forward on the couch. "My cubicle is full of pictures of me and Sammy, and whenever we're on video calls she walks into the frame!"

"I know, but I thought Sammy was your roommate!"

She shakes her head. "Oh, Joyce."

Lydia laughs, crosses her arms over her chest, and looks over at Erin. "You see what I'm dealing with here?"

They both laugh again at my expense, which is fine with me. I'm happy to be the rube if it helps them have a semicivilized conversation.

Erin is still shaking her head at me. "I mean, you're an archivist, Joyce. You interview families about their stories and are paid because you have a neurotic level of attention to detail. I assumed you'd catch on."

"To what? There weren't any clues! And besides, I was kind of distracted by my divorce."

"Look at you! Blaming it on your ex-husband!"

"I'm all for blaming anything you can on an ex-husband," Lydia says. "But that aside, Joyce is kind of dense in certain ways. For someone so smart, she misses a lot of clues along the way. At least, that's been my experience."

"Really? What else am I missing?"

Lydia shifts her weight on the arm of the couch, then waves me away as if my question isn't worth an answer. Something about that small movement causes her to lose her balance, and she flails for an instant against the cushions, before righting herself. "I've always been clumsy," she says, to Erin, without any embarrassment. "Joyce will tell you."

"That's actually not true," I say. "Lydia has always been the much more graceful of the two of us. She was the one who took ballet lessons the longest, and who took horseback-riding lessons, and who forced me to hike in the canyons whenever I came out to LA. But whatever. I'm the archivist. She's the revisionist historian."

She ignores me. "Well, I'll let you two get back to your conversation, the one you were having before I so rudely interrupted." She stands and straightens her pants, then turns to leave the room. "Nice to meet you, Erin," she says over her shoulder before shutting her bedroom door.

"WELL, THAT WAS SUPER UNPLEASANT," ERIN SAYS. "I DON'T THINK she likes me."

"Lydia doesn't really like anyone."

"Okay, but she *really* doesn't like me."

"People have always been unnerved by Lydia. The way she stares at them, takes them in, makes them feel like she disapproves of every fiber of their being. Even though that's not what she's thinking."

"I know what it is."

"It's not that."

"It is. It's always that." She shrugs, convinced that she's right. "It's because I'm fat."

"Oh my God, it's not that. I swear it's not that."

"People don't like fat people. Trust me."

I shake my head.

"You're not fat, Joyce. You have no idea the level of hate—of acceptable hate—fat people get. You can't possibly know what it's like to move through the world when you're my size. People judge."

"It has nothing to do with that."

"With what?"

"With being—"

"Say it."

"Heavy."

"Say it, Joyce. I want you to say it."

"Why?"

"Because it's just a word. It honestly would make me feel better if you'd say it. I've known you for almost two years, and I feel like that one unsaid word is a wall between us."

I squirm on the couch, then squeeze my lips shut, before finally relenting. "Fat." The word comes out like a sad sigh.

"There you go." She sits back on the couch, puts her feet up on the coffee table, and we both laugh, relieved.

"But seriously. Lydia doesn't even notice your weight. She doesn't see things that way. She doesn't see things, period."

"I don't believe that. It's like people who say they're color-blind when it comes to race. It's bullshit. People see fat people, and they don't like fat people. Even if it's unconscious."

"I agree with you. But Lydia's not like that. She's all about the underdog."

"Then why did she stare at me that way?"

"She stares at everyone that way. She's reading you. You're a jumble of shapes and colors and lines and shadows. It's how she processes things. How she relates to the world."

Erin shrugs, unsure of whether to believe me or not.

"If you knew how we were raised," I say, "it would make sense."

"How were you raised?"

I almost never talk about my childhood, especially with someone I work with and someone who is so much younger. It feels risky to voluntarily create a chasm of difference: not only with age, but with experience. I came from a sad family. Why go there? "We were exposed to lots of different kinds of people when we were kids, and that made us very compassionate about physical differences and challenges." I sound like a bad paragraph about diversity on a corporate or academic website. Title cards for this part of our family slideshow would include *Therapeutic Home Playgroups* and *Eleanor's Year at Fernald*—and the scenes and snapshots from that time play in my head: the parade of aides that came and went from our house—nurses who needed extra money, students who needed college credits. The holiday parties and picnics we went to at Fernald before, and after, Eleanor moved there: the wheelchairs, and leg braces, and metal crutches; the cacophony of nonverbal sounds, like an atonal symphony, that always played in the background; the smells—ammonia, urine, diaper, institutional cafeteria food—that were so strong Lydia and I would hold our noses until Louise gently pushed our hands away from our faces and told us to try breathing through our mouths instead. "Believe me: nothing fazes us about people's bodies," I tell Erin. "She's not judging you. That's just her affect."

"She makes me uncomfortable."

I exhale. "She makes *me* uncomfortable."

"How can you live with her?"

"It isn't easy. It's never been easy. It's always been hard for Lydia to make friends, especially female friends. She's a little—off." I remember how she used to try to connect with the girls at Hebrew school when we were younger, but eventually, she would always be dropped, left out of weekend get-togethers, bat mitzvahs, boy-girl parties. Maybe it was the dyslexia or the disabled sister who was wheeled into high holiday services once a year—and then the dead sister, the remembrance plaque Louise and Lenny bought for the Tree of Life on the wall outside the main sanctuary—that made her feel and seem so Other. Until she met Brad, she'd never really connected with anyone. "Her ex-husband was her longest relationship. That's a lot of pressure to put on a marriage."

"Actually, you're her longest relationship, right?"

"Right." A wave of guilt hits me when I realize I hadn't thought of that, the kind I always felt as a teenager when I went out with friends and left Lydia at home—upstairs, drawing, listening to music—before she left me and went to college. The kind I feel now when I'm talking about her to Erin—defending her, protecting her, excusing her—without going into too much detail.

"Has she been looking for her own apartment?"

"Definitely," I lie.

"Don't tell me: she hates everything."

"Everything. Too small. Too big. Too new. Too old. Too dark. Too bright."

"Maybe you have to give her a deadline. So she knows she has to be out by a certain date."

I laugh. "Lydia doesn't really do deadlines."

Erin stares at me. "Everyone does deadlines. That's how the world works."

"I'm not sure you understand what I'm dealing with."

"No. I guess I don't."

Someday I'll explain it to Erin—how she's always been in her own world, and how I've always been in mine, and how, even though we're living in the same apartment, sleeping in rooms a few yards away from each other, we're still in our own separate worlds. But for now, it's easier to let it go.

"We should leave soon, or we'll be late and there won't be any good tables left."

"You know what? I don't think I'm up for going out tonight," Erin says. "She kind of sucked the life out of me."

"I know. She does that." I ask her if she wants to order in instead, but she shakes her head.

"Another night." She gets up, snaps her puffy coat closed, and picks up her bag from the floor near the door, where she'd left it earlier. "I feel bad leaving you alone with her."

"She won't be here forever."

She pats me on the arm. "God, I hope not."

I HAD ASSUMED THAT LYDIA WOULD EVENTUALLY LOOK FOR A PLACE of her own, but after a few months shy of a year—it's October now—she doesn't seem to be going anywhere. Every few weeks, she does look at apartments—mostly online, occasionally walking through one or two in Cambridge or in Providence, where she's thinking of doing graduate work at RISD, where she went as an undergraduate—but nothing is good enough. She often texts me while she's in midtour with a realtor, showing me photos of whatever disappointing room she's in—kitchen, bathroom, bedroom— with the caption: *I. Can't. Even.*

I stare at the pictures, creep on some of them, looking for the flaws in design and decor that only Lydia can see. The way only I see the danger in the family photos I digitize. The fact that she's hard to please and I don't like conflict—I'd never, for instance, ask her what's wrong with the perfectly nice apartment she's texting me about or suggest that maybe she could learn to live with a tiny bit of imperfection—makes it a real possibility that she'll never leave.

At first, I think that's not such a bad thing: we're making up for all those lost years, and, all the cliches about endings and new beginnings notwithstanding, it was lonely living alone after Tom left. We take drives to the north shore and Cape Cod and Maine for the day to walk beaches, look at art, eat fried clams; we hate-watch TV shows everyone else loves while ordering takeout from our phones. There are worse things than having your sister as your long-term roommate, even if we're more Bette Davis and Joan Crawford in *What Ever Happened to Baby Jane?* than any of the *Little Women*.

But then the new people move in upstairs, and everything changes.

———

Walks in the Dark with Caroline

Last night just as darkness fell
like a blanket over Cambridge,
my friend Caroline and I
took our usual evening walk
along the river first, and then
down quiet side streets.
We love the smells
coming from someone's kitchen
or maybe a backyard gas grill:
steak, chops, fish.
Surf and turf?

Often we'll stop to breathe in the scents
of other people's dinners.
It might look creepy from the outside—
two people tiptoeing down a driveway to get a better whiff
of a stranger's cooking—
but we mean it as a compliment.

Sometimes though
what we smell
isn't to our liking.
I don't mean food-wise—
Caroline and I aren't picky eaters
and we like almost everything.
I mean the sickly-sweet artificial scents of
fabric softener or detergent
seeping out of
the dryer vents of laundry rooms.
Horrible.
An affront to us
in the otherwise perfect
night air;
a toxic slap in the face.
I try to keep Caroline
from throwing rocks at the offending house
or swearing at the people inside
to stop destroying our planet
but every now and then she gets one past me.

Then there's the gardening smells
which I hate—
spring days when landscapers have fertilized

or spread copious amounts of black-tar mulch
all along fence lines and under shrubbery
or put that disgusting fucking
fish emulsion
on front and back lawns.
I'll be so mad that I'll want to relieve myself
on their property—
How do you like this offensive smell?!—
which is fine with Caroline.
She doesn't try to stop me,
in fact, she even eggs me on.
Encourages me to do it.
So I do.
I haven't been caught
yet
but I know that someday
if I'm not careful
I will be,
and that will be the end
of my beautiful walks in the dark
with Caroline.

PART TWO

New World

The New People

Douglas, my landlord, stops by one afternoon in July to tell me that Upstairs Beth, the woman who rents the apartment above us—not Next Door Beth, who rents the first-floor unit in the back of the house, adjacent to ours—is moving out in a month. He owns all four rental units in the house but lives a few blocks away in a small, perfectly renovated ancient clapboard Colonial right off Brattle Street—prime real estate—and until that moment I realize that I've never thought about how little contact I've had with Upstairs Beth all these years. I used to blame it on the fact that she traveled constantly and was barely ever home, not to mention the fact that Tom and I were splitting up and not that into meeting people anymore, but now I have only myself to blame for not knowing more about her. *Where have I been?*

It's a bright hot summer day but Douglas wears a khaki field coat that looks like a safari jacket all year long and some kind of hat, usually one with a wide brim but sometimes a kind of woolen Irish newsboy cap. Depending on the day and his hat and my mood, he can either look extremely dashing or slightly deranged or somewhere in the middle. Today is one of those somewhere-in-the-middle days. He only stops by occasionally, maybe once a month or once every other month, so when I run into him on the lawn now after going out for an afternoon iced coffee, I wonder what he's doing here.

I also wonder if he's hot in that jacket. I would be. I'd probably be sweating and fainting with that ridiculous retro-*Esquire*-magazine getup, but as always, he's calm and cool and unflappable, deadheading the daisies in the flower bed in front of our windows, tucking the dried out flowers into his many pockets. He switched everyone a year ago to automatic electronic rent payments instead of checks, so he only comes by when there's a problem with someone's heat, or roof, or appliances, or some other kind of issue to discuss. When I see him, part of me always gets a tiny bit nervous—like I'm seeing a celebrity. *A celebrity who has the power to cancel my lease and ask me to move out in thirty days.*

"So, who are the new people?" I ask lightly, like they're going to be someone else's replacement neighbors, not mine.

"It's a couple—they're friends of a friend of mine." I assume he means his latest girlfriend—Douglas is always seeing someone new. "We were at a dinner party together, and when they said they were looking for a place starting in September, it seemed like they'd add a good energy to the house."

I'm not sure which came first—whether Upstairs Beth is moving out because Douglas wants these friends-of-a-friend-of-his to move in, or if she had already given her notice and the two facts are unrelated—and I force myself not to ask. I've always sensed that Douglas doesn't like gossiping, or anything that even remotely feels like gossiping. He doesn't even seem to want to get embroiled or involved in any domestic neighborhood drama—especially any potential disputes taking place within the house. Even though he's the landlord.

Like the time, the winter Tom and I moved in, when Next Door Beth and Ethan dumped their dead Christmas tree onto the lawn without even bothering to move it to the curb for pickup. *They opened their window and pushed it out of their apartment!* I told Douglas when he came to shovel. I'd noticed it the night before and inspected it in the dark with the flashlight of my phone, all the little pine needles peppering the snow and tiny strands of tinsel shining in the dark. Appalled, I expected him to agree that such a thing was unacceptable—*who shoves a Christmas tree out a second-floor apartment window instead of dragging it down the stairs?*—but he only grinned and shrugged and wiped his nose with his big handknitted mitten, a friendly winter garden gnome, before pulling the tree into the gutter without comment.

Today, though, knowing that the new people might have some kind of advantage over me makes me nervous in a familial, sibling-rivalry kind of way, and I can't help myself.

"I bet you'll like them better than us." I mime tears coming down my face in straight lines, like an animated emoji.

"Joyce," he says, smiling through his beard. "I don't have favorite tenants."

"Of course you have favorites. Everyone has favorites."

"If I did have favorites, they would be you and Lydia." He bows at the waist, and does a theatrical flourish with his hand, as if he's a Shakespearean actor genuflecting while holding a floridly feathered hat.

I blush at his little performance, even though I know he's lying, and even though I have no idea how old he is—with his shoulder-length gray hair that he either wears down or in a single neat Willie Nelson braid, he could be forty-two or sixty-two. The sum total of what I know about him is that he bought the condos years ago after his divorce—first the bottom, where he lived alone for a while; then the top when it came available; then later the other two—and originally planned to combine both units on the left side of the house into one big, fabulous apartment—he's an architect. But in the end, he rented out all the units and moved a few streets away. *I worried that this place would always remind me of that bleak period after my divorce*, he told me once when I'd asked him why he'd given up the possibility of a perfect duplex. *I wanted a clean slate.* I was still married then, and not yet familiar with that particular type of bleak period, but now of course I am. I'd give anything for a clean slate, too.

———

Porta-Petty

I'm having work done on my house
and the contractor put a Porta-Potty
in my driveway.
A neighbor complained
almost immediately,
saying it was an
eyesore and a blight to the neighborhood
even though it's temporary
(three weeks max, probably)
and even though she lives
behind our house and to the left
and could therefore barely see the Porta-Potty
without practically hanging out
an upstairs window or
standing on her roof.

———

When I tell Lydia about the impending change of tenants, she sucks her front teeth like there's food caught between them even though there isn't. Teeth sucking is both a nervous tic signifying nothing and a signal that something in our life is about to change dramatically and not necessarily for the better. Like the time Mr. Dennis picked us up one Wednesday afternoon for Hebrew school instead of Mrs. Dennis and the next day we found out they were getting divorced and dropping out of car pool and leaving the temple because, as I overheard Louise whisper into the kitchen phone one night, *Mr. Dennis likes men*. I'd thought that meant playing golf or going to brotherhood meetings at the temple or doing whatever other fathers did when they got together, even though Lenny didn't do any of that. Lydia's car-pool crush was Gabriel Dennis, with his tawny skin and perfectly maintained Jewfro, and at the time he was her only reason for living. The loss devastated her. Lydia's teeth sucking started then and never stopped.

In keeping with Upstairs Beth's history of extreme quietness, we barely notice when she moves out. But we do notice in the weeks and days after her departure that the New People are engaged in an extended and prolonged relocation operation. Lydia and I call it their *pre-move*.

"Don't people usually move in on one day?" I ask Lydia more than once.

"Not if you're control freaks."

The New People are what I, the resident Cantabrigian, call *Cambridge Folk*. He is slight, with big black glasses that telegraph a love of the mind; she wears her long, wavy gray hair in a loose bun and athleisure wear that makes it clear that wellness—physical and emotional—is a core value. I don't like them on sight. They seem fussy, entitled, privileged.

"Just like us," Lydia says.

Whenever they arrive for their pre-move, they park their ancient red Volvo wagon in front of the house. Their car is festooned with MIT and Harvard stickers, Obama and Elizabeth Warren stickers, and so many City of Cambridge parking permits on the front and back windshields that I wonder how it passes inspection with so little visibility. It looks like a prop car for a comedy about Harvard Square in the late 1960s.

Each time, I watch from my foyer desk as they unload the trunk and back seat, removing giant potted plants and long heavy boxes that look like window treatments, and always a red metal toolbox, and bring them inside. Sometimes Lydia comes out of her room and watches, too—both of us taking great pains to keep our surveillance activities hidden by turning off whatever lights are on and angling ourselves next to the windows instead of directly in front of them. But Lydia has never been all that nosy—she simply doesn't care that much about other people—so usually it's just me being weird, stealing glances through the blinds and thinking too long and too hard about what it all means.

By mid-September, even Lydia is curious. "What could they possibly be doing up there for a whole month before they move in?"

I suggest that maybe it's normal stuff: lining the kitchen cabinets with contact paper; hanging photos; installing shelves in the closets; giving the bathrooms an extra cleaning.

"None of that would take longer than a weekend," she says. "It doesn't make sense."

WE MEET THE NEW PEOPLE, FACE-TO-FACE, ON THEIR ACTUAL MOVING day, a warm late September morning. We're coming back from getting coffee at Simon's, which we do a few times a week together, and in the short time we're gone, a big moving truck has parked in front of the house. Three super-fit graduate students are now running up and down the ramps and up and down the lawn, and Lydia stops and stares so blatantly at them that I have to grab her by the elbow and push her out of the way toward the giant maple tree to make her stop.

"Dude," I say. "You're practically drooling."

"Sorry. It's been a while."

"I know," I say, stealing a quick glance, too. "But still."

That's when they—the New People—appear, hand-carrying their precious items. She is first up the sidewalk with an arm full of rolled yoga mats; he follows with a large and ancient-looking potted succulent and several coiled strands of ropes with pulleys attached over his shoulder. Their rubber shoes, the kind that separate the toes and look like monkey feet, squeak slightly on the sidewalk.

When they're close enough, Lydia waves. "Hi! Welcome!" she says, then leaves her hand up like something out of *Star Trek*. I pray she doesn't make a V with her fingers, like Spock. She does that sometimes, to mess with people.

They stop and smile.

"I'm Lydia, and this is my—well—this is Joyce. We live downstairs."

I step forward, about to offer my hand to shake, but theirs are too full of possessions to manage it. An awkward moment of what seems like curtseying but is really all of us balancing on the uneven cobblestone, with all the movers running around us, follows.

"I'm Stan, and this is Sonia," Stan says.

Lydia nods. "*Stahn*," she says, as if he is a former Soviet republic.

"Stan," he corrects.

Lydia sucks her teeth. "I like *Stahn* better."

I elbow her. "Yes, but his name is—"

"Stahn."

Stan looks at Sonia, who then looks at me for help. This happens when Lydia is around: no one ever knows what to make of her. I smile and make wide hostage eyes like I always do so people understand that I'm aware of their discomfort despite being powerless to do anything about it—*Yes, I know!*—and then quickly change the subject.

"So! Today's the big day!" I manufacture so much excitement that someone passing by might think I'm the one moving in.

"Finally." Stan pushes his glasses up his nose. "Sorry for all the hammering and drilling."

"We like things to be just right," Sonia says. "We're very particular."

For a split second, I think I catch Stan making hostage eyes at me, but I know it's probably wishful thinking. I want to know that other people suffer from close proximity to an annoying person, too.

"We're not particular at all," Lydia says. "We don't care about anything."

"She's kidding. Of course we care. But we're too lazy to change or fix anything." I decide not to mention her habit of moving the furniture around.

I could easily ask them a series of questions: where they've been living and how they know Douglas's friend; did they look at a lot of apartments before this one; what all the hammering was about and what all those ropes and pulleys are for. Like the archival projects I work on, I always try to get a baseline of information and facts about a family—or, in this case, a couple. But the head mover has a question, so Lydia and I take it as our cue to let them all get back to work.

"Nice to meet you, and we'll see you around, I'm sure!" Sonia says, waving as she heads toward the moving truck. I know by how fast she walks away that she's incredibly relieved to be getting away from us.

When they're both out of earshot, I glare at Lydia. "Why did you hesitate when you introduced me? Why didn't you tell them I'm your sister?"

"I don't know—I got nervous!"

"Now they think we're a couple."

"That's kind of funny."

"Is it?" The air is heavy with the smell of wet leaves, damp in the gutters of the house and matted on the edges of the street as we go inside. I watch her kick a path through them on the walkway even though she doesn't really have to. It's one of her affectations of being *back East*, which I find deeply annoying. "It's such a weird thing to lie about."

"Sometimes I get so nervous something untrue comes out of my mouth."

"Like a lie."

"It's more like a fib."

"Is there a difference?"

"To me, a lie is intentional; a fib is accidental. It happens in the moment—I blurt something out for no reason except anxiety. I can't help it."

"But you could have corrected yourself, clarified what you meant. It wouldn't have been a big deal to say, *Hey, I'm sorry if I was unclear, but Joyce is my sister, not my girlfriend.*"

"Nobody talks like that, Joyce."

"Like what?"

"Nobody says, *I'm sorry if I was unclear.*"

"Yes, they do."

"Not the people I know."

"Then the people you know don't care if they're unclear."

"I'm sure they care, but their speech isn't so formal. Or stiff."

"Whatever," I say with an attempt at nonchalance, but the word comes out all huffy and annoyed. Exactly the way I want it to.

"I know I could have corrected myself. In my own, less formal, less stiff words. But I didn't. And now it's too late. I'm locked in."

—

Mourning Our Maples
Every fall
I think about all the beautiful
maple trees
that used to line our street—
clouds of color above our heads,
yellow, orange, and red,
which marked the season.
Autumn was magical here
because of them.
I miss those trees
that were cut down three years ago
by the city
for no apparent reason.

That/Which
*That marked the season

Grammar Police
Are you kidding me?
Correcting someones grammar
who's sharing they're feelings is
not what Small World is for

More Corrections
*someone's
*their
*correcting bad grammar is exactly what Small World is for

The Noise

A week after the New People move in upstairs, the noise starts. The first night we notice it, Lydia looks up at the ceiling, then sucks her teeth. It's around dinnertime, but of course we're sitting in the living room with the TV on, switching back and forth from CNN to MSNBC, with no food in sight. We're like giant children, assuming that dinner will eventually magically appear, which it often does from one of our many delivery apps when one of us gets so hungry we almost start to cry.

"It's probably a dinner party," she says, pointing the remote at the screen. The television is muted, with the subtitles on, so we can simultaneously read the news and listen to the noise—which is a combination of heavy footsteps, talking and laughing, big thumping sounds, and a quiet period before the whole set of sounds repeats itself in the opposite order. "A housewarming. To show off all the pre-moving they did."

The second time, it's early evening again.

"Another party?" I say, knowing it can't possibly be. "Who has housewarmings in the middle of the week?"

"There's a lot of pre-moving to show off," Lydia says. She is not budging on her theory.

The third time, we know we're in trouble, but we still don't know exactly how much or what kind. Tonight, we're on the couch, staring at takeout menus on our phones—*Thai? Mexican? Vegan?*—while Lydia changes channels.

"Again with the noise," I say, looking up at the ceiling. There are the now-familiar heavy footsteps, the talking and laughing, the endless thumping sounds that come in weird, uneven waves, and then a quiet period. "It can't possibly be another party."

"I don't think it's a party."

"What else could it be?"

She stares at me. "Sex?"

"No way." I laugh nervously—*Oh God, please don't let it be sex, although maybe that would make our lives a little more interesting*—and then listen intently. Could she be right? The thumping sounds don't have any kind of sustained rhythm, no escalation and then sudden de-escalation. "It's definitely not sex."

"They could be swingers, Joyce. You have no idea what people do."

"And you do?"

"Yes. I do. I lived in California. People do lots of crazy shit. Not like here with all these uptight Puritan New Englanders."

The thumping picks up, then stops. We both stare at the ceiling, then at each other.

"A book group!" I say, like there's a prize in it if I'm right.

"Book groups meet once a month," Lydia says, "not every night. And most people don't thump with their feet when they discuss books. Even if they hate them. Which they almost always do. Which is why I'm not in a book group."

She's right. "Could it be game night? Bridge? Mah-jongg? Scrabble? Yahtzee?"

"Or some other kind of meeting?"

"You mean like Louise's meetings?"

She shrugs. "Some kind of support group?"

"Do support groups even exist anymore?"

"No idea."

"Louise's meetings didn't have so much movement." I'm thinking of the parent meetings, not the playgroups.

"Right. There was lots of talking but no moving around."

"And no laughing," I say as peals of laughter come through the ceiling and the windows, which are open a crack. I get up and close them, to muffle some of the mirth, but not all of it is blocked out. The noise—the voices and the movement—continues to seep in from places we can't see.

"Maybe it's some kind of business meeting. Maybe one of them works for a company that meets at night. Or they own a company that meets at night. What do they do?"

"I have no idea."

"Douglas didn't tell you?"

"No." He didn't.

"That guy," she says, shaking her head. "I'm telling you. He's useless."

———

Noise from the Apartment Above
Two students moved into
the apartment upstairs
and when they use
their Peloton bike
I hear every single sound
because the building is old and

everything everyone does
comes through the creaky wood floors
and thin walls:
voices/music/television/intimacy.
I hate to complain,
because people have worse problems,
but the noise from the apartment above me
has had a huge impact
on my life.
It's hard for me to relax now
when I'm home.
I bought a thick gym mat
and the people upstairs agreed to put it down
under the bike
to muffle some of the noise.
It helps a little bit,
but not much.
I can't take it and am now thinking
I'll have to move if I can't find a solution
to muffle the noise more.

When a Noise Is New
For me,
when a noise is new,
I notice it
and it bothers me more.
When I get used to the noise,
it bothers me less
and I almost stop hearing it.
But until that happens—until it fades

into a kind a background white noise—
it enrages me because I can't focus
or concentrate.
All I hear is the noise
and all I feel
is anger
about the disruption it's causing
and I become obsessed
with the person making it.
Why are they doing it?
Don't they know they're bothering people?
Do they just not care?
Some buildings have "rules"
about "quiet hours"
for home repair and parties—good luck with that—
and I doubt there's a Peloton-bike provision.
People don't like rules, as a rule.
I guess this is the price of living in the city.
I bet if I lived in the woods,
the silence would bother me too.

———

I keep wondering if I can say something to Stan and Sonia about the noise they're making. Politely inquire about the nature of the daily chaos above our heads. At night, before I fall asleep, and during the day while I'm working—or trying to, anyway, because I find the noise so unpredictable and intrusive that it's increasingly hard to concentrate—sometimes the noise is all day and into the evening; other times it's a few blocks of time during the day but quiet at night—I think about it. I imagine tiptoeing up the stairs and knocking lightly on the door, then asking either Sonia or Stan, whoever an-swers: *Hey, so what's up with the party every night?* I wouldn't say it that way. I wouldn't be flip and put them on the defensive. I'd ask super politely, with a big smile—less aggression, more benign curiosity—maybe even sugarcoat my question: *You guys sure are pop-ular! Do you have a housewarming party every day?* But then I realize: that would be weird. They're allowed to have people over. It's none of our business how bizarre we think it is that they have enough friends to never run out of people to invite. But whatever they're doing, why can't they all take their shoes off while they're doing it?

"Maybe they're repeating invitees," Lydia says.

"But why? What are they talking about every night? And what are they serving? If there's cooking going on up there, I'm not smell-ing it." I walk into the kitchen and stare at the ceiling, my nose in the air, though I'm not even sure if their kitchen is in the same place as ours. Still, I hear and smell nothing.

Again, Lydia shrugs. "No idea."

As much as I want Sonia and Stan to know that I'm registering the high level of foot traffic—that it's a big change from Upstairs Beth, who I now think walked across the apartment once a day, in slippers, the few days a month she was home, or hung from a zip line that transported her from room to room without her feet ever touching the floor—I'm afraid to start down that path. Once the rage genie is out of the bottle, there's no putting it back in.

"Yes, please don't," Lydia says when I bring it up later that week over "dinner," which consists of the two of us standing up at the counter next to the stove stabbing celery and carrot sticks and bagel chips into a plastic tub of supermarket hummus.

"Why not?"

She chews as fast as she can so she can answer. "Because let's not be Louise."

I stab the hummus again, then shove the celery stick into my mouth. She's not wrong, even though the two of us are basically being Louise right now by eating something we barely prepared while standing up. After Eleanor died and before she was fully engaged by the parents' movement for disability rights, Louise became slightly obsessed with the neighbors. Namely: with their tendency not to follow the city's rules and regulations to the letter.

"Remember how she would call the Neumanns on the phone every week when they put their trash out a few hours before they were legally allowed to?" I'm still embarrassed, decades after the fact, by the imperious tone she'd take when they answered—identifying herself on the phone as *Louise Mellishman*, as if there was another Louise who called to complain about whatever city ordinance they were breaking. "She would make them come out, bring the barrels back to their garage, and wait until it was time to bring them back out. Usually an hour later."

"And what about how she'd walk across the street when the Greens would park in front of their house, to complain that they were blocking her driveway. Which they weren't."

I cringe. The Greens were both elderly, but Louise didn't have any trouble making them move their car—in the rain, sleet, snow, or heat—when she had plenty of room to back out of our driveway. Rules were rules. They were meant to be followed. It was mortifying.

"I feel like we should apologize to everyone."

"Definitely. But they're all probably dead by now, don't you think?"

"Maybe. If they weren't, I'd write them all Sorry Notes." She stabs the hummus with a bagel chip that breaks in half.

"Can you imagine what she'd do right now about our situation?" I say.

"Actually, I can."

"So can I."

"It would involve going upstairs and knocking while the noise is taking place—a crucial piece of her investigative technique—to witness and ask the offender directly what the hell is going on, and then threaten to follow up with a call to the police when no satisfactory answer, or promise to cease and desist making the noise, is proffered."

"And then to follow through on the threat to call the police."

"Always. Louise Mellishman did not come to play."

So I keep quiet. Days go by, each one filled with a particular kind of noise, slightly different from the particular noise that came minutes or hours before. Every sound is a big, wet snowflake: unique and similar only in its ability to torture me, though I have no idea why they fluctuate so much—why some nights I think there's one or two people at the party and other times I think there could be upwards of ten.

Sometimes while I'm working, I get up and press my nose to the glass of the foyer window in front of me as discreetly as possible, which is to say, not discreetly at all—though I always shut my desk light off and dim my monitors to make myself less visible to the mystery people coming and going into the vestibule of our shared entrance, like I did during Sonia and Stan's pre-move. Usually, as I'm clicking through large files of photos and documents, organizing them as I go, I'll hear a car door slam and footsteps coming up the walk. Then there'll be a pause as they wait to be buzzed in, then the short trip up the stairs, then whatever sounds they make once they're up there.

Even with noise-cancelling headphones, I can still hear—and feel—everything: the movements, the vibrations, the energy. It eats at me in little bites. I find myself cataloguing each sound, qualitatively and quantitatively, to get a sense of the shape and patterns and possible reason for the noise: *several people coming up the stairs, early*

evening, talking and laughing; a single noisy person ringing our door-
bell by accident, then pressing the correct buzzer, then clomping up the
stairs, late morning; a group of people coming in together, laughing, and
clomping up the stairs, then laughing more, then clomping more, above
our heads in the living room, evening; individual people, one after the
other after the other, going up the stairs, staying an hour and a half, and
then leaving, throughout the day. What are they doing up there??

At the beginning, I resist the urge to take contemporaneous
notes, the kind that FBI types and journalists make in real time. But
by the second week, I have drained two pens of their ink. I write
things down in one of my extra Small World notebooks, which I
label NEW WORLD instead. A few times, I even try to capture the
noise with my phone's voice recorder, but it never works and only
makes me feel, when I listen to the unremarkable playback, like I'm
imagining things that aren't really there.

A FEW WEEKS AFTER THE NOISE STARTS, THE FOUR OF US RUN INTO
each other at our shared doorway—all crowded on the front step
with Whole Foods and Trader Joe's reusable nylon bags full of
bunches of sunflowers and wild daisies and long sleeves of flavored
seltzer cans. Sonia is carrying an amber growler of kombucha, and
Lydia has an armload of small pumpkins, even though it's still early
October. Since their arms are full, it's up to Stan and me to find
our keys.

"Looks like someone's having a Halloween party!" Sonia says.

"I love tiny pumpkins," Lydia says. "The only things I missed
about the East Coast when I lived in LA were Halloween and fall."

"They have Halloween in California." I'm always annoyed when
she makes LA sound like a foreign country. Which it kind of is, but
still.

Ignoring me, Lydia turns to Sonia. "I mean New England Halloween. *Real* Halloween. When you can wear a costume and it's not a hundred and ten degrees out." She shifts the weight of the pumpkins to her other hip. "Are you into Halloween?"

"I like the idea of it but not the reality," Sonia says.

"I don't know what that means," Lydia says.

"I don't like costume and artifice. It makes me uncomfortable. Like I'm being tricked."

"You mean, beyond the 'trick or treat' part?"

"Yes. Like I'm going to be taken advantage of. It makes me anxious."

"But you give out candy, though, right?" Giving out candy on Halloween has always been very important to Lydia.

"We prefer not to," Stan says. "Sugar kills."

Lydia sucks her teeth.

"Adults who love Halloween are so weird," I say, trying to take some of the pressure off them. "Almost as weird as adults who go to Disney World without kids."

Lydia pats my head, which she can do because she's five nine and I'm only five five. "Joyce is mad because Halloween is fun and Joyce is not fun," she says directly to Sonia again. "I mean, Joyce is great, and I love her, but she's no fun." We all laugh as she talks about me like I'm not there. "When I was at RISD, my boyfriend and I—this was during my experimental heterosexual phase of college—won the Halloween Ball prize for going as Rodin and *The Thinker*," Lydia continues. "I was Rodin, of course."

"Of course you were," I say.

"I like to control. Anyway. We stood there all night in one position while I 'carved' Brad, who was completely covered in bronze paint and makeup. It took hours to apply and even longer to remove. When we split up a few years later he still had bronze paint in some of his crevices."

"Lydia."

"We didn't even win anything, but it was fun. Halloween is fun."

It doesn't sound fun. I'm trying to picture Lydia carving Brad when Stan finally finds his keys and opens the door to the house. We all follow him into the vestibule with our bags. For a second I'm tempted to bring up the noise—to get it out in the open and put the whole thing to rest already—but before I can think of a way to say it on the fly, he and Sonia start up the stairs to their apartment. Then, right as Lydia finds her key, Stan turns around abruptly, and looks down at us from halfway up the steps.

"We should have you up for tea soon. Finally get to know each other."

"Oh. Yes," Sonia says, her face and voice flat. "Absolutely. We'd love that."

Lydia turns from the door and looks up the stairs. "Let's. But Joyce hates tea."

I glare at her. "This one!" I swat her arm to signal her to shut up.

"What?" she snaps. "It would be like if they invited us upstairs for drinks and I didn't tell them that I'm sober: they'd go to all the trouble of serving something I knew I wouldn't be able to drink. It would be rude—and weird—if I didn't say something before-hand."

Sonia shifts the weight of the growler of kombucha from one hip to the other. "Oh, wow. That's really great."

"What is?" Lydia says.

"That you're sober."

"Thanks. But I was only using that as an example."

I elbow her again, and this time she mercifully shuts up.

"Well, Joyce could have coffee," Stan says, thinking out loud. "Sonia and I don't drink it anymore—too activating for us—but maybe I could fashion a pour-over thing from a paper towel or cheesecloth or some kind of fine electronic mesh." The MIT sticker on the back of the Volvo is starting to make complete sense to me now.

"Hon, I've got an old Melitta cone and a Chemex contraption somewhere, saved from my single days." She grins, but he doesn't.

"Well, you don't have to hide it from me." He looks and sounds wounded. "If you want coffee occasionally, you should feel free to have it."

She pats his arm. "It's fine."

"Is it?"

She pats his stomach. "Babe."

He pats her hand as her hand pats his stomach. "I want you to be happy," Stan says, still patting.

"I *am* happy, hon!" She frees her hand from the patting and offers it in the form of a paw to his mouth, I assume for a quick kiss. When he licks it instead—a few times—like a tiny kitten lapping at a bowl of milk, I think I'm imagining it. Inside I'm screaming. Lydia sucks her teeth.

"Anyway!" I say. "Let us know when and we'll come up!"

"How about tomorrow?" he says.

"Tomorrow?" Lydia says.

We blink and stare at each other. "We've got that thing," I say.

"What thing?"

"That thing that we have. That we said we'd do. Tomorrow."

Lydia looks at me blankly, then turns to Stan. "Tomorrow works."

"Great," he says.

"Great," Sonia echoes, shifting her growler one more time as she heads up the stairs.

"Come up at four," he says, before following behind her.

"I CAN'T BELIEVE YOU SAID THAT THING ABOUT ME HATING TEA!" I whisper-yell, inside our apartment. We're in the kitchen, still holding our bags of groceries while Lydia arranges her pumpkins on the kitchen table. "And why did you say that tomorrow works? I was trying to get us out of it!"

"What did you want me to do?" Lydia takes a step back to admire her pumpkin arrangement like it's an art installation or a seasonal display at Whole Foods. "It was so awkward! They could tell there was no *thing. Tomorrow. That we said we'd do.*"

"And then you lied again! About being sober! You've never had a drinking problem!"

She shrugs. "It just came out!"

"I think you have a serious *lying* problem."

"I don't. I told you, I get nervous."

I drop the bags on the table, hoping to disturb her display a little. Or a lot. "But did you *see* the paw hand?"

"When he *licked* it?" she says. We both shake our heads and shiver. We are never closer than when we're mutually disgusted or horrified by someone disgusting or horrifying. "There's definitely something weird about their relationship."

"Maybe they haven't been together that long. He seems super insecure."

"Not to mention that she's older than he is. The first time I saw them I thought she might be his mother. Or his aunt." She regards her pumpkins, then picks up two of them and pretends they're kissing each other.

"You're so gross," I say.

She sticks her tongue out at me. "You're so uptight."

I take a few things out of the bags—avocados, cheese, Lydia's stupid kale chips that are always crushed when she opens the bag, various square boxes of sad frozen vegetable curries and burritos that we microwave and never finish. "They're probably upstairs right now talking about what a weird 'couple' we are."

"Who cares what they think!" Lydia snaps.

"I do. I care."

"Why do you give a shit, Joyce? Nobody cares what you do. Nobody even notices. Haven't you figured that out yet? You'd think, with the mother we had—who barely registered us—you'd get it."

"Thanks, Oprah."

"And promise me that when we go up there you won't do that thing where you ask them a million questions—that documentary-interrogation thing. I hate when you do that."

"No, I won't promise. This isn't a social call. It's a fact-finding mission. Don't you want to find out what the noise is?"

"Of course I do. But the *60 Minutes* routine stresses me out."

"Too bad."

"Then I'm not going."

"Good! I'll go alone."

"But I want to see their place, too!"

"Then stop being an asshole!" I hit her on the arm, she smacks me on mine, and suddenly we're in our old kitchen, with the turquoise Formica counters and cabinets and the giant flowered wallpaper, fighting over who ate the last Devil Dog without offering to split it. In seconds, we're back in the present, putting the food away in cabinets, on shelves, and in the refrigerator. Adults again, sort of.

"Wait till we tell them we're sisters," I say.

"Who says we have to tell them?"

"Lid."

"Let's mess with them a little," she says, laughing. "It'll be fun."

Upstairs

"S orry we're late," Lydia says the next day when Stan opens the door. "We got lost."

He blinks, tilts his head to one side like a dog trying to understand a person.

"It's one of my neighbor jokes," she says. When he tilts his head to the other side, she whispers: "Never mind."

I hand him one of Lydia's pumpkins, the one she agreed to give away, with the bad side facing me. "Thanks for having us!"

He brings the pumpkin up to his face and stares at it like it has eyes. "Hello, Mr. Pumpkinhead!" he says, his voice suddenly high-pitched and creepy.

Lydia laughs out loud. "What the fuck, my dude?"

"I'm Mr. Pumpkinhead."

"Are you, now," she says.

As we cross the threshold into the apartment, he points to our feet. "Mr. Pumpkinhead respectfully requests that you take your shoes off!" He's still doing the Mr. Pumpkinhead voice with the little pumpkin next to his face, like a ventriloquist act. "We don't wear shoes in the house!" Stan points down at his feet. "See?" He wiggles his toes inside his thick woolen socks.

I pull off my Blundtstones, and Lydia takes off her clogs. Mr. Pumpkinhead instructs us to leave our shoes on a long tray near the door, and as I walk away, I'm insanely jealous of them. *They get to stay.*

Once inside, I look around the entryway. I can't wait to see the upstairs version of our apartment—what's different and what's the same.

"I'll give you the tour." Stan puts the pumpkin down on the entry table as Sonia appears in the doorway of what I assume is their bedroom, since it's above mine. He walks past her into the room, motioning for everyone to follow, until the four of us—one real couple and one presumed couple—surround their bed.

Here, too, is the same turreted curve of three windows as downstairs and old painted radiator under a single window near the closet, the same full bath with concrete countertops and sea-glass-colored tile shower. Douglas's touches.

Then Stan leads us back into the hallway. "This is our little office," he says, as we follow him into a room with two long workstation-type desks against both walls, neither one with a chair tucked underneath, and all the shelving empty. "Still in progress," he says.

"What kind of work do you guys do?"

"Sonia's a healer," Stan says.

"*Real*ly," I say, making note of the books on one small shelf near the door—a fairly predictable "thinking healer's" mixture of Gabriel García Márquez, Ayn Rand, Bill Gates, Brené Brown, Elizabeth Gilbert, Deepak Chopra—unsurprising except for one wild card, Tom Wolfe's *The Electric Kool-Aid Acid Test*, and the many photos of Sonia mediating in nature and on distant mountaintops. It fits so far. "What about you, Stan?"

"I'm in tech. And sustainable farming."

"That's an interesting combination of things. What kind of tech and farming?"

Lydia points at me with a hitchhiker's thumb. "Here we go. Curious George over here."

"Stan helps me with my business," Sonia says, slipping an arm around his waist before leading us back out into the hallway so that I can't ask him anything else.

I can see Lydia in front of me about to enter the kitchen. "It's almost exactly the same as ours!" she says, waving. She's right. There's the familiar square island and cement countertops that we have downstairs, the delicate pendant lights overhead. More Douglas touches. But then I realize that instead of a wall between the kitchen and what is now Lydia's room, my old office, it's completely open up here. We both stare at the attached living room area, trying to get our bearings.

"Wow," Lydia says. "I wish our place was like this."

Sonia's eyes widen at the childlike envy in Lydia's voice—the unmistakable tone of wanting what you don't have. "It's loftlike up here, don't you think?" she says.

"It feels like a tree house to me," Stan says.

Now they're rubbing salt in Lydia's wound. "Why didn't Douglas tell us about this apartment?" she says to me, a flash of anger in her eyes. "We didn't even know it was available!"

I register her use of *we*. Even after ten months, it seems presumptuous. "Why would he have mentioned it? We already have a great apartment. Downstairs."

"Not like this," she says. She turns to Sonia. "So what's the deal with you and Douglas?"

"The deal?" Sonia says.

"Like, how did you get this place?"

Sonia shrugs. "He did a renovation of a friend's house, and we had dinner there all together when it was finished to celebrate. When we mentioned that we were looking for a place, he said he could help us. Douglas loves to help people." Her tone is either completely earnest or completely sarcastic, I can't tell which, and then she catches Stan's eye. They redirect us into the next room— the one right above our living room.

Instead of a normal space with a couch and a coffee table and a television, like ours, we're suddenly in a room with cubbies full of yoga mats and bolster pillows and support blocks and rolled-up Mexican blankets. Behind a half-folded rattan screen on the far side of the room are a padded treatment table and two leather swivel shrink-style armchairs facing each other: on another wall is a ballet barre.

Some kind of hybrid exercise studio/therapy office seems to have been MacGyvered out of thin air above our heads.

"*Holy shit*," Lydia whispers.

I scan the framed Buddha prints and the collection of Buddha statues on a shrine-like table: meditating Buddha, antique patina Buddha, brass Buddha. Then the table with ornamental incense on it, the Zen water fountain that turns on with a switch, more pictures of Sonia on foggy mountaintops. My eyes meet Lydia's, which are now wide open: I follow her stare to the wall behind me and see the ropes and pulleys and chains bolted to the wall that hadn't been visible from the living room.

"So *this* is what all the noise is about!" I say.

"What noise?" Sonia says.

I laugh out loud. "Seriously? *What* noise?"

Lydia walks over to the wall and, blushing, touches the hardware. Even she seems shocked. "What are you running up here?

Some kind of *yoga brothel*?" She looks from Sonia to Stan and then back to Sonia again, her mind putting all the pieces together. "Are you a *meditation dominatrix*?" She doesn't wait for an answer before stepping back and nodding. She's cool with it. Whatever "it" is. She's from California.

"This isn't a brothel," Stan says, totally tweaked. "It's a wellness studio."

"Oh, okay. Sure." She laughs again, then quickly considers the actual fitness possibilities. "Is this yoga or Pilates or barre? I've been dropping into different studios with ClassPass for my hip and ankle, but—"

"Uhm, Lid?"

"Sorry."

"You're welcome to come up anytime," Sonia says, looking Lydia up and down, assessing her. "I'm sure we can help you. I have classes and one-on-one sessions, and I do healing work as well, focusing on the emotional, the spiritual, and the physical. I'm also a medium and a medical intuitionist who can help figure out what's wrong when doctors can't. I help people find answers to questions they don't even realize they're asking."

Lydia claps her hands silently in front of her face like a toddler. "Oh my God!" She has gone from slightly horrified to all-in in under a minute. "One-stop shopping," she whispers.

"But this is *a house*, not an office building in a strip mall," I say.

"Meaning?" Sonia says.

"*Meaning* that our living room is right down there! Classes and clients, people coming and going all the time, is really noisy." I stare at Lydia for backup. "Right?"

"It doesn't bother me as much as it bothers Joyce, but we can hear it."

"Not to mention the fact," I say, saving what seems like the best for last, especially now that I'm apparently on my own, "it's kind of against the rules."

Lydia nods. "Joyce is a total rules follower."

I glare at her—*Why can't she ever take my side like a normal sister?*—and feel the sudden urge to call Douglas or the city to complain about the ordinances they're likely flouting up here. But I have a deadline coming up on the Maine project, and the last thing I need is a domestic drama like this escalating out of control. Instead, I inhale deeply, trying to find something benign to say. It comes to me on the exhale. "Despite the disruption to us downstairs, your work must be a gift to the people you help."

Sonia's face softens. She makes *namaste* with her hands. "It's incredibly gratifying. And humbling. Knowledge seekers, life seekers, love seekers—they are my purpose."

Stan beams. "You saved me." He turns to us. "I was a mess. My marriage was a prison."

"Isn't everyone's?" Lydia says, nodding and looking around at all of us, like she's waiting for an *Amen*.

"Babe. You saved yourself." Sonia holds up her paw hand, and Stan licks it like they are both cats. *I wish they would go outside and get lost like all the cats on Small World.*

It feels like we've all been pulled back from the brink of a potential social disaster, but then the kettle starts whistling like a screaming banshee, and Stan runs into the kitchen to turn the flame off, and I am awakened out of my temporary slumber of compliance.

"I'm sorry," I say, when he comes back to the yoga studio. The words come out of my mouth before I can stop them, like Lydia's fibs, except that mine are true. "But this isn't right."

"Joyce. Don't." Lydia waves frantically at me from across the room near the Peruvian blankets, then turns to Sonia. "Maybe you can put down some kind of industrial floor covering, something that will absorb the noise."

Sonia shakes her head. "Wellness studios need bare floors. You need to feel grounded, and your feet have to grip the wood." She scrunches her fingers as if they're toes.

"Come on, Lydia," I say. "Let's go."

She doesn't move. Her public betrayal feels like a gut punch. "Fine. Stay." My throat tightens and my eyes blur with tears. "But this is"—my mouth opens and for a few seconds before I find the right word nothing comes out—"bullshit."

I walk past the three of them and all the ropes and chains and pulleys, back into the hallway, to their door, where I'm reunited, finally, with my shoes, which I pick up but don't put on for the return trip downstairs. In minutes, Lydia will follow and come home, but it will feel way too late, like she's already chosen sides.

———

Navigating Filth

Did you know that Canada Geese
drop an average of a pound of feces every day?
I've noticed someone feeding them
at the historic Mount Auburn Cemetery
where I walk frequently.
There is so much goose-poop there already
it's hard to find a clean pathway
—intentionally feeding them is just making things worse.
A playground near me, in fact,
had to replace its grass
with astro-turf last spring because
the obscene amount of goose poop

had made the ground
too slippery
and had created an actual biohazard.
They may be majestic birds in the wild
but in a city setting they are unsanitary
and aggressive
and a health hazard for people and dogs.
Mourners should be able to
peacefully bury or visit their dead
without worrying about navigating filth.
Thoughts?

I Agree But . . .
I totally agree with you about the
unintended consequences of interfering with nature
and habituating wildlife,
but sometimes it is the loneliest people among us
who find solace in their connection with birds.
Pigeons and geese are annoyances to us
but for some, feeding birds in a park
or a playground
or even a cemetery
might be the only social interaction they have all day.
Who are we to deprive them of that?

Uhm
Harvard biology grad student here.
As noted above, with a slight correction,
a Canada Goose produces closer to

1.5 pounds of feces daily.
Do the math:
If you're feeding a flock of 20 or so birds
in a park or cemetery,
that's almost 30 pounds of new fecal matter
accumulating every day.
By comparison, for those interested,
a single pigeon produces 25 lbs. of feces a year.
A hundred birds will produce 1 ton of shit—literally—
before you know it.
I'm sorry for lonely people
but goose feces contain
E. Coli, Salmonella, Campylocabacter, Coccidia, and Giardia,
so if they're not careful, they'll be
lonely
and sick.

New World

Lydia and I don't discuss what happened upstairs. Instinctively we know to avoid it at all costs because it's too hot a topic to get anywhere near. At least for now. And maybe forever. She thinks I went full Louise, I think Lydia humiliated me by siding with my enemies, and now we have to figure out where to go from here. Solving the mystery of the noise has only increased my rage, because now I know that the people making it are basically criminals. Maybe not actual criminals in the true sense of the word, but definitely in the emotional sense of the word. In the sense that they are thieves, stealing my peace and quiet and making my life miserable without any remorse.

A quick Google search confirms my suspicion that the law protects people like me from neighbors like Sonia and Stan, who impinge on the right for "quiet use and enjoyment" of your home. But suing for damages is expensive, and to win I'd have to prove intentionality, and who besides Louise Mellishman would want to take that on? Not me.

They're definitely flouting rental-housing rules and neighborhood zoning laws, and yet: if I tell Douglas, I'll risk him seeing me as a tattletale. If I call the city and file a complaint using my name, it would get back to Douglas, who would then be held legally responsible for their behavior. Then he'd see me as a tattletale *and* a troublemaker and definitely ask me to leave. I don't want to be impulsive, and I don't want to escalate things to extreme Louise levels—I don't want to risk causing my own eviction—but letting them get away with what they're getting away with pushes all my buttons. Since going upstairs, the entire elevator panel of grievance and retribution in my brain is completely lit up.

At first, Lydia and I manage to go about our business—working, eating, reading, doom-scrolling, watching the news, streaming some new show that we're simultaneously bored and fascinated by— sometimes we even leave and drive out to Concord or Lexington for vegetables and apples and cider donuts—despite what we now know is going on upstairs. During the day at my desk, when people are going to and from their various wellness sessions and private lessons, and in the evening, during the classes Sonia holds above our living room, I make notes in my NEW WORLD notebook, about when and what I'm hearing. My notebook is a police log; it feels like my duty to document every infraction.

Before the noise, sitting on the couch at the end of the workday, looking at my Small World feed for poem-worthy posts, used to be like having a drink or a cigarette. All the lost cats being found, movers being recommended, information about where to get the best pet-safe ice-melt and back-saving snow shovels being shared was deeply relaxing. But those peaceful moments enjoying my neighbors' questions and complaints are gone. Instead, I picture what's going on above me. The six or seven people heading up the stairs to their apartment. All those running shoes or hiking boots or Birkenstocks or clogs being removed and hitting the tin shoe tray by their front door. Does Stan use his Mr. Pumpkinhead voice every week to make sure they follow the rules?

Now I see them traipsing down the hallway, then over into the yoga room, dropping their bags and zippered fleeces and athleisure-wear vests and jackets on either side of the doorway in neat piles before entering Sonia's sanctuary, the laughter in advance of the fun they're about to have as they choose mats or unroll the ones they've brought with them from home, slung across their chests or behind their backs like soft little bayonets. Here comes the sound of blankets being laid on top of those mats, of six or seven bodies dropping to the floor, lying down, flopping around to release the tension in their muscles, and finally, the long stretches of relative quiet while Sonia walks slowly between mats, giving her corrections, as yoga teachers do: *tighten this, raise that, relax these.* I can't hear her words from here, but the low thrum of her voice passes through the floor and right into my head. When I close my eyes, that sound is oddly calming, almost hypnotic. Though I choose not to document that one tiny benefit in my NEW WORLD notebook.

A FEW DAYS AFTER THE ABORTED TEA DATE, LYDIA COMES OUT OF HER room around dinnertime and joins me on the couch. The October sky is ink black on the other side of the windows, and cold air seeps in through the spaces between the old mullioned frames and casings. Class has started upstairs, and we both sit and listen. We're keeping vigil with the noise, as if witnessing it together will confirm its existence and maybe make it go away.

"You're not wrong," she says. "It *is* weird. All these people coming over all the time."

"I hate it. It's making me crazy." It's the first time we're talking about the situation, and I can feel little bubbles of rage moving from my chest to behind my eyeballs. "Doesn't it bother you at all?"

"It's getting to me, too, a little bit. I'm trying to figure out why."

"Because it's annoying?"

"Because it reminds me of something." I wait while she finds her words. "I think it reminds me of Louise's meetings. Of not being invited. Of not being included. It's the same feeling." She turns to me. "Don't you think?"

"I hadn't thought of that."

"Seriously?" She looks at me like I'm crazy, and I can't blame her—how strange is it that I didn't make that connection? That I didn't realize that I'm being triggered by feeling left out. But then her face softens, like she's at the top of the stairs, playing with our toys. "We're there, but we're not there."

I'm there now, too, remembering the odd relief of invisibility. How not having to be present has always made things easier: the freedom to observe without the pressure to participate. Wasn't that one of Tom's complaints, too? That I was here but not here?

"We *could* be there, though," Lydia says. "We're adults now, right?"

"Well, kind of." My lame joke falls flat, even to me.

"You know what I mean," she says. "We're not children anymore. We have choices." She leans back, looks at her fingers. There's paint under the nails and on a few of her fingertips. She stares up at the ceiling again. "We could be included if we want to be."

I don't like where this is going. "But we don't want to be. That's the point." I stare at her. "Right?"

"I don't know. Maybe."

"Maybe?"

"I mean, why not? Why can't we be?"

"Because!" Isn't it obvious?

"Because we're not joiners the way Louise was? Because we don't like people? We can change our destiny."

"Because they're making our lives miserable! Joining would condone their behavior, not get them to modify it."

"She's making *your* life miserable. Not mine. We're different. Which means we experience things differently. Our fates aren't necessarily the same."

"What does this have to do with fate?"

She picks at the paint on her nails and shrugs. "I guess it has nothing to do with it. But I've been thinking about my destiny lately. Being back here reminds me of all the things I missed out on. All the things I was left out of."

"We were both left out."

"I know. But I was left out even more. Because I was so difficult."

The scorekeeping and hairsplitting never ends. Neither of us got much attention in our family, but the fact that she got less than I did means she wins. "So?"

"So—I want to be included now. I want—community. Connection."

"Join a temple. Or a church. Or take a class."

She stares at me. "I want to take *her* class."

"Lydia."

"It's upstairs, which makes it super convenient, and she teaches everything I love. Plus there's the added bonus of the medical-medium stuff."

I glare at her.

"What's the big deal? It's just a stupid class."

"You can't be serious."

"Jesus, Joyce. It's just yoga."

"It's not just yoga, and you know that."

"I didn't even say I definitely want to take it. I'm still only thinking about it."

I can't believe we're having this discussion. Lydia is, after all, a guest in my apartment, a very long-term guest, even though she could find her own place any time. But she's family—the only family I have—and I've wanted her to feel completely at home. Shouldn't her gratitude for my extended hospitality include, at the very least, basic loyalty—which I would define right now as siding with me over the people who are making my life miserable?

"You're just jealous," she says, with a big shrug. "For some reason you don't want me to be friends with Sonia."

"Wait. Now you want to be friends? I thought this was about yoga." She wants me to react, to take the bait so that we'll get in a big fight and she can feel justified in taking the class.

"Why are you so negative? And why do things have to be so black and white with you? Sonia and I ran into each other yesterday and started talking, and she couldn't have been nicer. She was telling me how much good her class could do me. Why does it have to be such a big deal if I decide to go?"

"Why does she care so much if you come or not?"

"She thinks she can help me."

"Help you with what?"

"With some of my stuff!"

"*What* stuff?"

She pumps her hands open and closed again. "With my stiffness. My aches and pains. My back. You know. I'm getting old!"

"Bullshit," I say. "You're not old."

"I'm older than you are."

"What does that have to do with anything?"

"She knows a lot. She was a physical therapist before she even became a yoga teacher."

"How do you know?"

"It was in her bio, I think, on her website."

"She has a website?"

"Everyone has a website, Joyce."

"I don't."

"Okay, everybody except you." She shakes her head. "Anyway, she understands problems in the body."

"*What* problems?" Lydia, to my constant annoyance, has never looked better. In fact, she looks better now than she did in her twenties or thirties. Not that I saw her much during those years, but still.

She shakes her head. "No problems. Never mind."

"Then why the sudden and overwhelming urge to betray me and take her class? You know how I feel about what's going on up there!"

"Because pursuing something I want that you don't want shouldn't be seen as a betrayal. And because I'm lonely." She stares out the window. In minutes, we start to hear the buzzer and the door of the vestibule opening and closing after each person comes in and heads upstairs. "Aren't you lonely?" She looks at me but doesn't wait for an answer. "I feel like I've always been alone. And that I'll always be alone. Maybe that's my true destiny, my true fate. Maybe that's the true meaning of *Mellishman Luck*."

Flugue State

I don't want to think about Lydia's loneliness and aloneness. Or my own. How I secretly share her belief that I, too, am forever fated for a solitary postdivorce future, a life lived in the shadow of grief. Isn't that what Louise modeled for us? How Mellishman Luck must be silently endured; how a thin strand of stoicism can hold the few good pearls of your life together. Lydia and I both inherited that necklace. It's the thread that connects us. That proves we're unlucky, in life and in love. *Of course we're meant to be alone. Who can stand us?*

I also don't want to acknowledge my growing suspicion that Sonia has been put here to drive a wedge between us. A third person. An instrument of triangulation. If she can split us, she can get what she wants. But what could she want that she doesn't already have? She has the better apartment upstairs; a thriving career; a dude, such as he is. What else is there?

Maybe Small World will provide the answer, or at least a clue. I search for references to Sonia Flugue—her name on the mailbox—in the app, hoping to find where she used to teach and maybe even figure out why she's not there anymore. Did she get into trouble with a studio? With a student? Is that why she's working out of an apartment—the apartment above my head? Why else would someone hold classes from home unless they had to? There must be a story, a tiny piece of gossip that will solve the puzzle.

But there's nothing. "It's like she's hiding her classes," I say to Erin when she comes over later that evening.

"Or maybe it's an exclusivity thing. You only hear about her through word of mouth. Which makes you feel like an insider."

"We heard about her through the ceiling. Which makes us *actual* insiders."

"Speaking of *we*," she says, scanning the apartment, "where is she?"

"Who cares," I say with a shrug. I have better things to do than stalk my sister's whereabouts. "I have no idea. She left a little while ago. I'm just glad she's out."

I invited Erin over on this night, at this time, because I want her to hear the noise from tonight's class, to experience it firsthand, in real time. I want her to understand what I'm dealing with while I try to work at home. How distracting it is. How much it's affecting my ability to concentrate and focus and produce. Which could be a really dumb thing—admitting to your manager how much you're struggling to focus—but I can't help myself: I need her to know. And since I'm getting my work done despite the adversity, telling her could even work in my favor. It could make me look good.

I position her on the couch with a drink and then sit down next to her. We wait. It doesn't take long. I elbow her. "There it is. It's starting." The vestibule door opens and closes; there's clomping up the stairs, footsteps above our heads as the studio fills with students. "You hear it, right?"

Erin rolls her eyes at me. "Joyce. Chill."

In a few minutes, there are more sounds. All kinds now. I narrate them like I'm the Tour Guide of Aggravation—*Here we have the mats being unrolled onto the floor; that's the sound of bodies landing on those mats and starting to stretch; now we're coming up on some weird kind of jumping-jack warm-up thing, which makes no sense since it's yoga.* My rage surges like adrenaline.

"You see what I'm up against, right?" I say.

"I do."

"Doesn't it suck?"

"It totally sucks."

"But why is she teaching from home? Why doesn't she teach from a studio like a normal person?"

"Maybe she doesn't want to pay taxes," Erin says. "Or maybe she likes the freedom. No one to answer to; no one looking over her shoulder all day." She elbows me now. "Isn't that why you like working from home?"

"Haha. But seriously. I think it has more to do with hiding the class itself. For safety. Kind of like how I hide my Small World notebooks."

"What Small World notebooks?"

Oops! I wave her away, then tell her only about my private obsession with the app, how much I love reading all the weird, sad, funny posts, not about the poetry part. *TMI.*

"I'm on there, too," she says. "Not a lot, but once in a while. When I forget the holiday trash pickup schedule or when I want to know the best place to get a Christmas tree. Isn't everyone?"

"I guess. But I can't find anything on her on there. She's a mystery."

"Have you posted?"

I shake my head quickly. "No. I never post. And I would never post about this. She'd know my name."

"Well, she doesn't know my name." She taps her phone until it lights up, then opens the Small World app. "What should I write?"

IN THE TIME IT TAKES US TO WALK THE FEW BLOCKS TO THE BAR AT the Sheraton Commander, her post gets a few responses.

"Three," I say, checking the site as I hoist myself ungracefully up onto a stool and slip off my puffy coat. Erin slides onto the banquette. "Now there's four."

We stare at our screens, then at each other. Nothing to see here. Three people endorse her but don't know what studio she's with now; the fourth person mentions that she's teaching from home and includes a link to her website: Flugue State. I flag down the waiter to give him our drink order while we both scroll.

> "'Clients are welcomed into private classes after a screening call to ensure our goals as teacher and student are in healthy alignment.'"

"So it's like an interview," Erin says. "I'm good at those."

When our drinks arrive—my red wine, her pink wine—the first sip warms me and calms me; my circular thoughts slow and fade. I sit back and close my eyes. I could talk about this all night, but I won't. *Joyce's attention to detail was an asset for the archiving projects she worked on, but disturbing when she would become fixated on things. I observed moments when she wouldn't, or couldn't, let things go. While I can't say that Joyce was a stalker, I can't say that Joyce wasn't a stalker.*

I'M TEARING UP AT ONE OF ERIN'S BAR MITZVAH SLIDESHOWS. SHE'S showing it to me on her phone, letting me watch it as a treat because she's had a drink, and because I've had a drink, and because she wants to cheer me up and distract me from all the noisy-upstairs-people talk. I go from crying-crying when Eric Handelman thanks his parents and his grandparents, both Holocaust survivors, for all their love and guidance over his thirteen years, to crying-laughing into my big cloth napkin when he and his friends Beyoncé their way through "Put a Yarmulke on It." That's when I realize that someone is standing at our table. At first I think it's a waiter, giving me time to collect myself before interrupting. But no, it's Lydia.

She explains that she was walking by and saw us from the sidewalk, through the window: definitely a fib, since we're sitting in the back of the restaurant, which isn't anywhere near the window. Her cheeks are flushed, and she's glowing. I want so much to ask her where she was, but I refuse to give her the satisfaction of my nosiness. I know she'll use it against me someday.

"Don't worry. I won't stay long," she says, in her cropped yoga pants and running shoes, already slipping out of her orange down jacket. Her chin-length hair is up off her face in a little scrunchie.

Erin stares at me and rolls her eyes. "That's what you always say."

"True," Lydia says, then motions for her to scoot over. "There's room for me next to you—that way they don't have to bring an extra chair."

Erin moves about an inch, then goes back to her drink.

"Aren't you going to ask me where I was?"

I shrug. "No."

"I was out. I took a barre class. In Harvard Square."

"Good for you."

Within minutes, Erin has signaled for a second round. Lydia, well into my previously untouched glass of ice water, has somehow managed to change the topic of conversation. To me.

"See, it's very important for Joyce to be liked," Lydia tells Erin. She states her opinions about me the way sisters do. Like they're facts. "Not just liked, but loved. Adored."

"No, it's not," I say.

"Of course it is. It's probably the most important thing to you. You can't take it when people don't fall in love with you instantly." She turns to Erin and tilts her head, like she's sharing a secret. "Joyce is warm. Everyone loves Joyce. They always have."

Erin looks at me, pats my hand across the table. "That's because she's so loveable."

"Which is why the situation is making her so uncomfortable. She told you what happened with the new people upstairs, right?"

"A little bit."

"She doesn't like that she got mad about their secret yoga studio." Lydia stops to grab and chew a handful of crunchy, spicy chickpeas from the bowl on the table and then wipes her hands on her lap. I slide my napkin toward her, hoping she'll use it, but she ignores it, and me. "Normally, I'm the blurter. But this time our roles were totally reversed. I was shocked."

"Tell me more."

Lydia snort-laughs. "Joyce kind of lost her shit."

"I did not lose my shit."

"Joyce, did you lose your shit?" Erin says, trying to keep it light.

"I most certainly did not lose my shit."

"Yes, you did." Again she turns to Erin. "Joyce is a real rules follower."

"That's what makes her such a good archivist."

"What they're doing *is* against the rules," I say. "If not actually illegal."

"Okay, but you got really bent."

Erin looks at me. "Did you get bent, Joyce?"

"Joyce can't laugh at herself right now because she feels like I'm attacking her."

"You *are* attacking me."

Erin shakes her head at me from across the table. "How do you live with her?"

I nod, then sigh. "I don't know."

"Then why did you ask her to move in with you?"

"I didn't see it then. I think I was in denial."

"Jesus, Joyce. That's a big blind spot."

"Huge."

Lydia leans forward, interested in this fascinatingly rude person we're talking about. "Wait, what did I do?"

Erin laughs out loud. "Look. Your sister is upset because the people who moved in upstairs are really disturbing her. This is her home, remember. Where she's trying to get over the end of her marriage. Where she's living, as an adult, with you, her older sister, for the first time since childhood. Where she does her work. And they are breaking the rules with fucking yoga classes and psychic readings and a whole bunch of other services that they should be offering from a commercial space. And they are *loud*. I heard it myself tonight. So I hardly blame her for losing her shit and getting bent."

"She's a medium, actually, not a psychic," Lydia clarifies. "Isn't that cool? We should all get readings. Separately, or together. Or both!"

"See this is exactly what I'm trying to explain to you," Erin says. "You're talking about all of us getting a reading, but this is your sister's home. Her haven. And the new people upstairs—especially the person from whom you're suggesting we get a reading—are disrespecting her space and her feelings. When you make fun of her for reacting to what they're doing up there, it's hurtful. Because now *you're* disrespecting her feelings."

Lydia shrugs. "Our family doesn't understand feelings. Hasn't Joyce ever told you what it was like growing up with a disabled sister?"

Erin slowly turns around in her chair and stares at me. "No, she hasn't."

"You didn't tell me you were gay, and I didn't tell you about my childhood," I say. "Same thing."

"Not really, but whatever."

"Well, then I'll fill you in," Lydia says. "Unless Joyce and I were bleeding or dying, our problems—as bad as they might have been, or as bad as they may have seemed at the time—didn't really matter. Because our problems weren't as bad as our sister Eleanor's. My dyslexia. Joyce's stutter. Those things didn't compare."

Erin looks at me. I've never mentioned my stutter, either.

"Which was true." Lydia pauses, nodding. She's there right now, in the kitchen, or the living room, after school, holding back tears about being made fun of for her reading or having stuck up for me about my stutter. "Eleanor's problems *were* really bad. She *did* have it worse than we did. Much worse. And Louise, our mother, had infinite patience for Eleanor, who was in a wheelchair. For us: not so much."

"Eleanor died when she was ten," I say. "I was eight and Lydia was twelve, and we never really talked about it. As a family. Or even between the two of us."

Erin shakes her head. "Wow."

"To be fair, the rules thing isn't really Joyce's fault," Lydia says. "We had rules growing up. We had to have rules. And we had to follow them. Because if we didn't put our toys away after we played with them, if we didn't do everything the way Louise told us to— there was a system in place for everything we did—meals, going places in the car, having friends over, not that we had friends over very much—then Eleanor could get hurt. The rules kept Eleanor safe. And they kept us safe."

"Safe from what?"

"From Louise's temper," I say. "There was no room for carelessness, or thoughtlessness, or childishness—for being normal kids. There was too much at stake. The consequences always felt so dire."

Erin takes a small sip from her drink, then wipes her mouth with her paper cocktail napkin. "So maybe the fact that the people upstairs aren't following the rules makes Joyce feel *un*safe."

Lydia nods, then leans over across the table and pokes me on the arm. "Do you feel unsafe, Joyce?"

I start to laugh, reflexively, out of habit, the way I always do when she makes it clear she wants to end a fight with a big joke at my expense, but suddenly, unexpectedly, my eyes fill with tears.

"Oh, babe," Erin says, right before I cover my face with my hands. "I think we touched a nerve."

———

Injured Bird
We found an injured baby blue jay
under the tree out front.
Another blue jay keeps checking on it.
Did it fall out of the tree?
Is the bird checking on the fallen bird
its mother?
Does anyone know what to do for
a little bird that can't walk or fly?

Frantic Parents in the Fullness of Time

Lots of baby birds jump out of their nests
and flail on the ground
before they learn to fly
much to the dismay of their
worried-bird-parents.
Some die, but some don't,
and hard as it is not to intervene,
we need to let nature run its course.
If your baby blue jay is injured,
there's not much to do except hope
that it didn't break any little bird-bones.
It might just be disoriented
like we would be if we fell out of a tree.
Assuming a cat doesn't eat it first
it'll eventually get up and go about its business
the way all birds do
living long enough to
become frantic parents themselves
in the fullness of time.

Ambush

Late in the afternoon, a week or so after our disastrous tea date, Sonia and I run into each other in the vestibule: I'm leaving for my daily walk along the Charles to clear my head and she's coming down the stairs. I flash a fake smile, then eye the door with intent.

"Confession," Sonia says with urgency, to stop me from moving forward. "I heard you just now and ambushed you."

"Thank you?" I say.

"I'm sorry about last week. I realize that you were blindsided by the studio."

"That's an understatement." I'm not in the mood to be conciliatory today.

"We probably should have told you before we moved in."

"Or not built it."

"Well, what's done is done."

"Is it?"

"Oh, Joyce. I've come to make peace. Or amends. Or to try to, anyway. I thought I'd give you a little time to cool off, but maybe I didn't wait long enough."

"That's a nice gesture, but what really needs to happen is for you to make less noise. I work from home."

"So do I."

I roll my eyes. "Yes, I know."

"We'll try to figure something out. Maybe carpeting on the stairs to absorb that noise. Possibly something in the studio itself that would be consistent with the feel of the studio and its aesthetic— nothing too institutional or gym-like. Practicing in a home environment is the point. I'll look into it, I promise."

I'm surprised she's offering a possible solution, though with all the caveats I doubt that anything will come of it. I force myself to appear positive, so I don't react again in full-Louise mode. "That's a start. I guess."

"I'll get Stan on it. He loves to have a project. Does Lydia like having a project?"

"I'm the one who does." I sidestep the partner part of the question, and I also don't tell her that my favorite kinds of projects— Small World poetry and watching Erin's slideshows—aren't the home-improvement do-it-yourself kind. "It's a great distraction."

"From what?"

"From everything."

"I like my 'everything,'" Sonia says. "But I get it. Life is hard. No one has it easy."

"Some people do. My mother used to say that when people tried to tell her otherwise: *Some people actually do have it easy.* It was her version of the perfect fuck-you."

"I take it she did not have it easy?"

"She did not."

She waits for me to say more, but when I don't, she laughs. "Okay. But yes, I'd agree with your mother. Some people do have it easier than others."

I smile, suddenly and unexpectedly at ease in her presence.

"Why don't you invite me in for a few minutes so we can start over," she says.

For some reason, I agree. Sonia steps in and looks around. "Quite a different layout down here," she says. "Not as open, but I like it. It's cozy. Walls keep people contained. It makes us feel enveloped, and safe."

It's weird, in a good way, to be talking to someone new. I spend most of my time with Lydia these days, and I'm not sure I can call what we do "talking" at this point. After almost a year together, and until the stress of a week ago, the two of us have been like an old married couple with our nearly silent drives or walks and our brief, excruciatingly dull exchanges about groceries, the temperature of the apartment, television, and dinner. Now there's a potential friend—who also happens to be a wellness and spiritual guide— living right upstairs. Maybe Lydia is right. Why should I deprive myself of an opportunity for community and connection just because she's making my life miserable with her noisy illegal business?

"It *is* a great apartment," I say, "and I'm certainly lucky to be here. Lydia moved in after my divorce, and hers. She felt the urge to come back east after not living here for a long time." I'm trying to imply that she traveled back and forth to make our long-term relationship work, which isn't entirely untrue if you think of our family. "Everyone says you regress when you get divorced, and it's true. I certainly have."

"So did I," Sonia says, nodding. "I moved back in with my parents many years ago for a while after my marriage ended."

"My parents are gone, but I never would have moved back in with either of them anyway. They were very good people but definitely not the comforting types. Neither is Lydia, I suppose, but then neither am I. It's who we are."

"Sometimes we marry our parents."

"Lydia and I aren't married."

"Stan and I aren't married, either. I'm never doing that again. I meant that sometimes we choose partners who, in some ways, remind us of our parents. The good and the bad parts of them."

I can't help but laugh at the lie and the truth. "That would be me."

Except for my dinner dates with Erin, and one or two other old friends I stay in touch with, I'm so out of practice socially that it's taken me this long to remember to offer Sonia something to drink. But we're out of everything. "All we have is seltzer or water."

"Nothing stronger?"

I shake my head apologetically.

She raises an eyebrow. "I have something stronger." She stands up and points to the ceiling. "Let's go upstairs. Stan's out, too."

I GRAB MY PHONE AND FOLLOW HER UP TO THEIR APARTMENT, SLIP-ping my shoes off and onto the tray at their door like I did the last time. She walks barefoot into her kitchen and over to the refrigerator and takes out a cold bottle of pink wine. Not usually my thing—too sweet—but I nod enthusiastically anyway when she offers to pour me a glass. The wine quickly and completely frosts both stemless glasses, and it's so unexpectedly pretty that I'm reluctant to touch mine. I know my fingerprints will instantly ruin its perfect opacity.

It's strange to be here—like I'm doing something behind Lydia's back. Which I am. Yesterday we had that big fight about her wanting to take Sonia's class, and only a week before that we were up here for the first time. It feels like a month has passed. I grab a coaster for my wine from the island, and that's when I see it—a watercolor card partially sticking out of an envelope with Lydia's unmistakable handwriting on it: *Sonia and Stahn.* I feel my blood pressure shoot up. Without even having to read it, I know what it is: a Sorry Note. *Apologizing for* my *behavior!*

"Lydia slipped it under our door," Sonia says when she sees me register the envelope. "Stan and I—I mean, *Stahn*—were so touched. It was very sweet of her. Nobody writes paper thank-you notes anymore."

I don't know if I'm more shocked that she wrote them a combination thank-you/Sorry Note, or that Sonia has so good-naturedly accepted Lydia's preferred pronunciation of Stan's name—but Lydia has that way with people sometimes: getting them to go along with her reality instead of forcing herself to accept theirs. I can tell from the way Sonia stands there, looking at the note, that she's waiting for me to say something conciliatory about that visit, which is completely galling, but I decide to do it anyway. She's accepting Lydia in all of her weirdness. That's something. A meaningful concession. The last thing I want is for them to complain to Douglas that I'm a problem, or even a buzzkill to the newly reconfigured energy of the house that he was hoping for. The whole thing could completely backfire and set up another possible scenario: where I'd be the one who would have to leave.

"I'm sorry about last week," I say. "I can be super rigid."

"I understand." She picks up our wineglasses, and I follow her over to the couch.

"Sometimes I want to shake myself and tell myself to chill out, but I can't."

Sonia leans back and tucks her legs up underneath her, crisscross applesauce. "You started to say something downstairs about your projects providing a great distraction. A distraction from what? Work? Your relationship?"

"Sure. Both," I say. "But don't most people feel that way? Everything comes at a cost."

"It's up to us to decide what is too high a price to pay."

Sitting here in their much-envied open-plan living room that Lydia and I don't have downstairs, unprotected and uncontained by walls, I feel vulnerable, but in a good way. The sun is golden behind the trees in the mullioned windows, and the amber glow of the light—and the wine—make me realize how long it's been since I talked about personal things. Something I didn't even know I was craving until this minute. *I am lonely*, I suddenly realize. *I'm so lonely.* What I couldn't admit last night to Lydia when she asked me, I'm now able to admit to myself.

"Sometimes I wonder what my true purpose is," I whisper.

"Isn't everyone's true purpose to love and be loved? To be in service to and to take care of those who need us most?"

"I suppose."

"You suppose?" Sonia laughs. "I assume Lydia is an important piece of your purpose."

"She definitely is."

"How long have you two been together?"

I look out the window, then blow air out of my cheeks like a cartoon liar. "We've been living together for almost a year, but we've known each other longer." Much longer. "What about you and Stan?"

"Together for a while; cohabitating for the first time here."

"So: not long!"

"Long enough!"

I feel like we're both speaking in riddles. I resist the urge to reveal the truth about our "relationship"—Lydia would kill me if I did so without her knowledge. She'd consider confiding in someone she wants to be friends with but who I said she couldn't be friends with to be the ultimate betrayal, so I play along. Which isn't that hard because Lydia is indeed an important piece of my purpose. On some level I've known that she moved back for a reason, even if neither of us knows exactly what that reason is yet. She's put herself, and me, in the position of finally revisiting our childhood—the loss of Eleanor, of Lenny, of Louise—with adult eyes, which we've both spent most of our lives avoiding. Why else would she have come east? Why else would I have invited her to move in with me? What else could possibly explain her staying longer than either of us anticipated even though she could, at any time, live on her own?

"It's just that Lydia is a lot of work."

"Too much work?"

"Maybe. I wonder sometimes."

"I would wonder, too. I sensed that there's a great chasm. Deep similarity and connection in some ways; extremely opposite in other ways."

"Boy, you're good," I say. She's perfectly described our relationship as sisters without even knowing it.

"It's what I do: I read people. I don't know how to explain it other than to say that I have a sense about these things. Remember I told you that I'm a medium."

"I thought that meant you see dead people."

Sonia laughs. "I hear them, sort of. Which is a whole other thing." She shifts on the couch. "But I also see living people. By which I mean, I *really* see them."

She's staring at me in the late-afternoon light. I'm embarrassed to admit that I'm enjoying the weird laser beam of her attention; growing up feeling ignored and unseen and perpetually misunderstood makes me vulnerable to this kind of person—the kind of person who senses what I want and need and gives it to me. It hasn't always turned out well. I wonder if this time will be different. I hope this time will be different.

"Well, it's no surprise then that you have a devoted clientele up here."

"I wish you were part of that clientele. I think yoga up here would help you a lot. Especially with some of your issues."

I straighten, take a sip from my glass. "What issues?"

"Your stutter."

"My stutter?" I shrug. "I don't have a stutter."

"When you were both here that day, I thought I picked it up. Granted, you were extremely stressed. But I know what I heard. A hesitation more than a stutter, to be clear, but still."

I fold my arms across my chest and look out the window, saying nothing. The trees are electric with color. I wish they could stay that way forever.

"Oh no," Sonia says. "Look what I've done. I was trying to be helpful, but I've made you incredibly nervous. Which will only make the stutter worse, am I right?"

I smile again, trying to be nonchalant, but my face is hot with childhood shame, and inside I'm dying. I'm wondering what gave me away. Almost no one knows about my stutter—it's practically nonexistent now; I have so thoroughly overcome it that sometimes even I forget about it, the misery of when I could barely make it through a sentence without getting stuck, usually on *S*s and *M*s. Regular school and Hebrew school, all those awful girls and nasty boys tormenting me for years with *Here's J-J-J-Joooooooooyce!* Like Ed McMahon introducing Johnny Carson.

"Look, I don't have a stutter." I'm suddenly flushed with a sense of danger. Why did I agree to come upstairs and let my guard down with someone I barely know and instantly disliked? Even though I didn't say too much, I've said more than I should have. Regret completely overwhelms me, and I stand up. "I should go."

Sonia stands too and squeezes my hand. "Don't worry. Your secrets are safe with me."

I'm sobering up quickly now. "Nothing I said is a secret." It sounds defensive, like a lie. "Lydia knows that she's difficult; she knows that living together is a challenge. For both of us."

"Of course she does," Sonia says.

"Listen. Sonia."

"Yes, Joyce."

I look at the yoga studio through the glass doors, dark now with no class in session, and think of several things I don't want to say. I put my glass down on the island. "If you could figure out some new flooring in there, that would be great."

She seems surprised by my change in tone, by the sudden return to that pesky unpleasant topic—*the noise*—as I walk past her through the kitchen and toward the door in my stockinged feet. Leaving this sister-apartment for the one downstairs, where my sister is probably waiting for me by now, I think I hear her say behind me:

What a namastake.

LYDIA IS ALREADY HOME. SHE'S PICKED UP DINNER—PAD THAI AND some kind of soup—and set the table. I see the containers stacked on the counter from the foyer, where I drop my phone on my desk. The shoes I've carried downstairs I leave near the front door on my way to the kitchen.

"Where were you?" she says. "I'm starving. I got home almost an hour ago, but I didn't know where you were." She stares at me. "Why weren't you wearing a coat? Or shoes? It's freezing out."

"I was upstairs."

"Up*stairs*?"

I feel like a criminal. I tell her how Sonia ambushed me in the hallway; how she wanted to make the peace; how we came in here briefly to talk. "When she realized we didn't have any wine, we went upstairs."

"And?"

"And we had a nice talk. I guess. I'm not really sure."

"What does that mean?"

"It got kind of weird, so I left."

"Weird how?"

"She—she said something about my stutter. I don't know how she picked it up. I haven't stuttered in a long time." I sit down at the table. "Have you heard me stutter the whole time you've been back?"

"No."

"So why would she say that?"

"I have no idea."

"You didn't say anything to her about it, did you?"

She stares at me, pissed. "Why would I do that? We've only talked one time since the incident upstairs."

"I don't see how she could know about it."

"Well, I hate to say it, but it proves that she is what she says she is: some kind of medical intuitive. A health medium." When I don't agree with her benign interpretation, she moves on. "So then what happened?"

"That's when I left."

"On a bad note?"

"On an uncomfortable note."

She shifts her weight. "Like there's an uncomfortable note, and there's a Louise Mellishman note. Which is it?"

"Somewhere in the middle."

"Great. Another scene."

"I'm sorry. I tried. I didn't expect her to bring up something so personal and sensitive. I barely know her, and suddenly she's talking about my stutter! Which is totally gone!"

"Mostly gone."

I stare at her with my mouth open. "What does *that* mean?"

"What's the big fucking deal, Joyce? Sometimes you hesitate between words. Or you open your mouth and nothing comes out for a few seconds, like you did just now. There's no shame in it."

"Easy for a nonstutterer to say," I manage to say without hesitating or stuttering. Which feels like a miracle, since all this talk about my stutter has made me completely self-conscious and tense about talking for the first time in years.

"But back to you going up there," she says, shaking her head in confusion. "I thought you hate them. That they're the enemy. You made it sound like my not leaving immediately with you, and staying behind to smooth things over, and telling you that I want to take her class, were Shakespearean-level betrayals."

"I don't hate them. It's that I don't trust them. It's the sneakiness of what they did: moving in and building a yoga studio above our heads when it's so clearly illegal. Then her bullshit about putting down some rugs and maybe some kind of flooring—*if* it doesn't interfere with the studio's *aesthetic*. That's never going to happen."

Lydia puts two water glasses on the table.

"What do *you* think?" I say. "Do *you* trust them?"

"It's not up to me. How we deal with the situation is up to you. This is your place, and I'm just a guest. I don't really have any rights. Which isn't fair."

"Of course you have rights. We're adults now. We both have a say."

"It doesn't feel that way. You were super rude that day. It was totally embarrassing. Louise Mellishman embarrassing. I didn't really have any say in that."

"Yes, you did. You apologized for my behavior. I saw your Sorry Note in their kitchen."

For a second, she looks caught. "I had no idea you were going to go rushing up there the minute I'm not home after basically calling me a traitor for expressing interest in her class. I didn't want this to turn into a big thing. I want to live in peace, without stress."

"So do I, Lydia. But what they're doing is wrong. And I'm sure it's illegal. I'm not going to get a lawyer or do anything, but I know I'm right. No one on this street—in this neighborhood—has a home business like this. With people coming and going, individually and in groups. It's absurd! Am I supposed to pretend like it's all fine and normal when there are ropes and chains hanging from the wall?"

"I don't know!" she says, throwing her arms out and shrugging with comical exaggeration. "Maybe for once you could keep your disapproval to yourself. I mean, we live here. And now it's awkward."

"That's not my fault! I didn't build a fucking yoga studio in our living room. I would just like some normal upstairs neighbors, that's all."

"No one's normal, Joyce."

I turn toward the window by the long oak table we eat at. Dusk has mostly fallen, but there is still a glimmer of light coming through the branches, making the yellow and red leaves on the trees almost glitter and glow before the sun slinks away for good.

"At least you'll be happy to know that I kept your little charade going. I didn't let on that we're sisters."

She shrugs. "Gee, thanks."

"Not that I even understand why we're doing that."

"It just happened. I didn't plan to mislead them, but once I said it, and once I didn't correct it upstairs, it was too late."

"It's never too late to correct a lie."

"Then feel free to fix it. I thought it would be fun to have a private joke, just the two of us."

I feel my heart soften a tiny bit. The idea that she wanted to share a secret with me makes me hate myself for being so strident. *I have to start being less of an asshole.*

"You're right," I say. "I'll stop. Let's eat."

"I'm not hungry anymore." She gets up, puts her unused plate and glass back in the cabinet, then walks to her bedroom. I hear her door close. Alone in the kitchen, with the little light on over the stove, I make myself a plate of noodles, then put the rest of the uneaten food in the refrigerator. I'll eat at my desk, in the foyer, and watch people walk by on their way home from work; then I'll go through a few hundred photos on the Maine project and go to bed early.

I won't know it then, but later, when I'm asleep, Lydia will paint a Sorry Note for me, then tiptoe across the apartment to slip it under my bedroom door. *I'm sorry I got mad and ruined dinner*, it will say. Like the one upstairs, and like all the other Sorry Notes she wrote when she was little, it will ask to be forgiven for something that's not her fault.

———

Inconsiderate Noise
I've lived on what used to be
a quiet sreet in
West Cambridge.
I say "used to" because
recently
two families with young children
moved in
and destroyed the peacefulness of the street.
I agree that kids have a right to be kids

to make noise when they play
but screaming and shouting constantly
at the top of their lungs
and running up and down
other people's driveways
and lawns
is inconsiderate.
I blame the parents mostly
who let their children
treat the street like a school playground
where it's recess all day every day.

An Underlying Feeling
I hope you won't be offended if I say,
with compassion and kindness,
that you may be deeply unhappy.
If you search for the cause of this unhappiness,
the self-knowledge you acquire
will likely be
transformative.
You may find
that the noise will cease to bother you
and that it will
instead
fill you with joy.

Camp Fantastic

Louise hires students from area colleges to help with Eleanor—young people studying to become social workers and physical therapists, teachers and nurses. They come over in shifts, on mornings and afternoons, nights and weekends, to bathe and feed and change her. Louise is always there—she almost never goes out—so she, too, lifts and wipes and washes and brushes Eleanor. Sometimes we come home to Eleanor out of her chair or special scooter chair and on the living room carpet, doing a new kind of therapy—"patterning"—where Louise and an aide are moving her body slowly to stretch her tight ligaments and tendons, in the hope that, eventually, it will be able to mimic those movements on its own. Muscle memory. It doesn't seem to work—nothing does, really, but Louise never gives up. There is always a new therapy, a new drug, a new theory being tested in other countries that she hears about. Help is always right around the corner.

"It's so unfair that Eleanor has to live in a world that wasn't built for her and that doesn't want her," she often says.

"Maybe we should stop trying to force a square peg into a round hole," Lenny will say.

"Meaning what? That we should put her in an institution?" Louise's voice rises, and her eyes widen in horror. "I'm not sending her away."

"But that might be the best thing for her. And for everyone."

"You want to warehouse Eleanor because it would make things *easier* for everyone?"

"Louise. We have two other children. They need our attention, too. What about Joyce's stutter? And Lydia's reading. What about them?"

The mention of the fact that you and Lydia exist—that you two also have needs—never fails to overwhelm her and send her into a panic that, once ignited, cannot be calmed by Lenny, who's lit the match. It isn't until you and Lydia are weeping and crying and the three of you are following her through the house, begging for forgiveness and pledging your undying support to the cause of keeping Eleanor at home no matter what, that she finally calms down.

WHEN YOU'RE SIX, LOUISE ANNOUNCES ONE EARLY JUNE EVENING over dinner that she's found a special summer camp for Eleanor.

"It's in the Berkshires. And it's only for handicapped children." She puts her napkin on her lap and looks around the table, gauging your collective level of enthusiasm. So far, it's not yet matching hers. She tries again. "It's called Camp Fantastic, and it looks *amazing* in the brochure. I mean, can you *imagine*?" Her eyes blink back tears. "A place for kids like Eleanor? Created and built *only* for them?"

Lenny puts his fork down. "Louise. Eleanor's in a chair. She needs constant care. She's going to sleep in a bunk and do arts and crafts?"

Louise pulls open the metal tab on a can of Fresca, pours it slowly into a tall glass filled with ice, then waits for the fizzing to stop before adding more. "It's a special camp, Lenny. All the kids need that level of care."

"I don't know. It doesn't sound safe."

"Trust me, it's safe. I've done my research."

"So you're saying we'd put her on a bus and pick her up in two weeks like it's nothing?" When she shakes her head no, Lenny pushes himself away from the table, crosses his legs, and wipes his mouth with a paper napkin, the kind Louise buys in bulk for her weekly meetings. "Then what are you suggesting? Tell me. I'm all ears."

"I'll go with her."

He nods. "I see. This is already a done deal. Which means, as usual, this 'discussion' is a charade."

Louise sips her Fresca and ignores her food. If we were on the porch or at the picnic table in the backyard, she'd be reaching into her purse for a cigarette right now. But she never smokes inside, so all she can do is sigh and endure Lenny's questions.

"I know the camp director. Through Fernald. His name is Alan Bloom. He started it a few years ago for his son who died recently. Alan's philosophy is to treat the handicapped campers like people, not problems."

Lenny nods. "Of course I want Eleanor to be treated like a person, not a problem. But how is that possible at a rustic camp in the middle of nowhere?"

"I convinced Alan to let me come for the week. I promised that they'd barely know I was there—that I wouldn't interfere in the activities and how they do things. I told him I'd get the office organized in return for the favor."

"And he believed you?"

Lenny wants to laugh—so do you and Lydia—but Louise doesn't have time for jokes. She's too excited. "They hire young camp counselors—college students from all over the country. There's music and art and nature and swimming—everything you could ever want for Eleanor to experience."

"She experiences a lot of that here," Lenny says.

"I mean away from here, with new people."

"When does it start?" Lydia asks.

"Beginning of July."

"So in a few weeks," Lenny says. When Louise nods, he points across the table. "What about Lydia and Joyce? Will they be going to camp, too?"

Louise looks at you, and for a moment you sense a hint of guilt, as if she'd completely forgotten about that detail—that you two need to be occupied during summer vacation, too. But the shadow of regret passes quickly, almost instantly, across her face. "They'll be fine here."

"For a whole week?"

"They don't need me the way Eleanor does."

Don't you, though? Sure, you can be occupied with puzzles and games, crayons and coloring books, with beads and pot-holder-weaving projects and pastels and watercolors. You can spend a few mornings in Lenny's waiting room, and an afternoon or two at friends' houses. But who will feed you? Who will help you with baths and shampoos? Who will put you to bed and ask you if you have any problems?

And so the conversation goes back and forth between them, right in front of you and Lydia, like you're not there, which is nothing new. At some point the two of you slip away from the table, put your plates quietly in the sink, then slide open the bottom freezer door. You remove two ice cream sandwiches from an already open box and walk quickly through the dining room to the porch and then out to the backyard, where you unwrap them in the growing dusk.

Lydia stares at her ice cream sandwich before she eats it like she's never seen one before.

Later that night, when Louise puts you to bed and asks Lydia if she has any problems, she says she does.

"How do they get the ice cream inside the ice cream sandwich?"

Louise thinks for a few seconds, then says something about an automated machine and a conveyor belt full of bottom cookies, and a nozzle that squeezes vanilla ice cream onto them before another machine puts the other cookie on top as it continues down the belt to be wrapped in paper and boxed up and frozen. You have no idea if that's really how ice cream sandwiches are made, or if she invented the whole thing so that she could give Lydia an answer, but it sounds good.

Then she comes and sits down on your bed. "What about you, Joyce? Do you have any problems?"

Your mind is still full of the magical conveyor belt, covered with ice cream sandwiches, ready to be assembled and wrapped and boxed for everyone's freezers. "Who will take care of us when you're gone?"

The question, so similar to the one that is asked of her at meetings by tortured parents, you realize years later, spooks her. She sits up, looks at you and Lydia, and smiles. Something—a solution—has occurred to her.

IT'S A HOT, SUNNY JULY MORNING WHEN YOU LEAVE FOR THE BERK-shires in Western Massachusetts. It takes a while to get Eleanor ready and to get the car packed for the trip—she has never gone away like this before, and neither have you, so you're all nervous about how it's going to go. Because she loves the Captain and Tennille, you put her favorite album on so she can listen to "Love Will Keep Us Together" while you wait. When the song starts and she flaps her hands, you kneel in front of her chair and lightly tap your palms on her bony little knees. The only thing she loves more than music is Patty Cake, so you play your own version of it with her: you clap your hands, then pretend to clap her hands, then take both her hands in yours for the rolling part. *Patty cake, patty cake, baker's man. Bake me a cake as fast as you can. Roll it, and pat it, and mark it with an* E. *Then put it in the oven for Eleanor and me!*

Before the game is over, Lydia comes into the living room with a small stuffed elephant. She crouches down, too, then touches the elephant's trunk to Eleanor's nose. "Nose kiss!" she says. When you both take turns touching your nose to her nose, she makes her happy sounds and pats both of you on the hair. Then it's time to go.

Once you're on the road, Louise continually checks the rearview mirror. Eleanor is supported with extra pillows from all of your beds and extra straps from the garage for the long drive—your own makeshift version of an adaptive vehicle. Somehow, miraculously, the almost-three-hour drive goes off without a hitch.

"This is us!" Louise says when she pulls off a paved road onto a dirt road after you pass a hand-painted wood sign: CAMP FANTASTIC. She stops at the "reception area," which is a dirt path in front of a small wooden shack with another hand-painted sign that says OFFICE stuck in a patch of dried grass. Louise puts the car in park, opens her door, and tells you to do the same—to get some air into the back seat for Eleanor by catching whatever tiny breeze might be out there.

"I'll be right back," she says to the three of you—and then, to

Eleanor directly: "They'll take good care of you." And then she's gone, up the rickety wooden stairs and straight through the door of the office shack without even bothering to knock. Louise always moves through the world like it's expecting her.

The heat creeps into the car fast. It feels like you're parked on top of a furnace or a firepit. You can smell the dirt and the grass, and the sound of a soon-to-be hot summer day buzzes in the trees. In Louise's brief absence, and without music or some other kind of entertainment or distraction, there's an awkward silence—you and Lydia look at each other, and then at Eleanor. You check her straps and adjust her pillows, use a paper map from the glove compartment to fan her face. Then you look out the windows again.

Neither of you knows what you're supposed to do—you're almost never alone with Eleanor. Louise doesn't ever outsource any of her caretaking to you two, and without her constant narration of the world around Eleanor, the sudden silence makes everything seem unknowable. *Does she understand you? Like you? Love you?* You think she does. You're sure she does. But you often get shy and tongue-tied, and you think Lydia does, too.

Lydia stares out her window and then at you. Buses are pulling up behind you and young counselors are pouring out of the office in T-shirts and shorts, helping get wheelchairs, and then campers, off each bus. It's nothing like the few times you've visited Fernald—no institutional protocols, no brick buildings and college campus–like grounds, no nurses in white dresses and caps and shoes, no doctors in white coats and skinny ties. This is a free-for-all. Chaos. Except that everyone is laughing and yelling and having fun.

You look at Lydia. "When is she coming back?"

"Soon." She's lying. You both know she'll be in there talking to everyone, buttering up the staff so that they'll treat Eleanor well. But because of the heat, it isn't long before Louise comes down the wooden stairs with two young men, teenagers or college students— one black, one white—on either side of her. She opens the back door of the car, and you and Lydia slide out while Louise tells the counselors how to undo the straps that have been keeping Eleanor immobilized in the back seat since you left home.

She hands you her keys. "Open the trunk for me so they can get her chair out, okay?" she says.

The keys are cold in your hand as you walk around to the back of the car, careful not to get your new white Keds dusty on the dirt path. Lydia comes, too. You try to pull the chair out yourselves, and when you can't, one of the counselors takes over, lifting it onto the ground and opening it up in one swift, smooth motion. Even if they aren't trained professionals like at Fernald, or experienced like the aides that help out at home, they've opened enough wheelchairs this summer to know what they're doing. In seconds, Eleanor is out of the car and in her chair, with Louise right behind her, pushing her up the path. The counselors follow.

"Let's go see your bunk!" Louise says, leaning over the back of the chair so Eleanor can hear her.

You and Lydia stand next to the car, watching them all get smaller and smaller.

"Should we wait here? Is she coming back for us?"

You shrug, then look around at the trees and the sky. As usual, you have no idea what to do with yourselves.

At first, you think you should get your stuff out of the car— maybe you'll be going to a bunk, too?—or had you overheard correctly something about a nearby motel? Since you're not sure, you assume it's safer to wait for instructions. Not wanting to do the wrong thing, and, having no idea what the right thing is, you each get something out of the bag in the back seat to do while you wait: you get a Nancy Drew book, and Lydia takes a pad of paper and a small box of thick crayons. Then you sit on the steps to the office. The wood is rough on the backs of your bare legs, and Lydia tells you not to fidget. "You'll get a splinter." Every time someone comes up or down the stairs, you move your knees, inching closer to the railing, but no matter how small you try to make yourselves, you still feel like you're in the way.

Someone—an adult—finally sees you.

"Are you here for camp?"

It's a man, big-haired, bearded, barrel-chested, in a tie-dyed MIT T-shirt and leather sandals. He's older than the counselors, like someone's uncle—like Uncle Murray if Uncle Murray had let himself go and become a hippie instead of an orthodontist.

Your tongue gets heavy, and you freeze.

"My sister is here for camp," Lydia says.

He smiles at you. "Welcome to camp, sister!"

"Our other s-s-sister," you say.

His eyes register your stutter. "Who's your sister?"

"Eleanor."

"And you are?"

"Joyce."

He turns to Lydia, and she tells him her name.

"Well. You must be the Mellishman Sisters. Your mother has told me a lot about you."

No one has ever called you that before, has ever seen you as a cohesive unit, connected, related.

"Really?" Lydia says.

"You sound surprised. You don't think she talks about you behind your back when you're not around?"

You both shrug shyly, until he laughs. "That was a joke." He sits down on the steps next to you. "Your mother has said very nice things about you."

"Like what?" Lydia says. You stare at her, shocked that she asked but secretly glad she did. You want to know, too.

"Well, one of you likes to draw and paint, and one of you likes to read," he says, looking at both of you as if to divine the answer. "My guess is that you're the artist, Lydia."

Her eyes get wide, and she blushes. There's a thrill at feeling seen, which you can't help but instantly envy. "How did you know?"

"I'd like to say that I'm gifted, but you're holding the art supplies, while your sister here is holding a book, which means she's the reader." He turns to you. "What do you like to read, Joyce?"

You shrug, then go quiet.

"You can talk. I'm not going to bite you."

His words sting, and your eyes instantly fill with tears the way they always do when someone makes fun of you. If that's what he's doing, which isn't even what it feels like.

Lydia sits forward, on the edge of the step. "Joyce stutters."

"Yes, I know. And who cares?" He smiles, then puts his big hand on your shoulder. "I mean, look at where you are. Everyone here has something." He points at the buses still disgorging campers and wheelchairs. "Some kids can't walk; some can't see or hear. You can be yourself here. No one cares."

Satisfied with his answer, Lydia nods and leans back. "So what's your name?"

"I'm Alan. And this is my camp."

WHEN LOUISE RETURNS, ALREADY TAN IN HER MADRAS PLAID SHORTS and sleeveless button-down blouse, she finds you on the office steps with Alan.

"You've got some cool cats here, Louise," he says.

"Those are my girls!" Her voice lilts with pride in a way it never does at home, one that makes it sound like you're close and have fun together all the time—like you're actually the Mellishman Sisters, as Alan called you—which of course you aren't and you don't. Lydia looks at you. It's years before her teeth-sucking starts, but this would have been the perfect moment for it.

Alan asks about Eleanor, about whether she's settled in her bunk, and if the accommodations are to her liking. "And yours," he says, winking at you. He already knows who's boss.

"It's perfect." Louise's eyes light up as she takes in all the activity going on around you. "It's like real camp."

"It *is* real camp."

She sits down next to Alan, and sighs, her whole body seeming to relax in that one released breath. "All I've ever wanted is for Eleanor to be included. I can't tell you what it feels like to know that she will be here." She turns to Alan. "I think this is the first time I've ever felt this."

"Felt what?"

"Relief. Like she's normal."

Alan's eyes flicker. "I don't love that word, but if you mean that here, she's the norm, then you're absolutely right."

"That's exactly what I meant. I'm overwhelmed, and a little tired from the drive." She exhales again and looks around—beyond the dirt path and the buses, to the woods, and then up to the sky. Her eyes fill with tears. "It's amazing what you've built here. It's a kind of utopia."

Someone is playing a guitar and laughter wafts through the trees, tall evergreens, that surround you. You don't know what *utopia* means, but you do know that you feel a little calmer, too.

"Well, clearly you haven't seen the bathrooms yet," Alan says, "but if you can overlook the horror, I think you'll see that this place will be a great experience for Eleanor."

There's a pause in the conversation—Alan and Louise look at each other and then at you and Lydia, like they're trying to figure out what to do with you, but Louise is not someone to leave things like that up to chance. She's used to planning out the day to the minute.

"Time to head to the motel." She motions at the two of you to stand up.

You and Lydia hop down the stairs into the dirt. Maybe there's a pool there and a Howard Johnson's nearby with grilled cheese sandwiches and orange soda.

"You trust us with Eleanor?" Alan says, standing now, too.

"I guess I have to."

"I guess you do." He pats her on the back. "We'll take good care of her."

"You better."

He laughs. "Believe me. The last thing I want is for Louise Mellishman to come after me. But don't forget: My son was here, too, once. Briefly."

She lowers her eyes. "I know."

"Look after your mother," he says, putting one hand on your head and the other on Lydia's head, then squeezing lightly like they're two cantaloupes, as he walks you to the car. You climb in the back seat and watch Louise and Alan talk for another minute or two before they say goodbye.

THE THING IS: LOUISE DOESN'T NEED YOU TO LOOK AFTER HER. BACK in the car, pulling away from Alan and the camp office, the tires of your paneled station wagon crunching and popping on the dirt road, you head to the motel, a few miles away. Rimmed with tall pines, it's an L of single-story units, all with red doors and shutters and an air-conditioner sticking out of each window. Louise parks in front of the office, goes to check in, and comes out with a key on a long brown plastic diamond-shaped holder: *11*. She moves the car in front of your unit, opens the trunk, and you and Lydia get your stuff out and wait for her to unlock the door and let you into the room.

Inside, it's musty and hot—two double beds with brown bedspreads that have a kind of sheen to them, brown wall-to-wall carpeting, brown paneling, and a thick phone book on the bureau that has a big brown television on top of it. Louise puts her suitcase on the bed closest to the bathroom, and you put yours on the other bed, which you'll share. It occurs to you as you watch Louise put her shorts and skirts and blouses into the drawers that you've never stayed in a hotel room together. That you've never been alone with Louise without Eleanor until now. Then she tells you both to change into bathing suits so you can all go to the pool.

You and Lydia splash alone in the water—it's oddly empty on this Thursday before July Fourth weekend—while Louise sits on a lounge chair, legs oiled, sun hat and big sunglasses on, with a thick paperback bestseller on her lap that she never opens. On top of the book is the newspaper opened to the crossword puzzle, and a blue ballpoint pen dangles between her fingers like a cigarette. Instead of reading or filling in the little squares—in ink—and checking off each clue as she completes it—she stares off into space. You follow her eyes to see what she's looking at, but there is nothing there, really, only a rusted chain-link fence, and the pines, and the highway beyond it.

Lydia climbs out of the pool first and spreads a towel on the hot cement next to Louise's chair. She lies down on it, on her stomach, and watches her wet gray footprints start to fade and disappear almost instantly in the heat. You do the same thing, and by the time you lie down, your wet bathing suit is almost dry.

Lydia sits up, cross-legged, and looks at Louise. "Are you sad?"

Louise smiles. "No! I'm happy!"

"Why are you happy? Don't you miss Eleanor?"

"Of course I do. But I know she's going to have fun at camp."

You're confused. "How?"

Louise pushes her sunglasses up onto her head so that her thick brown hair frames her face in waves. Her mouth tightens. "I don't understand your question."

You can feel your tongue get heavy behind your teeth.

"How will she have fun if she can't swim or do arts and crafts?" Lydia says. Then she looks at you to make sure that's what you would have said if you could have said it yourself.

Louise flips her sunglasses down over her eyes and opens her book. Later, you will come to know this series of movements as what she does when she doesn't have an answer for you—or when she doesn't want to answer you. But back then, before either of you are even ten, sitting on thin motel towels around a cement pool without Eleanor for the first time ever, you assume you've asked a stupid question. A question so stupid it doesn't even deserve a response.

YOU'D THOUGHT THAT THE WHOLE POINT OF CAMP FANTASTIC WAS for kids like Eleanor to be on their own—in the care of Alan and the counselors—away from the watchful eyes of their parents. Hadn't Louise told you in the car that the camp's mission is to foster independence and a sense that people with disabilities aren't the problem—people *without* disabilities are the problem because of their inability to accept disabled people and make room for them?

And so you're surprised the next day when Louise tells you to pack towels and a change of clothes in a plastic tote bag. You've been in your bathing suits since early morning, waiting patiently for her to take you to the pool again—you never ask her directly for anything—after she makes herself a cup of instant coffee with the in-room hot plate.

"Are we going to the pool again?" Lydia asks, unable to take the suspense any longer.

"We're going to camp!"

"What about the pool?"

"You'll go to the pool there."

"With the other kids?"

"Yes, with the other kids." She's packing her own bag now, too.

"But you said families aren't supposed to go to camp." Even then, you're questioning things, trying to get them to add up and make sense. Alan had said that, too, when you'd sat on the stairs with him—that they would take good care of Eleanor.

"They'll make an exception for us."

"Why?"

"Because I'm here to learn." Louise touches her earrings, checking to make sure both silver hoops are still there—more a nervous habit than anything else. "Maybe there's a new way of doing things for her that I don't know yet. Anything's possible."

It's already hot and sticky when you follow Louise to the car. You climb in the back seat, roll the windows down, and sit on your hands until the leather cools down enough to not burn the backs of your thighs. Louise pulls the car away from the motel, and as you leave the parking lot and edge out onto the road, you can see the pool behind the chain-link fence, through the trees. You thought you'd be spending the week together, on vacation, the three of you, for the first time—you, Lydia, and Louise—while Eleanor was occupied, and you can't help feeling tricked now. Other kids are already there, splashing in the turquoise water, their parents watching in chairs. As the hot wind whips your hair against your face and into your eyes and mouth, you think about how Louise always promises you things, but in the end, Eleanor gets everything.

LOUISE DIDN'T KEEP HER PROMISE TO YOU, BUT SHE KEEPS HER promise to Alan. Back at the camp office, she parks the wagon on the side of the building, then grabs her purse and keys. The tote bag is for you both to take. She's going to work in the office—to get the place organized, she says, as she fixes the strap on Lydia's bathing suit top and makes your hair into a fresh ponytail.

"Alan will take you to join the rest of the kids."

You and Lydia are standing on the dirt path, each holding a handle of the canvas tote bag, when Alan comes out. Same beard and hair, same shorts and sandals, different T-shirt.

Lydia strains to read the letters while her lips move, sounding out the words. Years later, you'll find out that she's dyslexic, but at the time she seems like a slow reader. Between that and your difficulty with words that start with *st*—neither of you wants to read the long word on his shirt out loud.

"Steppenwolf," he finally says. You stare at him blankly. "Great band." He points at his shirt, and you both think he's going to sound out the letters and turn it into a teaching moment the way most people do—but not Alan. "Ketchup," he says, rubbing the second *p* with a wet finger before giving up and accepting the stain. "I'd change into a clean one, but lunch is a free-for-all—you'll see—so that one would get dirty, too. It's pointless to try to look decent here."

You scuff along on either side of him in your shorts and tank tops, the soft slap of your rubber flip-flops quickening as you try to keep up with him.

"You hear that sound coming through these white pines and firs and balsams?" he says, not waiting for you to answer. "Those are happy sounds. The sounds of kids having fun. That's why they're here. Why we're all here." You nod obediently. "What do you two Mellishman girls do to have fun besides wheeling your sister around?"

"We're not allowed to wheel her around," Lydia says.

Alan stops, puts his hand on her shoulder to steady himself on one foot, then digs at the sandal on his other foot to free a stray pebble from inside his shoe. "That's why we locked your mother in the office, gave her a mound of phony paperwork to make her way through. Busy work," he says, back on both feet and walking again. "Time for the Mellishman Sisters—all three of them—to have some fun away from the boss."

The pool is long and rectangular, cut into a field surrounded by a bigger rectangle of cement and, beyond that, grass and a chain-link fence. Nothing fancy, but you love it immediately. It's late morning now—the sun is already coming out from behind the clouds, making the line of wheelchairs along the edge of the pool shine and shimmer, sometimes blinding you when the rays hit them a certain way. The pool is full of kids splashing, with life preservers on, surrounded by counselors, who are everywhere—on the cement; on the grass just beyond the pool; one or two are even in the trees.

Alan motions for you to follow him. "Louise tells me that Eleanor loves the water, so let's take her for a swim," he says, kicking his sandals off and pulling his T-shirt over his head on the way to her chair. She has a new sun hat on to shield her face—a floppy one with big orange and yellow flowers that you and Lydia picked out for her at Filene's before the trip—and her skin is white with a thick layer of suntan lotion. You and Lydia bend over to give her a nose kiss, then you each take a hand to pat-pat-pat. She smells good, like Coppertone.

Alan crouches down to talk to her—he tells her that this is his camp, that he's so glad she's here, that you're all going to have fun in the pool. Then he motions for you to push her chair. You both grab a handle and look at each other, then at him. You're not sure if you're doing it right.

"Perfect form," he says, nodding his encouragement. "Follow me."

IT'S THE FIRST TIME YOU'VE EVER PUSHED ELEANOR ANYWHERE. IT suddenly seems totally weird that Louise never really lets you near her, considering how she's always with you, on almost every outing, trip, and errand. For all her belief in inclusion, it's all for Eleanor's benefit, not yours. Pushing her across the grass to the cement area by the pool is hard, especially in the heat, and in flip-flops, but Alan pretends not to notice how much you're both struggling. He waits for you to get there—to where he's standing, now holding his sandals and looking for a free spot to put them—then shows you how to set the brake on the wheels.

"Good work, Mellishmen. Or Mellish*women*," he says. "I'll take it from here." He picks Eleanor up—her small body in his arms, her skinny legs dangling from under his elbows—while you watch. You've never seen anyone else besides Lenny or Louise take her into the water, either at the beach or at a pool—not even one of the regular aides. "Meet us in the water in two minutes," he says over his free shoulder as he walks away.

You find an empty spot on the grass for your tote bag and towels and slip off your shorts and tank tops until you're standing there in your one-piece bathing suits. Then you watch as Alan and a counselor slide into the pool—the counselor first, then Alan with Eleanor still in his arms—dunking her slowly in the blue water, giving her time to get used to it. You and Lydia look at each other. For all your complaining about not being included, you're suddenly not so sure you want to be. The pool is super crowded, with lots of other kids like Eleanor and their counselors, and it makes you nervous that she's around so much splashing and yelling. Like something could happen to her. It seems easier to watch and wait from afar.

As if reading your minds, Alan calls out to you: "Come hang out with me and this little mermaid!" You both do as you're told, walking quickly over the hot cement and then slipping into the pool, but then you both get awkward and shy. You're afraid you'll do something wrong, or worse, that you won't do anything at all: you're not used to being hands-on helpers. Not that there's anything you really need to do and not that Alan is even asking you to help. When you and Lydia go stiff, standing in the barely waist-deep water with your arms crossed in front of you like you're cold even though you're not, he smiles and tells you to relax. *Be here now*, he says. *Just be here now.* You're not sure what that means, but you think it means that it's okay to show Eleanor your dead man's float and to dog-paddle in circles around her in the water that she loves, on this perfect summer day.

When it's time to get out of the pool, Alan asks you to put a dry towel down on the seat of her chair while he and the counselor carry her out of the water. He tells you to lift this, then wipe that, things Louise never asks of you, and so you do those things and then crouch down in front of her while Alan puts a new layer of Coppertone lotion on her little arms and legs and back and shoulders. Eleanor's hands tap your hands, and your head, and your hair. You look up at her as if seeing her for the first time: you're not sure if it's the sharp sun in your eyes or all the chlorine, or the fact that she seems to love it here at Camp Fantastic, but you don't think you've ever seen her happier.

Alan dries himself with a towel, wears it around his neck so that it hangs down over his shoulders, and motions for you both to push Eleanor back toward the bunks so she can be changed before lunch.

"Since you're here," he says, "and since you've been doing such a great job, how about being counselors-in-training? If you learn enough this week, you could come back next summer for pay. Wait—how old are you guys?"

"I'm almost ten and she's six," Lydia says.

Alan laughs. "Okay. Well, *junior* counselors, then. Like my son. He'll be five next year and I'm definitely going to put him to work."

EVERY DAY, YOU HELP IN THE POOL, YOU HELP AT THE CRAFTS TABLE with paints and big crayons; you help in the music room handing out bongo drums and tambourines and pots and pans and wooden spoons. You help in the dining hall—giving out extra napkins, and clean bibs, and racing back and forth to the kitchen to refill water pitchers, then walking slowly, concentrating as hard as you can not to spill them on the way back to the tables where everything is served family-style. Each morning, when Louise drives you over from the motel and reluctantly goes into the office, you and Lydia race to find Alan, and then Eleanor. You can't wait to see her in this new place, and learn from him what to do and how to do it.

By the end of the week, you're tired and sad to leave. But you're filled with a strange sense of excitement as you drive away from Camp Fantastic toward home. You helped. You were involved. You were included. For the first time, there had been a place for you in Eleanor's world.

Trick

What are you going to be for Halloween? It's coming right up." Lydia's standing next to me at my desk, flipping through a file of Maine photos paper-clipped to typewritten letters and old recipes and faded maps. It's been well over two weeks since our fight about me going upstairs after I'd told her she couldn't, and as usual, we've been avoiding the topic of Sonia and Stan and the noise. There's always an elephant in the room, a thing between us, that makes it hard, if not impossible, for us to be close. First it was Eleanor. Then it was geography—three thousand miles of land and a five-hour flight. Now it's this. I'm starting to think there will always be something that will get in our way. Including ourselves.

"Nothing." I swivel slightly to look at her. I hate Halloween— the dressing up, the enforced creativity, the pressure of not eating the candy you collected and the shame when you do—and have refused to participate in it as an adult since college. I've never understood the allure of group infantilization.

"Of course. Stupid question." She sits on the edge of my desk, still looking at the pictures. I want to tell her to be more careful with them, but before I can, she notices that the photo she's looking at is the one that's up on my monitor.

"Oh, wow." She leans across my desk, glancing from the photo to the enlarged image on the screen. "Show me what you do and how you do it. I realize I don't really know what your job is, on a granular level."

I sigh, then look at my phone to check the time. I can tell she's trying to be nice, trying to be overly friendly, though I'm not sure why. I want her to know that I don't have all day for her sudden interest in me after ten long months of barely engaging me in conversation about anything other than how much she hates whatever show we're watching or what we should do for dinner.

I take the snapshot from her hand and point to it, without touching it. "This is Margaret Smythe, and her sister, Emily, and their brothers, Roger and Admiral. Yes, the boys are twins. And yes, his name is really Admiral." The siblings, in down jackets and wool caps, are all standing on a mountaintop—one they've clearly hiked to the top of together—and have posed for a group photo, probably using the old-fashioned method of setting a self-timer on an actual camera. Behind them are sky and clouds and a steep cliff drop down to land. "We scan everything and then digitally edit and restore." I point to the screen now. "I cropped a little over here on the left, cleaned up the creases that were in the original photo, and adjusted the color a tiny bit to account for fading and aging."

She nods, looking from the photo to the monitor. "But what's this?"

I pretend I don't notice what she's pointing to. "What's what?"

"This thing behind them." She looks at the photo again to be sure she's right. Which she is. "It looks like a rope." She leans closer and runs her finger lightly across the screen.

"Oh, that." I nod. "Yes, it's a rope."

She stares at me. "You're being super weird, Joyce."

"Am I?"

"Did you add that to the picture?"

I shrug. "Maybe."

She starts laughing, covering her mouth with one hand and pointing at the screen with her other. "You added *a rope*—like *a safety rope*—behind the Smythe siblings? As if a rope would even keep them from falling off the mountain?" She's laughing so hard that tears are coming down her face and she almost falls off the side of my desk. "Joyce Mellishman: trying to keep people safe, one photoshopped picture at a time."

I refuse to laugh, even though she's right: I'm completely ridiculous.

"Don't they notice when you add things?"

"No. Because I always remove whatever I add before I deliver the project." Or, I *almost* always remove them. Every now and then I'll leave something in—something tiny and barely noticeable, unlike this mountaintop rope, which Lydia saw right away. It's my tiny little revenge moment for how they tempt fate and allow family members to be put in danger.

She gives me back the file and wipes her eyes one last time. "Anyway . . . back to Halloween. I had stupidly asked you what you were going to be, since of course you're not going to dress up as anything."

I can tell she's waiting for me to ask her what she's going as, but I refuse to.

"I'm going as Laura Ingalls Wilder," she says.

I can't even. "Because?"

"Because it's easy. It's a prairie dress and ankle boots. Target has a whole line of those dresses now. They're like the hot new thing, which I totally don't understand. I don't think I've worn a dress since third grade, but I'll get one later when I go there—everyone says that they still have a great selection of full-sized candy. I want to get ours before they run out."

"Who's 'everyone'?"

"Oh, all the weirdos on the neighborhood app Small World."

I swallow. "You're on there?"

She shrugs. "Every now and then. Like I was in LA. But only for important stuff, like who has the most Halloween candy left. I have to get a ton of *extra* candy to make up for certain neighbors who don't believe in sugar."

"We don't usually get that many kids on this street."

"You never know. There could be an unexpected rush. Good weather. I checked."

She could be right. The sun has been out all week, and the sky has been that crazy perfect fall bright blue—if we're lucky, it'll stay cool but not too cold for the rest of the week. But it's the complaint about the upstairs people that surprises me most. "I would have thought the fact that Sonia and Stan don't do Halloween would be a dealbreaker for you. But I guess you still want to take her class and be her best friend."

"It almost was a dealbreaker. But nobody's perfect, right?" She says this like she's an easygoing, forgiving, nonjudgmental person, and like I am, too. "At least the neighborhood kids have us to pick up the slack." I stare at her, my face blank. "Okay, at least they have *me* to pick up the slack. I'll turn on all the lights to attract as many kids as possible. Because you know they'll turn *their* lights off upstairs and pretend to be out. Which, to me, is the epitome of cruelty and selfishness: depriving children of their right to have fun and be happy. At least one night a year."

"Maybe Sonia is having class on Halloween," I say, with barely muted disgust. "A special *Yoga Spook Fest*."

Lydia looks up. "I doubt it."

"Why not? Halloween falls on a Tuesday—and she always has class on Tuesdays."

She shrugs, then slides off the desk. "Who would take yoga on Halloween and miss out on all the fun?"

DESPITE THE MULTIPLE UNITS IN OUR HOUSE, IT'S THE TWO FIRST-floor apartments that are mostly responsible for taking care of trick-or-treaters, though usually everyone—except Upstairs Beth, who was always away—gathers in the vestibule and opens the door together for each group of kids that comes up the walk, then holds out multiple bowls of candy to grab from. Some take as many treats as their hands can hold, but often the younger ones, shy and overwhelmed by all the activity and too many choices, freeze and don't take any. That's when I bend down and drop one or two or three pieces into their pumpkin bags and apologize for having too much candy to pick from. *As if,* I always mouth to the grown-ups in the vestibule, then snort. The next day, every November first, Next Door Beth and Ethan always dump their carved pumpkins out their window into the leaves on the lawn below, where they will "naturally compost themselves"—that's what they actually say. This drives me crazy, naturally, but Next Door Beth and Ethan always give out full-sized candy bars—Snickers, and sometimes the double pack of Reese's cups—so I let it go.

Later, when I'm done with work for the day and scrolling through Small World on the couch as a brief reward, I see the app's ad:

HALLOWEEN IS COMING!

Don't forget to let your neighborhood know that you want to be on our Ghost and Goblin Tour™! Have great decorations? An impressive selection of candy? Are you offering nonfood treats

for children with allergies and other diet-limiting conditions? Add
your address so that people will know you're in on the fun and
to ensure that you'll get lots of spooky little spirits ringing your
doorbell!

Unbelievable. When we were young, we all went out into the
cold black night without a plan, wearing weird homemade costumes
and ringing the doorbells of whatever houses appeared to be giving
out candy. It was trial and error in real time. Sometimes the houses
with lights on didn't answer the door; sometimes a friend insisted on
ringing the doorbell of a house that was dark in case they changed
their mind; but there was never an "interactive map" to plan and
optimize our candy collection route.

I assume that Lydia will be doing both—decorating the out-
side of the house and giving out candy—considering how she
spent part of the weekend lugging the big pumpkins we'd bought
at a farm out in Lincoln into the kitchen and carving them on
the table covered in newspaper, putting votives and tea lights into
them, then arranging them outside on the steps, waiting for the
big night to light them up. Halloween is her Christmas.

Instead of turning the map announcement into a poem, I consider
doing what it says and adding our address. Why not? Just because
I hate Halloween doesn't mean I should deprive the neighborhood
kids of Lydia's candy and enthusiasm. I'm convinced she was punk-
ing me earlier about the Laura Ingalls Wilder costume and will really
dress up in something brilliantly designed and constructed that she's
been secretly working on for weeks, though I haven't seen any signs
of that, and I know that she would never leave a crucially important
Halloween costume to the last minute like this. I'm about to swipe
and tap to add our address, when I think: *Add Sonia and Stahn's
apartment instead.*

My evil idea completely delights me. In fact, it erases the bad mood I've been in all day and all week brought on by the distraction of the noise itself and the added tension between Lydia and me because of it. It reminds me of the old days, when people would send HairClub for Men brochures and porn magazine trial subscriptions to people they couldn't stand by filling out a blow-in card with someone else's address. Life was so simple then.

But this is simple, too. While I can't add Sonia and Stan's address and apartment number from my account for obvious reasons, I can click the icon of our whole house and add a note in the "special instructions":

Press the buzzer for Apt. 4 really hard so that Laura Ingalls Wilder can hear you from her little house on the prairie!

If I'm caught, which I won't be, because they're not even on Small World, I'll say the apartment number was a typo. Fat fingers. Plausible deniability. I'm so tickled that I'm tempted to knock on Lydia's door to share the news of my brilliant practical joke, but then I remember she's out. And besides, it's probably better to keep this to myself.

———

So Much for the Honor System!
We left two big bowls full of candy
on our front steps
for trick or treaters
then went out
to a friend's birthday dinner.
When we came home

both bowls were gone.
By which I mean:
the actual bowls.
Not just the candy in them.
They were two of my oldest and most favorite bowls—
one I always use for mixing cakes and cookies,
and one I always use for salads.
So much for the honor system!
Next year I'll just leave candy out
in paper bags.

Another Story
I bought a big plastic black and orange bowl
at Target
a long time ago
and I have the opposite problem.
Nobody steals the bowl
because it's so ugly
so instead they steal all the candy.
They really shouldn't be so greedy
but that's another story.

Better Idea
How about actually staying home and
giving out candy
in person
like a good neighbor?!
If you have to leave,
turn your porch light off

and don't put a bowl out
for kids to take too much candy from
or steal
so that you can
complain about it later on
Small World.

———

Two days later, on Halloween, I make sure to finish my work early, by a little after five. Our street never gets foot traffic before six o'clock—even the littlest ones, dressed as princesses or puppies or Hershey's Kisses and held by their parents, wait until then. I use that hour to straighten my desk, change into warm socks and a warmer sweater, and double-check that the front lights are on.

At about five thirty, Lydia comes out of her room in a light blue tiny-floral, nearly full-length prairie dress, and black Doc Martens lace-up boots. The dress—with its ruffled high-neck collar, flouncy tiers, and big balloon sleeves—is as hideous as I'd imagined it would be. No. It's *more* hideous.

"Look!" Lydia says, slowly turning and twirling, when she sees me staring at the dress. "It ties in the back!"

"Wow" is all I can think to say.

"I know, right? Isn't it awful?"

"So you know it's ugly."

"Of course I do."

"Then why are you wearing it?"

"Because I don't want to upstage the little kids coming to the door with their adorable costumes! It's their night. Halloween isn't about me anymore. It's not about outdoing all my art school friends and winning some dumb costume contest. That said, I can't wear normal street clothes—I refuse to not observe the holiday in some small way. This is my version of wearing an ugly bridesmaid dress to a wedding so as not to upstage the bride."

I start hearing the buzzer in the vestibule and people coming in—as I'd suspected, there *is* a class tonight. The clogs and boots are making their way up the stairs, and then, in minutes, the people in them are right above our heads. We both look up at the ceiling as the sounds of shoes coming off and movement into the studio space increase.

"I told you." I can't help myself. *It feels so good to be right.*

"Well, I mean, I guess if you're not doing Halloween, you might as well have class."

I nod, then take a few steps away to check Small World: my note is still there. Then I check the time: a few minutes past six. Class has started. I watch Lydia putting the finishing touches on a giant wooden salad bowl filled with candy. "Full-sized," she says, drawing out the *iiiiiiiized* for as long as it takes her to walk past me into the vestibule.

I grab my phone and join her out there, watching as she lights the candles in the jack-o'-lanterns on the stoop before coming back inside. For some reason, we're the only ones in the vestibule, which is weird, so I check my email. Sure enough, I find a thread that includes Douglas and all the residents in the house explaining that Next Door Beth and Ethan are meeting out of town friends for dinner in Somerville, and Upstairs Jen and Mike have gone to their house in Vermont. They thank us for doing Halloween in their stead and promise to be here next year.

"IT'S JUST US TONIGHT, I GUESS," I SAY TO LYDIA AS SHE PLAYS WITH the stupid yoke on the front of her dress and reties the back of it so that it's a little tighter. Then she picks up the bowl of candy and stands guard at the door.

Voices and peals of delighted laughter are coming from the street now—we press our noses up against the cold glass of the vestibule door and stare out into the blackness, then step back and look at each other excitedly as a steady stream of kids and parents wearing glow necklaces and holding glow sticks head down our walk and up the stairs. I've never seen so many trick-or-treaters here!

Instead of the buzzer going off in our apartment, right near us in the doorway, I hear and feel the distant vibration of the upstairs buzzer. Sonia and Stan's buzzer. *It's working.* Several kids press their doorbell at the same time, leaning against it with all their weight, buzzing and buzzing and buzzing.

Lydia opens the door and greets everyone—"Hi, Buzz Light-year!" "Hi, Hermione!" "Hi, Thomas the Tank Engine!"—and offers the bowl of candy to each one until they make their selections. No sooner does that group turn around and go down the stairs than another group is coming up the stairs, pushing and pushing and pushing the upstairs buzzer. Each push is like a jolt of oxytocin to my brain. I could not possibly be happier.

This happens repeatedly—Lydia greeting everyone and offering the bowl of candy, me echoing her comments and waving goodbye—until finally, in between two large packs of trick-or-treaters, Stan comes rushing down the stairs into the foyer.

"Hello, Stahn," Lydia says. "Will Mr. Pumpkinhead be joining us for tonight's mischief and merriment?" she says in the same high, creepy voice he used to make us take our shoes off, hoping he'll do the same.

"Mr. Pumpkinhead is not available right now, Lydia."

"Why not?"

"Because Sonia's trying to teach up there, and she can't because of all this noise!" he finally whisper-yells in the Mr. Pumpkinhead voice. Surprised and embarrassed that he was so easily bullied into compliance, he straightens his posture and looks at the two of us like we're up to no good. "Why do they keep ringing our doorbell?"

"I don't know!" I say, with faux astonishment. "For some reason it's the only bell they're ringing tonight! Which is ironic because *you're* the only people in the house who don't celebrate Halloween!"

"Can't you tell them to stop?"

I blink at him, feigning confusion. "You want *us* to tell *children* to *stop* their trick-or-treating?"

"I want you to tell them to stop ringing our bell!"

"Oh, we can't do that," I say.

"Why not?"

"Because it's Halloween, Mr. Pumpkinhead! It's their night, not ours. Plus," I say, pointing to Lydia's prairie getup, "does it look like she's dressed as a *dream killer*?"

"But Sonia's in the middle of teaching a class!"

"Well, maybe next year she shouldn't have class on Halloween," I say, "and you guys should join the fun down here instead, *like good neighbors.*"

Stan is about to turn and go back up the stairs, when he squints at the door instead. He moves closer to it as a bunch of children start ringing the bell—their bell—and then he opens it.

When they all scream, "Trick or treat," he manages a big fake smile. Then he reaches for Lydia's salad bowl of candy and offers it to the group—two devils, one race-car driver, and an organic avocado (stickered for proof)—as if the full-sized candy largesse is his own supply.

"I have a question for all you little ghouls and goblins!" he says, in the Mr. Pumpkinhead voice. "What's making you press our bell so much?"

"You're on the map," says one of the devils.

"On what map?"

"On the Ghost and Goblin Tour trick-or-treat map."

He looks at Lydia, who stares back blankly. "I don't know anything about a map."

A parent who has overheard the exchange steps up with a group of younger children. He takes out his phone and shows Stan: on the screen is an orange map with little pumpkins all over the streets. I bite my lip, then silently retreat into the dark shadows of the vestibule.

"It's Small World, the neighborhood app," the parent says, explaining how houses sign up to be included so that they'll get more trick-or-treaters.

"But we didn't sign up for that. We don't want more trick-or-treaters. We don't want *any* trick-or-treaters!" I cringe when I realize he's said the quiet part out loud.

"Maybe someone else signed you up, then. The note for your house says to press the buzzer a lot 'so Laura Ingalls Wilder can hear from her little house on the prairie.'"

All the air leaves the vestibule and my lungs as Stan turns toward Lydia, who then turns to me.

"Yes, that's clearly what happened," he says, nodding. "Laura Ingalls Wilder's sister signed us up. How very thoughtful of her." He hands the bowl of candy back to Lydia, glares at me, then walks quickly up the stairs.

———

Trick or Treat Apology

I want to apologize
to the teenagers
wearing costumes
who rang my doorbell last night.
At the time,
I was annoyed
to see kids so big and tall
who were clearly in middle school
or high school
trying to get candy.
I scolded them,
telling them they were
too old
to be trick or treating.
I was so wrong.
I hope they keep
the children still inside them
alive forever.
Age is just a number.

The Turkeys

The turkeys are always emboldened by fall. I often come upon a pack of them, a creepy prehistoric posse, taking their time crossing a lawn or driveway or soldiering down a walkway to someone's backyard, uninvited, or in the middle of a street, forcing cars to stop until they've made their way to the other side. Maybe it's the cooler weather, the sun moving across the sky and sinking behind houses and trees earlier in the day, or maybe they like that short lull between afternoon and evening, when people are still finishing up at work and haven't yet spilled out on the streets and sidewalks to walk or drive home to start dinner.

I usually walk before dusk, right when the light is starting to fade. There is something breathtakingly sad to me about that time of day, something that has always reminded me ineffably of childhood: the loneliness of it, the lost innocence of it, the unbearable endlessness to it. The sky, before the light disappears completely, seems to be holding its breath until it just can't do it anymore and it surrenders so that darkness can finally fall. Sometimes on my walks, in the quiet of the in-between time, before people have left their offices, when nearby students are still in the library studying or kill-ing time in their dorm rooms before dinner, I feel the veil drape over me, the memory, from so long ago, of waiting at home in the dark-ening house, for Louise or Lenny to come home. He was at work, and she was so often out, either visiting Eleanor at Fernald, or, after Eleanor was gone, working on behalf of other families. I still can't articulate—not in words, not in found poetry from Small World—how lost I feel every day, at this time.

———

Fearful
I hate coming upon a group of huge turkeys
when no one's around.
I wish they would just stay
in the woods
or on farms
or wherever their natural habitats are
instead of roaming around loose
like something out of Jurassic Park.
They just don't belong in the city.

I Would Rather See a Turkey
I'm more afraid of people
than of animals
to be honest.
While groups of huge turkeys
kind of creep me out
I would rather see a turkey

or any kind of wild animal
on a deserted street
than a stranger.
People are the problem.
Not wildlife.

Boundaries

It's because people feed turkeys that
they come into our neighborhoods and
cross the streets
running the risk of getting hit by cars.
That's why maintaining boundaries is so important.
The more time they spend around people
the more they lose their fear of them
and become increasingly aggressive.
If you come upon scary turkeys,
make it clear that you're the boss,
make noise,
swat at them with a broom,
turn a garden hose on them.
If they don't try to attack you,
just ignore them until they go away.
The problem with animals becoming habituated
to our urban world is that sometimes
we have to re-establish the power hierarchy
to maintain safety—
theirs and ours.

———

It's afternoon, cold and full of soft light, as I snake behind the old seminary buildings of what was once the Episcopal Divinity School but is now Lesley University, the well-kept lawns and campus grounds off Brattle Street, on the edges of Harvard. It's quiet and still, and for once, I see no turkeys here. But I do see something else: a familiar bright orange jacket. Lydia. She's far enough away for me to watch from a distance without being noticed. Instead of calling out to her, or catching up to her, like a normal person, I stop and wait for the distance between us to increase. I continue slowly behind her, like I'm stalking her. Which I kind of am, even though I have no idea why. In the same way that Lydia feels locked in after she lies—or fibs—I feel trapped by my evasive maneuvering. It already feels too late to self-correct and chase after her instead of creeping behind her in silence.

There's something different about Lydia in the outside, in the wild—I sense it, which is why I think I stop myself from saying hello, from catching up and walking together somewhere—down to the river and around into Harvard Square, in the last of the day's light. She's a stranger out here. Maybe she's always been a stranger. Maybe I've never really known her, except in childhood, those few years we shared a room, but even then, she was inscrutable. Maybe I was, too. Maybe I still am.

I tell myself to go up to her—*Say hello, before it's too late!*—but I don't. I step back and move behind a tree. Now I'm really locked into this evasive course of action. What do I think I'll see her do? What strange secret behavior do I think I'll catch her engaging in? She stops on the grass, to the left of the Longfellow House, the big yellow Colonial that once was, the National Park Service sign outside informs visitors, George Washington's military headquarters, and sits down. Or tries to. Because when she lowers herself to the ground, she loses her balance and collapses in a heap of limbs, legs and arms. A few seconds later, she rolls over, sits up, then looks behind her, trying to figure out what, if anything, she tripped on.

She lies back down, by choice this time, flat now in the dry cold grass. The sky is getting gray. Dusk is coming. She closes her eyes and extends her arms out to her sides. If there were snow on the ground, she'd probably make a snow angel, but instead she brings her knees up to her chest and rolls her hips back and forth a few times, stretching, the way they did in a yoga class I once took but never went back to because, well, I didn't want to go back. She stops and looks up at the trees and the sky, then starts to get up: first making it to both knees, then waiting until she's ready to push herself up from there.

I'm about to sneak away from the tree, to retrace my steps back home, make a clean getaway, when I see them: a line of turkeys heading straight toward her. There are six or seven or eight of them, their feathers puffed out, their giant black tails fanned. This is why one of the collective nouns for them is *gang*. They're a gang of gangsters ready to surround and attack.

I'm not sure what to do. I'm paralyzed by my own paralysis, my secretiveness for which I have no logical explanation. I could still correct myself—all I have to do is pretend I came upon her now on the grass, before trying to ward off the turkey threat—but I don't move. My feet feel planted in the ground like stakes. Maybe the turkeys will walk right past her; maybe they'll cross Brattle Street the way they so often do, holding up traffic until they make it to the other side of the sidewalk, then head down Hawthorn Street to Mount Auburn, to Memorial Drive and the river. Maybe she'll be spared.

Before I can yell out to get her attention, the strutting turkeys start making sounds. She turns and freezes, then looks around for someone to help her or someone else for the turkeys to fixate on.

But there is no one on the grass, and no one walking by on the sidewalk. It's one of those strange moments in the rhythm of a city when it seems suddenly and completely empty; a wrinkle in time, as if the Rapture has taken place. I keep waiting for Lydia to run away, especially when the turkeys catch up to her and surround her, but except for shouting at them to try to shoo them away, she doesn't move.

I finally manage to get unstuck and run toward her, calling her name, yelling at the turkeys to scare them off. Which works. By the time I'm by her side, breathless and awkward from panic and fear and shame for waiting so long to take action, the turkeys have mercifully moved on. Now blocking traffic, four at a time, like the Beatles in the middle of Abbey Road, they are crossing Brattle Street on their way to the river. Normalcy resumes, and once again, there are people around, and the world is back in motion.

"Thank God!" she says. She grabs onto my arm and I pull her up. "Where did you come from? How did you even see me?"

I shrug, then swat at the dried leaves on her back and pick a few out of her hair from when she was on the ground stretching. "I was doing my usual route," I say, turning to point back toward the brown stone campus buildings, "and I saw the turkeys marching in formation across the grass. I knew they were up to no good."

She shakes her head, still a little stunned. "I went out for a little walk, to meditate in nature and find some peace, and instead I get attacked!"

"If I were faster, I could have made it over to you sooner."

"I was fine. I would have gotten away. Luckily I'm still incredibly quick and flexible."

I laugh. I think she's kidding until her expression makes it clear she's not. "But you fell," I say.

"No, I didn't."

"Yes, you did."

"When?"

"Just now. In the grass. I saw you."

"I didn't fall."

"You toppled. Before the turkeys."

"I lost my balance."

"And then you had a hard time getting up."

"Bullshit."

I laugh. "Fine. Never mind."

"How did you even see me? And so what if I did? What's the big deal?"

"It's not a big deal, but you made such a big deal about being so flexible, that I felt compelled to correct the record."

"Okay, you win, Joyce."

"I'm not trying to win. I just want us to be honest with each other."

"I'm not being dishonest with you. You're always so suspicious of everyone. You're convinced that everyone is sneaking around, doing bad, secret things behind your back."

I can't help but laugh. *She's right. That's exactly what I think.*

"Why is that?"

"I have no idea."

"Seriously. Why do you distrust everyone?"

"I wouldn't say I distrust *everyone*. I don't trust *most* people. It's just how I am."

"Well, I'm not 'most people,' and you don't seem to trust me. But you've always been this way, and you're this way now, so I guess I have to accept it."

THE WIND IS PICKING UP, AND THE SUN IS ALREADY GOING DOWN. I zip my jacket to my chin and pick her bag up from the grass, then hand it to her. She puts the strap over her head and wears it on her hip, like a bike messenger, then brushes herself off. We both walk slowly across the lawn toward Brattle Street.

"Should we go home?" I say, knowing we're heading in the opposite direction for that. "Or should we take a detour into Harvard Square first, maybe go to the bookstore or get coffee? If you want to." I assume she'll say no; she always says no.

"Sure. I'll go."

It feels like the temperature dropped ten or twenty degrees since I left the house, and now, not far from all the stores, as the streetlights flicker on, I'm freezing and dying to take refuge inside, anywhere that's warm. "I know where we should go," I say, and a few minutes later, we're at tiny Winthrop Park, where people still smoke pot and play guitar, and where Grendel's Den is. We both waitressed there at different points in high school and during and after college, and it's one of the few places left from the old days. Heading inside and down the stairs, leaving the last of the late-afternoon light behind us at the door, my eyes are still adjusting when Lydia walks over to the two empty stools at the end of the bar. It feels like a million years since I was picking up drinks for my tables with an apron full of cash and coin tips.

"We're the only ones here," I say.

"I guess we're early. Unlike when I worked here. I was always late."

"Me too."

"Are you going to have a drink?"

I shrug. "Probably not. I have work to do later."

"Me too."

The bartender arrives—he's tall with short gray hair and sleeves of tattoos on both arms—and asks us what we're having.

"Harpoon," I say.

"Same," Lydia says.

We both laugh at our lack of resolve, then I raise an eyebrow. "Look at you, having a beer!"

"It's gluten-free!"

Sitting there in the quiet of the bar, I realize that we haven't been out together since Sonia and Stan moved in. Their presence disrupted whatever rhythm we'd gotten into—the occasional morning or afternoon walks into Harvard Square or Porter Square, or Davis Square in Somerville, for coffee and pastry, or for Thai or Indian food at night, sometimes the Sunday paper to share the *New York Times* crossword puzzle. Maybe this is another new beginning; a way to restart things after all the stress of the past month.

When our drinks come, tall glasses of deep amber beer, we wriggle out of our jackets and let them drape over the backs of our stools. I lift my drink, she lifts hers, and we clink the glasses. But something happens to Lydia's between the time we touch rims and her first sip: suddenly there is the sound of shattering glass and the splash of beer everywhere.

"*Shit*," she says.

"No problem," the bartender says. "I got it."

"The glass slipped right out of my hand," she whispers, as I wipe my shirt with my hands first, and then with my tiny cocktail napkin. She stares at her fingers, like they don't belong on her body. Like they're someone else's.

I jump up and reach for the roll of paper towels that's now on the bar, dabbing at myself and then at her. She seems stunned by all the activity going on around her. While I'm wiping up the counter, the bartender comes out from behind the bar with a dustpan and brush. He kneels between our stools and sweeps up the broken glass, then takes a quick look at our seats to make sure there's no glass on them before we sit back down.

He pours Lydia another, but she doesn't touch it. She wiggles her fingers, looks at the tops of her hands and then the bottoms. They seem to be working, but they betrayed her once; now she's afraid to trust them again.

"Well, that was embarrassing," she says.

"At least you weren't drunk when it happened," the bartender says.

She smiles. "That's what's so embarrassing. I'm not drunk. I'm not even tipsy. But I'm sorry that you had to clean this up."

He's staring at her, and then me. "You're sisters, right?"

"We are," I say. "Though I've never really seen the resemblance."

"Neither have I. We look nothing alike," Lydia adds, clearly grateful for the distraction and the chance to change the subject. "But here's the big question: Which one of us is older?"

"Be very careful how you answer that," I say, though I know what his answer will be. Lydia has always looked and seemed much younger than me.

He points to Lydia. "You're older."

"Well, if I hadn't dropped my glass like a senior citizen, you might not have said that."

He's staring at both of us again, back and forth, his eyes mapping our faces. It feels a tiny bit creepy until he says, "I feel like I know you guys."

"And we're not even wearing matching *I'm Divorced!* necklaces," Lydia jokes, like he's trying to pick us up.

"She's kidding. We don't have *I'm Divorced!* necklaces."

"Though we are divorced."

"From other people."

"Not from each other."

"No, seriously," he says. "You two look really familiar."

I explain that we grew up nearby. And that we both worked here, a long time ago. None of that seems to help. He names places we might have in common, where our lives could possibly have intersected and overlapped—junior high school, high school, church, sports, college, AA—but still nothing connects.

"Nope, sorry," Lydia says, turning back to her drink and then to me. It's starting to feel like a cheap party trick.

"Wait," he says. "Did you have a sister at Fernald?"

We look at each other, then at him.

"She was retarded, right?" Before we can answer, he shrugs apologetically. "That's not the right word now. Now it's 'developmentally disabled,' I think." When we don't respond, he shakes his head. "Never mind. I'm probably confusing you with someone else."

"No. That's us. That's our family," Lydia says.

"My brother was there."

"Who's your brother?" I ask.

"Stevie. Stevie Stepanian. He had Down syndrome. I'm Jimmy."

We turn to each other in disbelief. "You're Stevie's brother?" I say.

"Well, was," he says. "Stevie's been gone awhile. He died about fifteen years ago."

We lower our eyes and say how sorry we are. "We used to go to your house on Christmas Day," Lydia says. "We're the Mellishmans. I'm Lydia, and she's Joyce."

"I know. I remember."

"And your parents?" I ask.

"Gone."

Lydia nods. "Ours too."

"Luckily Stevie went first. Which sounds like a strange thing to say, but all my life my parents worried about who would take care of him when they weren't around anymore."

"Well, you could have," Lydia says. "There's nothing like the love and care of a sibling." She smiles slyly at me, and it takes me a few seconds to realize that she's trying to pay me a compliment.

———

Even after Eleanor dies, your family stays involved with Fernald. All the parents Louise and Lenny remain friends with—the Stepanians, the Spellmans, the Fialcos, the Pierces—have developmentally disabled children who are already well into their twenties. Sometimes you hear your parents talking about whether it's better to lose a young child, the way they did, or to worry about an older child outliving them, the way most of their friends do.

Louise is in charge of the annual dinner dance for the Fernald League, the parents' advocacy group, and for the ad book that goes along with it. In the afternoons, when she gets home from whatever meetings she's been at, she makes calls, and after dinner she makes calls to other Fernald parents, helping to pull everything together before the big evening event that's always held in the late fall, at the Armenian social hall on Mount Auburn Street in Watertown. It's the most fun night of the year for Fernald parents and their families and friends: the women wear long dresses and high heels and have their hair teased; the men wear dark suits and wide ties. The one time that you get to go—the year after Eleanor dies—you and Lydia wear matching sleeveless floral maxi dresses: hers is blue, yours is pink. The third dress, the one that Eleanor would have worn, is yellow.

The highlight of the dinner dance is a big raffle, and the grand prize is always a brand-new car, donated by one of the local dealerships—the owner of which usually has some personal connection to the cause—either a sibling or a cousin or a friend's sibling or cousin has a physical or developmental disability. Every fall, you and Lydia are sent out into your neighborhood to sell tickets to the raffle, walking the nearby streets together, but you go up to each house separately. You're both shy, and it seems easier not to witness each other's fumbling sales pitches.

You approach each house slowly, your shoes crunching on the dry brown leaves that cover the sidewalks and driveways and stairs, then ring the doorbell. It's always chilly and windy while you wait with your little booklet of white tickets in one hand and your envelope full of dollar bills in the other hand, secretly hoping that no one will answer. But someone usually does. When they crack open the storm door, you force yourself to try to get your words out.

Would you like to buy a raffle ticket for the Fernald School for Retarded Children? That's what the families call it, and that's how you're supposed to phrase the question, but sometimes, depending on the vibe from the person opening the door, you stammer out the pitch, getting stuck on the *f* and the *s* in the middle of the sentence. Sometimes you don't even get that far. Your mouth opens and closes like a fish's, but nothing comes out—not even air—and you end up showing the booklet of tickets to the person so that they can read what's written on the front of the booklet themselves. Usually that's enough to take the pressure off you and you're able then to get most of the words out—*Would you like to buy a raffle ticket for the Fernald School?* Or: *Would you like to buy a ticket for retarded children?* Or sometimes even just: *It's for retarded children.* Most people buy one—maybe, you think, because they assume from the way you talk that there might be something "wrong" with you, too—some don't. When your friends at school talk about selling Girl Scout cookies, it never sounds as hard as this.

For a few years, you get together with the Stepanians on Christmas, always going to their split-level ranch in Framingham on

Christmas Day because you, as Jews, don't celebrate it. You and Lydia are always cold in the back seat on the drive there, with your dresses and tights and patent leather shoes that Louise insists on out of respect for "their holiday," and even though you don't really know anyone there—you're always the only kids—you're glad when you finally arrive. You love seeing people's Christmas trees, all the ornaments and tinsel and lights, all the presents waiting, or just unwrapped, underneath. You wish that Christmas were your holiday, too.

From the outside, their house is a plain ranch, half wood and half fake brick, but on the inside it's like a movie set: all red and black, Chinese-style lacquered furniture and accessories everywhere, like the Chinese restaurant you always go to. Chinese decor is Mary's obsession. They are both warm and welcoming and attractive—Mary with her chin-length brown bob and high cheekbones; Steve with his gray beard and his sparkly blue eyes—and they both love their two boys: Jimmy, who's still in high school, and Steve Jr.—Stevie—who's in his twenties.

Stevie lives at Fernald, but when he comes home for Christmas, he takes over the paneled finished basement, standing behind the black vinyl bar with the Schlitz beer wall clock lit up and all the little bowls of snacks on the counter. Stevie is obsessed with Elvis. He dresses like Elvis and plays a toy guitar like Elvis and sings Elvis songs. On Christmas, Mary and Steve make sure the record player is set up and that Stevie has all his Elvis records so he can play them, one after the other, for all the guests: Elvis DJing an Elvis hit-a-thon. Everyone who arrives comes downstairs to greet Stevie and admire his shirt and his pants, and all the great music he's playing and singing to, before going upstairs for dinner. Steve pours drinks from behind the bar, and helps Stevie change the records when he gets too excited or is too busy dancing. He always kisses his head or his cheek. *My boy*, he says, beaming. *My beautiful boy.*

Stevie's favorite part of Christmas Day is when Jimmy comes down to the basement. He loves Jimmy almost as much as he loves Elvis, and Stevie always gives him a huge hug when he appears. Jimmy always hugs him back and tells him that he loves him and misses him when he's gone. You and Lydia look at each other when they do that—two siblings expressing their love and affection for each other—and then you look away.

At night, when you're all back in your separate rooms and spaces, distanced and disconnected from one another, you'll think about how visiting Stevie's family is like being in another country and not understanding the culture or the language. Their behavior is utterly foreign to you. Years later, when you're older and have known more people and have seen some of the world, you'll realize that what you saw those Christmas Days was a happy family, and that the thing missing from yours that you could never name—the language none of you spoke in your country—was joy.

The Class

I 've been thinking of what to get you for Christmas—or Hanukkah," Erin says, "even though it's still a ways off."

"Besides a promotion?" I say, grinning like a goofball. "I'm kidding. But not really."

"I'm working on that, too. Though I was talking about something more immediate."

"Like a raise?"

"Like: I could check out the class upstairs."

I sit forward on my chair. "Seriously?"

"I've witnessed the noise in real time, here, with you, so I understand, as your manager and as your friend, how distracting it is for you when you're trying to work at home. But now I want to go up there and see for myself what's going on. I went to Sonia's website again, and we've exchanged a few emails to *assess our suitability as teacher and student*, and there shouldn't be any problem. I've done a ton of yoga, and despite my size—which of course I didn't mention—I'm very fit."

"You have no idea how happy this makes me."

"I do have some idea. I know how you get. I think part of what's distracting you is the mystery: the not knowing exactly what they're doing up there. Even though you kind of know what they're doing up there."

"Classes. And one-on-one body work. And readings."

"Right. You need specifics. Visuals."

My head is exploding. "You'll take pictures?"

"No, Joyce. They'll think I'm a narc or a perv if I do that. I meant verbal pictures. Firsthand descriptions. That kind of thing."

"Of course. That would be amazing." Already I feel my brain calming at the thought of knowing more than I do now. Erin's right—it's the lack of details that makes me most anxious. That, plus the actual noise itself. And how they're doing what they want up there, with total impunity, as if no one lives below them. Even though we do. I do.

It seems that we're the only ones affected by the noise. I broach the subject with Next Door Beth recently when we run into each other dumping our recycling into the big blue bin in the backyard shed—and with Upstairs Jen and Mike when we come in at the same time with groceries. Both times I ask gingerly if they've noticed what's going on with all the visitors. But because Lydia and I are the only ones directly below Sonia and Stan, none of them seem to know what I'm talking about, or care when I inform them that there are classes and private lessons going on in the house. *An actual business right upstairs, with people coming and going throughout the day and evening!* No one seems to understand that, at best, it's extremely disturbing, and at worst, it's illegal. Their reactions, or lack thereof, make me rethink my impulse to complain to Douglas. He'd probably shrug in his safari jacket, tip his hat to me, then drop off an eviction notice the next day like the sneaky little garden gnome that he is.

IT'S THE SECOND WEEK OF NOVEMBER WHEN THE TUESDAY-NIGHT class that Erin plans to go to comes around. She arrives at the apartment a little after five thirty, with her workout clothes already on under her big puffy coat. As always, when she walks in, she looks around for Lydia, though after she crashed our drinks date at the Sheraton Commander and the three of us had a semipleasant, if not very interesting, conversation, Erin seems to be more tolerant of her. Still, when I tell her that Lydia already left for her barre class and won't be home until later, she smiles with relief.

"Good. One less thing to worry about."

"Are you nervous?"

"Not nervous. Curious. Very curious."

"Me too."

"Maybe I'll get a good vibe, a cooperative vibe, a collaborative vibe, that will give us a clue about how to deal with her more constructively."

I can't help but bristle. "More than I have been?"

"You haven't done anything wrong! I just mean: it's always good to get another set of eyes on a problem."

"Like when you show me one of your slideshows before it's done."

"Right. When I'm stuck because I don't know how many shots of cousins in matching yarmulkes I should include."

"Like is ten enough or do you need twenty?" We both laugh. "Always twenty," I say. "You can never have too many pictures of kids in color-coordinated matching yarmulkes."

"Good to know." She checks her phone. It's five minutes to six. She stands up, picks up her rolled mat, and I open the door. She steps into the foyer and gives me a little wave before turning toward the stairs to their apartment.

"WELL, THAT'S NOT AT ALL WHAT I EXPECTED." ERIN WALKS IN SLOWLY
and puts her mat and her puffy coat down near the door. "She was
very welcoming. And very kind. I'm pretty surprised, to be honest."

I wish she sounded apologetic to be delivering this news, but I
wave her toward the couch anyway. "Tell me everything."

"When you go up, Sonia stands at the top of the stairs, greeting
everyone—*namaste* and all that. Right away she went overboard
in making me feel comfortable, which, like I said, surprised me.
I hadn't mentioned my weight when we spoke on the phone. On
purpose. I wanted to catch her off guard, see how she'd react."

I raise an eyebrow. *Sonia's manipulation strikes again!*

"We all got on our mats, sat quietly, or stretched out, and it was
tight in there, but there was room. There just wasn't a *lot* of room. I
could tell that my size, the space I was taking up, was a concern for
some people. Maybe not a concern, but they were noticing it. Feel-
ing it. Which is fair. I mean, it was a very small space for that many
people. How could they not?"

"So you felt weird? Nervous? Out of place?"

"I'd say I felt *awkward*. I definitely felt awkward."

"I'm sorry." Like Louise used to say, *The world wasn't made for
Eleanors*. It wasn't made for Erins, either.

"Right before the first pose, I stood and started to roll up my
mat—I really thought it would be better if I left, since I was starting
to get a few looks from people. But Sonia convinced me to stay. *All
bodies are welcome here*, she said. *The space will accommodate you*.
And you know what? It did." Erin nods, swallows, and her eyes fill
with tears. Then she puts both hands over her heart. "It was an incred-
ibly kind thing to say. People chilled out, and the class went on. The
space accommodated me. The space accommodated everyone."

I shift on the couch, annoyed. Erin wasn't supposed to get in-
veigled. She was supposed to *expose* the inveigling.

"I hate to say it, Joyce, but she knows her stuff. Her directions for each pose were clear and easy to follow, and the corrections she made on me were super smart. Crazy smart. She even identified my back problem—I'd broken it skiing a million years ago. There's no way she could have known that, but somehow she did. She understands the body, or senses things about the body, exactly like she claims to." When I roll my eyes, she shrugs. "I know. I'm sorry. I went in there expecting to hate her—to co-hate her on your behalf—but I have to say, I didn't."

I make a big fake happy face. "Well, then, thanks for nothing!"

"Actually," she says slowly, "it wasn't a total waste." She sits forward on the couch, and sighs. "Joyce—Lydia was upstairs. She was in the class."

The door suddenly opens, and we both turn. It's Lydia. She's got leggings on and a big scarf wrapped around her neck, and she's carrying her mat and her orange jacket.

"I was at my class," she says slowly, carefully, her eyes going back and forth from me to Erin again, trying to figure out what we're talking about and if I know.

"What a coincidence," I say. "So was Erin."

Lydia sucks her teeth.

"But then, of course you know that." My cheeks are hot with the rage and humiliation of trusting someone and realizing you've been duped. I feel my tongue get heavy, like I'm little again, but I try to ignore it. She's wanted to go up there since this whole thing started. She doesn't care about me, or our life down here, about how they've invaded our peace and quiet with total disregard for our feelings—my feelings. I stare at her, my eyes filling up with tears. "Why? Why would you do that to me?"

"I didn't do it *to* you. I did it *for* me."

"But why?"

"Because her classes were really helping me."

"Class*es*?" I say. "Plural? This wasn't your first one?"

Lydia says nothing.

"How long has this been going on?" My voice is shrill, like I'm trying to put together the pieces of an affair.

"A few weeks, I guess. Maybe longer. Probably longer."

"So on the nights when you've said you're going out to your 'barre' class, you really went upstairs to take Sonia's class and then came home and lied to me about it?" She shrugs. "A stupid yoga class was really that important to you?"

"And a few private sessions. And a reading—which I had to cancel because of an appointment, so that doesn't count."

"Wow. Nice," Erin says, shaking her head in disbelief. She stands, picks up her coat and her bag and her mat. "I think it's best for me to go now so that you two can work things out in private." She waves goodbye, then lets herself out, shutting the door silently behind her.

"You're right," Lydia says when we're alone and I'm still blinking, trying to figure out how I didn't notice all her missing time from the apartment. "I shouldn't have lied. I should have told you the truth."

What she thinks is a concession does nothing for me. "No. You shouldn't have gone at all."

A FEW MINUTES LATER, THERE'S A KNOCK ON THE DOOR. WE BOTH know who it is before Lydia goes to answer it.

"Can I come in?" Sonia says.

Lydia hesitates. "I'm not sure. I'll have to check with Joyce."

I turn so that I can see the two of them at the door.

"Can she come in?"

"I think we should all clear the air," Sonia says.

I shrug. "Fine. Clear the air. Be my guest."

Sonia walks in silently, her long hair in its usual loose bun, her soft white flowing pants making it look like she's floating over to the couch instead of walking on legs. *If only she made so little sound moving around upstairs.* I glare at Lydia as we follow behind her and all sit down.

"I'd offer you something to drink, but I think Joyce would kill me," she says, laughing a little, trying to lighten the mood. But I'm having none of it.

"You're right. I would kill you."

"Joyce. Lydia told me that Erin is your friend, who I assume came upstairs to find out more about my practice out of loyalty to you. To let you know if what I do is legitimate, and good, and true, and I think she found out that it is—and that I am indeed all those things. But in that well-meaning reconnaissance mission, she discovered something else entirely. Something unexpected."

"*Lydia!*" I say, the way Seinfeld used to say *Newman!*

"Yes. Lydia. So I'm here to make the peace. Again."

"Why? It didn't work last time. You've done nothing about the noise, which continues to make my life a misery."

"I've ordered sound-mitigation-flooring samples. They're on their way!"

I shrug, not sure I believe her. "You lured me upstairs and tried to extract secrets out of me. Which I don't have. And then you talked about my stutter. Which I don't have."

Lydia rolls her eyes at me. "Dude, seriously, what is the big deal about this? You used to stutter. Sometimes you still stutter. Why is it such a secret?" I ignore her.

"You make it sound like I seduced you," Sonia says.

"You kind of did. Almost. But it was all a manipulation. You were trying to befriend me so that I wouldn't complain to the city or to Douglas about what's going on here."

She stares at me, blinking with incredulity. "Why on earth would you do that?"

"Because. It's. Illegal."

"Well, I'm very sorry to disappoint you, but Douglas doesn't have a problem with our studio."

"I don't believe you."

"Joyce, he takes my classes."

Lydia nods slowly. "He does. He was there tonight. And I've seen him upstairs before."

Another betrayal; another gut punch. First Lydia, now Douglas. My sister *and* my landlord! Is nothing sacred or safe? "How can he not care about what's going on here? How can he let this go on? He owns these units. It's his responsibility to make sure everyone follows the rules."

"Joyce, this is Cambridge. Also known as the People's Republic of Cambridge. The home of antiwar protesters, civil rights fighters, and acid-tripping folk-music lovers. People pride themselves on being free thinkers. Disruptors. Rule-breakers. Douglas is just excited to have finally found a yoga class he likes. Architecture has been very bad for his back."

I shrug, then roll my eyes. *Whatever.*

"Maybe if you came up and tried a class, or did a reading with Lydia, you could move past this."

"Past what?"

"Your past. You're carrying a lot of emotional weight. I feel it."

"We should do it, Joyce. Maybe we'll learn something about ourselves and about each other. Maybe it will be the thing that finally changes our relationship."

AFTER SONIA LEAVES, LYDIA GOES INTO HER ROOM, AND I GO INTO mine. I'm tired of trying to make her understand my point, my side, the obvious wrongness of her cavorting with the enemy— my enemy—behind my back. I'm tired of trying to get her to see me. It's not working. It hasn't worked this whole time. It's like childhood all over again: Nothing I want or need matters. Tonight, after this humiliation—knowing now that for weeks she's been sneaking around, secretly going upstairs for classes and triangulating with Sonia, not to mention Douglas being up there, too, which means he never would have sided with me if I'd been stupid enough to complain to him like he was a normal landlord—something inside me shuts off like a switch.

In my room, away from Lydia, after the first flush of anger and embarrassment passes, an oddly settled feeling, a cool kind of deadness, takes its place. I'm done. I've reached the end of the line with Lydia, finally. I've tried all these months to make up for our lost years, but it's pointless. Those years are gone. And they're never coming back. We're not meant to be close. I feel it now; I know it; I accept it in my bones. It's how Tom must have felt when he told me he was leaving: how tired he was of trying to reach me, of trying to make me care; how exhausted he was by my ambivalence. *You don't love me*, he'd said. And even though he knew I did, it didn't matter anymore: *You don't love me enough.*

Lydia doesn't love me enough. Neither did Louise. And neither did Lenny.

It's barely nine o'clock when I get undressed, turn on the little lamp next to my bed, and shut the big light off. Then I get under the covers and shut the little light off, too. In the dark, I think about how I would answer Louise if she were here right now, asking me if I had any problems. If she'd asked me last night, I would have said: *How do I get my sister to love me more?* Tonight, I would say something else: *How do I tell my sister who doesn't love me enough that it's time for her to go?*

I DON'T NEED ONE OF LOUISE'S MADE-UP ANSWERS TO TELL ME WHAT to do. I get up and write to Lydia on a piece of white printer paper, folded in quarters to look like one of her old Sorry Notes, and tell her that I think it's time for her to move out.

I know it'll probably come as a shock to her, but I don't care. I want my apartment and my life back. I want my solitude and my privacy, and I want to copy my Small World poems into notebooks and not have to hide them for no other reason than I don't feel safe around Lydia. I want to finish grieving my marriage and processing my divorce, and I want to pick up where I left off with building a new life for myself. Whether I stay on here in this apartment or choose to go, too, because of the noise, I have no idea. But I do know that it's time for Lydia and me to separate.

On the front of the folded card, before I slip it under her door, I cut and paste a photo of the painting of the two us that's in the living room that I print out from a photo of it on my phone. It's not great quality, but it doesn't matter. She'll either notice the now-tied shoelace on my sneaker that I photoshopped in—and understand its message—that I'm protecting myself, trying to keep myself safe—or she won't.

———

In the Middle of What I Thought Was Nowhere
I saw a sign today
in a neighborhood I don't usually go to
that pointed to a new Dunkin Donuts,

but nothing was there.
I walked around a few corners
down a few blocks.
Still nothing.
I hadn't even planned on having a donut
but the idea was planted in my head
and now I was walking
in the middle of what I thought was nowhere
craving something I didn't even know I wanted.
On my way home I stopped at the Dunkin Donuts
near my house,
which I call "*My* Dunkin Donuts."
(Isn't that what everyone calls the Dunkin Donuts near them?)
It was right there, like I knew it would be.

PART THREE

Out of This World

New Project

The Wednesday morning before Thanksgiving, Erin and I meet at the EverMore office in Harvard Square. She has a new project for me: a rush job, mostly digitizing and organizing a tranche of photos from an old family-run camp in Western Massachusetts into a memory album—with the slim possibility of a legacy video using existing film clips and new ones that would have to be shot quickly.

"But the video is unlikely."

"That's what you always say." I put my bag down on the floor and slip my coat off, letting it drape over the back of my chair so that my phone and credit cards fall out of the pockets onto the rug.

"I know, but this time I mean it."

"That's what you always say, too."

She ignores me as I pick up my belongings. "The client's father is ill, and he wants to give it to him as a gift. But there isn't much time left, so the mini-doc probably won't happen."

"With or without the video, it's kind of bad timing, don't you think?" The thought of dealing with a difficult family situation right now—a family preparing for the loss of its center when I've got so much going on with my own difficult family situation—worries me. "I mean, it's right before the holidays."

"You're not even cooking, Joyce. Or hosting. We are, and Sammy doesn't want you or Lydia to bring anything." She looks up at the wall clock. "I have two more meetings today before I can get out of here, so let's get started already."

If I hadn't found out about Lydia's betrayal, I would have wanted to make our first Thanksgiving together in years a memorable occasion at our apartment, even though for her, Thanksgiving is not Halloween. She doesn't care about any of it—the turkey, the stuffing, the table decor—she'd much rather eat a peanut butter sandwich and work on a collage in her room. Still, I would have downloaded a million recipes, emailed myself brining instructions and tips for the best gluten-free piecrust and corn bread stuffing; I would have gleaned from lurking on Small World where to get everything premade at the last minute in case I ran out of time. I would have put together a little schedule for myself—shopping, cooking, serving, cleaning—in one of my fake-poetry notebooks. But when Erin asked us to join her and Sammy, I was grateful for the invitation. Now we can walk over, eat, and leave. No shopping, no cooking, no cleaning up. No pressure to manufacture familial meaning in the holiday, or in our relationship.

"But what about all my other work?" I say, trying, and failing, not to whine.

"You're practically done with the Maine project. I took a look at it last night and the family album was really good. The text was historically comprehensive and engaging. Well organized and beautifully arranged. The draft of the video script was excellent. Moving, even. Once it's shot and recorded and the cards are in, it'll be great."

"Really?"

"You sound surprised."

"I am. I didn't really get them as people, or as a family. It was kind of a struggle relating to them. By which I mean: I couldn't really relate to them."

"Well, you'd never know it from what you produced. I think they'll be really happy with it. I'm really happy with it."

I exhale and sit back in my chair. I'm always shocked and relieved to find out that I haven't done a terrible job and won't be getting fired anytime soon. But then I remember the photoshopped pictures: the gate by the swimming pool, the soda cans, the leash on the dog, the rope. Because it was such a vast project and there were so many images—and because there seemed to me to be an egregious number of near-death situations—I took a chance this time and left them all in. They deserved it.

"And with a few small edits, you'll be all set." She clears her throat.

"Like?"

"Like, you're probably going to want to remove the gate near the swimming pool and that ridiculous 'safety' rope on the mountaintop."

I cringe. "Okay."

"But since I'm scared to death of dogs, you can keep the leash in, and you can leave the soda cans, too. Drinking beer before night skiing and snowboarding is dangerous, so your corrective here is good for the client, legacy-wise."

"Sorry."

"I'm surprised you didn't fix any of the kids-in-the-backs-of-station-wagons and teens-in-the-backs-of-open-Jeeps. There were so many opportunities for—"

"Vehicular accidents?" I laugh, finally. "I know. I was going to add a few seat belts, but I didn't want to get greedy."

"Do you always do this? Fix the photos to make the people in them less unsafe? If you do, I've never noticed before now."

I'm surprised and relieved to hear the kindness in the question and in her voice. "Sometimes. Most of the time. But I always take them out before I turn a project in."

"Why didn't you do that this time?"

"I got careless."

She shakes her head. "No, you didn't. Joyce Mellishman does not get careless."

"I don't?"

"I think you wanted to send a message by correcting those pictures, even if nobody else got it besides me. That life is precious. That we should watch out for each other. Take care of each other. And that people shouldn't be so fucking stupid and reckless."

I smile, even though I suddenly feel awful. "I'm so embarrassed," I whisper. "I shouldn't have done that. I guess I've felt like everything shifted when the new people moved in upstairs. It's been a little destabilizing."

"I think it shifted when Lydia moved in. Though I have to say, I'm glad she came because now I understand you more. Without her, I never would have known anything about your family. Your quirks make so much more sense to me now."

"But things were calm when it was just the two of us, before they came. Before Sonia lured her up there. Though Lydia was willing to be lured. She knew that going up there would really get at me."

"Maybe not."

"Do you have a sister, Erin?" She shakes her head. "My point exactly. This is what sisters do. We mess with each other, make each other jealous, punish each other for reasons we don't even understand."

"But what if she was being truthful? What if she really wanted to work with Sonia because she really did want her help?"

"Help with what?"

"I don't know exactly, but I get the feeling that something's off with her."

"Of course something's off with her. She's Lydia."

"I mean physically. Something about her seems—fragile. Maybe Sonia was helping her with that. With whatever issues she's having with her body."

I sit back in my chair, then look out the window. From the third floor of the building on Story Street, I can see people on the sidewalks, dodging one another, dressed for winter. I think of Lydia slipping off the arm of the couch the night she first met Erin; the day I saw her fall in the grass at the Longfellow House, right before the turkeys came at her; how the glass of beer slipped through her hand later that same day at Grendel's. I feel my stomach drop.

"Do you think something's wrong with her? Do you think she's sick?"

"No." Erin shakes her head quickly. "I'm sure it's stress. She moved east, moved in with you, made a big mess going behind your back with Sonia. All I'm saying is that maybe she was being honest with you when she said she needed help with the toll all of that has taken on her."

I bite my lip. So maybe this wasn't the best time for me to have finally told her to move out.

———

Relocate/Evict
I need to
safely relocate/evict
carpenter bees
without using chemicals—
they're beneficial pollinators

needed for our ecosystem.
Looking for tips on how to
gently and humanely
encourage them to leave
and go somewhere else
before they destroy my shed.

———

"You didn't."

"I did." I tell her about Sonia's visit after the class, our conversation after that, how I slipped a note under her door before I went to bed. "It's kind of the chickenshit method of confrontation, but it's the best I could do."

"So then what happened?"

"Nothing. We haven't talked about it since."

Erin cannot understand how this is possible—how we can be moving around the same apartment, making coffee, working at our desks, running into each other before or after our walks, and occasionally overlapping in the kitchen—without talking about it. But it doesn't seem that strange to me. It's a variation on our usual behavior, our superhuman ability to ignore things that we don't want to deal with.

"Not to brag, but we're really good at compartmentalizing."

"Clearly," she says. I know she doesn't mean it as a compliment.

Before she goes into another meeting and I pack up my things to head home, she emails me the details about the new project from her laptop and tells me to take a look at everything before Monday's client meeting.

"But today's Friday."

"I know what day it is, Joyce," she says, walking me out. "I'm sending him your name and contact information, too, so he'll have it. He's super cute—I saw when I Googled him. Gideon, whose last name I forget—so you can thank me later."

———

Pie Parade
If you're baking pies
for Thanksgiving
please—take a photo
of what you make
and post it here in the comments
to inspire holiday cheer in others.
Neighbors: click the "like" button on the pies
you think are the best
and we'll post the winner of the
"First Annual Best Small World Thanksgiving Pie Contest!"
(Note: No tarts, cookies, cakes
or other non-pie desserts.
This is an all-pie thread!)

This Feels Discriminatory
Why exclude other baked goods?
Maybe some people can't eat pies
and can only, for dietary reasons or allergies,
eat non-pie desserts.
You should be more dessert-inclusive.

No Jack and Jill

D o you want to go shopping together?"

It's Friday, the day after Thanksgiving, to which we brought nothing and left with nothing—Lydia hates leftovers—except for almost a quarter of an apple pie that Erin insisted I take home. *Twist my arm*, I'd said, and carried the big wedge wrapped in tinfoil, still warm, in the deep pocket of my puffy coat. We barely spoke, Lydia and me, at dinner or on the walk home—the air clear and cold; the sky dark—we'd gone over at dusk, around four, and eaten at six. Erin's parents came in from Vermont, where she's from, and Sammy's brother had driven up from Connecticut. It was a nice group: part family, part chosen family.

"Her parents aren't really into me," Erin said to us in the kitchen as she and Sammy carved the turkey and took rolls and stuffing and bottles of wine to the table. "I think it's because Sammy's normal size and I'm not. They can't understand what she's doing with me."

"They're not into the whole gay thing," Sammy clarified. "That's why they're not here."

"I wonder what Louise would have done if one of us were gay," Lydia said when we were a block or so from our apartment.

"She probably wouldn't have even noticed."

"Unless it was Eleanor. Then she would have started a parade."

Today, when she stands in my bedroom doorway, I'm folding laundry and thinking about how I have to fix the Maine photos and familiarize myself with the new project—I need to read the client's profile; look through the forms he sent in through the website; get a sense of what to ask regarding scope and existing materials that need to be digitized, restored, archived. I'm not thinking about shopping with Lydia.

"What do you need to buy?"

"Well, Joyce, it's almost Christmas, and today's the first official shopping day of the holiday season."

"I know. But who are you shopping for?" Having a small family, or almost no family, has its positive holiday aspects: a short gift list. It also has its negatives: no one to buy presents for. Except each other, in our case, though I'm not sure I want to give her anything this year except a going-away present.

She sits down on my bed. "Good question. It's not like I have any friends these days."

"What about your upstairs friends? Or do they not celebrate Christmas, either?"

"Sonia's Jewish, but Stahn is not, so they do both."

"Good for them."

"Well, you asked."

"Well, I don't really care. I would think you would know that by now."

"I already have the gift I'm giving you—besides my gift of moving out," Lydia says, redirecting me. "It's kind of a combination Christmas and thank-you present."

I turn to her and stare. "Do you want to finally talk about it?"

"About what? About me leaving after overstaying my welcome by almost a year?" She shrugs. "Do we have to?"

"No, we don't *have* to. But maybe it would be good to. So it doesn't become a thing."

"It won't become a thing," she says. "I came, I stayed, I'm leaving. I'm grateful you let me live here so long, even if I never did tell you that in so many words. Until now."

I want to ask her why she did stay so long, where she's going—what she thinks our lives will be like after she moves out—but, as usual, I decide not to go any further. We've taken a step. We've broached the topic, acknowledged the most basic aspects of the truth. Isn't that good enough for now?

"I hope we're doing Hanukkah before I go," she says. "For old times' sake."

"If you want to."

"Of course I want to! Don't you? We haven't had a Hanukkah together since"—she moves her head back and forth as if to shake the answer loose—"high school. Not even. I think we stopped doing real Hanukkah after Lenny left. Which means early junior high school."

"It's not really Hanukkah without the Banner, so maybe we should skip it." I can't believe how well this new attitude of not giving a shit is working. The less I seem to care, the harder Lydia tries to get my attention. Has it really always been this easy?

"No!" Lydia almost howls. "We can't skip it!"

"Okay." I go back to my folding and leave Lydia staring at me, waiting for an answer on the shopping trip. Which turns out to be a *no*. I'm just not in the mood.

———

Golden Lab Looking for a Home

My name is Joey
and I am looking for a new home
because my family cannot keep me.
I'm a good dog
and though it takes me a while
to feel comfortable with new people
once I do,
I feel right at home.
I am not a particularly snuggly dog,
and sometimes I bark too much
for no reason,
but I like being petted
and taken out for walks
and I like to watch TV
especially movies or shows with
families and dogs in them,
and I don't shed much.
I also used to like sleeping on my family's bed at night
like a person
but I don't have to do that if you don't want me to.
If you can't take me in,
maybe you know someone
who can help me find a new home
and a new family
to care for me.

———

The Banner is made from heavy oaktag-shaped dreidels that spell out HAPPY HANUKKAH, in English on one side and in Hebrew—

חמש הכונה—on the other side, all held together by little brass brads so that it can expand and contract for hanging and storage. Every December, Lenny takes it out of the bottom drawer of the teak banquette in the dining room and brings it into the living room with a roll of Scotch tape or masking tape. You and Lydia love watching him tape the letters up, one by one, above the entrance to the hallway. Louise always wheels Eleanor in so she can watch, too.

When you're little, Hanukkah is eight nights of bliss: eight nights of coming home from school and waiting to light the candles in the kitchen; eight nights of closing your eyes when Louise goes into the hall closet and pulls out three little wrapped gifts—one for Lydia, one for you, and one for Eleanor—and puts them into your open hands; eight nights of squealing when you unwrap the one big gift that starts the holiday—usually a doll for you, a big box of pastels or paints for Lydia, and a stuffed gray elephant for Eleanor—and all the little gifts for the remaining seven nights: coloring books, an Etch-a-Sketch, bags of marbles and sets of jacks, new records for the record player.

Every year there's an extra special gift for all of you to share, like an Easy-Bake Oven or a Lite-Brite with all the little colored pegs to plug in. Even though Eleanor can't help with the baking or with the pegs, she's always in the kitchen with you, watching and listening to you describe your progress, the way Louise teaches you to do: *Just talk to her like you talk to each other.*

You and Lydia never narrate what you're doing when it's just the two of you in the kitchen—*I'm cracking the egg now! I'm mixing up the batter! I can't wait to eat this!*—but you do that for her. Once the tiny chocolate cake is baked by the heat of a single light bulb, or the Lite-Brite reveals the magic of what you've made with all those plastic color pieces—a sailboat, a clown's face, a blue house under a tree and a big yellow sun—you make sure she shares in the joy of it: you take turns feeding her small bites of cake and wheel her over to the Lite-Brite so she can see it. Sometimes, when it's all over, you and Lydia sit down in front of Eleanor's chair and put your heads in her lap, and she pats your hair a few times with her hand or her stuffed elephant. It's not quite a hug, but in a way, it's better.

Lenny insists on documenting everything with his movie camera—you and Lydia playing with the cheap clear dreidels that open at the top and are filled with drugstore gold chocolate coins; lighting the normal-sized candles in the big menorah and the little candles in the child-sized menorah that Louise let you buy one year from the temple gift shop when you were still members. Later, he'll take pictures with his Kodak Instamatic, directing the three of you to squish together so he can get all of you in the frame. The flare of the flash always blinds you for a few seconds and you and Lydia complain endlessly. Eleanor moans and blinks, too.

Hanukkah is also when Louise buys matching pajamas for the three of you. You know she secretly wishes that she could include herself in that yearly holiday ritual, but back then matching mother-and-daughter clothes aren't as easy to find the way they are now, in catalogues or online. You'd have to sew matching clothes yourself if you wanted them, and Louise doesn't have the patience or the skill for that kind of thing. Instead, she goes to the Carter's store for stretchy cotton floral tops and bottoms or soft flannel nightgowns which she never bothers to wrap as gifts. She hands them out, still in their plastic factory wrapping, tells you and Lydia to go upstairs and change; then she opens up Eleanor's pair and wheels her into her bedroom for her wardrobe change. When you come back down, the sight of the three of you dressed the same never fails to still Louise's perpetual motion into a moment of silent reverence. She always takes this first group picture herself: she picks up Lenny's camera, poses the two of you on either side of Eleanor, fixes all your hair barrettes, then tells you to kiss Eleanor on the cheek until the camera flashes.

Lenny then tells Louise to get in the picture, that he'll take one of the four of you. At first, she demurs, but before you know it, there she is, right behind Eleanor. Always behind Eleanor.

———

Alert: Urgent!
People in our neighborhood
still have their
Halloween decorations up.
Pretty soon it will be February
and they will still have their
Christmas decorations up too.
Maybe if people were fined for
these aesthetic offenses
we would all be better off.
I honestly find it extremely depressing to see
old dead pumpkins rotting on stoops
so long after Halloween that it's almost Thanksgiving!
Get it together, people!

———

Later that afternoon, I walk into Harvard Square alone. The sun is already on the other side of the sky, dropping down on Church Street, across from the brick dorms on the edges of Harvard Yard, even though it's only three o'clock. Dusk is coming earlier and earlier as we approach the winter solstice—and the only plus side to the ever-shorter days is that once we reach it, the tables will turn:

instead of losing a minute of daylight every day or two, we'll start gaining it. I go into the Coop for a cool notebook for Douglas even though he doesn't deserve it, then to Cardullo's for some of Erin's favorite Vermont chocolates and a really good bottle of Pinot Noir for Sammy, then to Harvard Book Store. I buy a few paperbacks and cards, though I have no idea who they're for—for Lydia maybe after all? For me if I decide not to give her anything?

Afterward, at a new café I've never heard of and have never been to, I sit at a table by the window, fogged with steam from everyone's hot drinks. I watch people in long wool coats and thick parkas and hats, carrying shopping bags, walking along Massachusetts Avenue across from the front gates of Harvard Yard. Most of the students are already gone for winter break, flying home to their Christmas trees and their big, festive holiday dinners with parents and siblings and cousins and friends. Imagining other people's families—their turkeys, their hams, their bowls of spiked eggnog, their candles and tinsel and piles of gifts wrapped and waiting next to fireplaces— always feeling like I'm on the outside looking in—seems like an impossible habit to break. Not that I've ever tried. If life—and my job—have taught me anything, it should be that every family is a mille-feuille of pathos and neuroses, sins and secrets. Someday I'll stop assuming that everyone except me grew up feeling at home in their homes.

I unzip my jacket and then hear tapping on the glass: it's Lydia. I stare at her, wave, and before I know it, she's miming that she's coming in. Inside, she moves my shopping bags off the extra chair to under the table, then sits down across from me. I offer to go up to the counter to order, but she takes out her phone and orders two hot chocolates through the café's app.

"Do you remember when Louise tried to get you to do 'Jack and Jill' with her and you wouldn't?" she says, apropos of nothing.

The story was lore in our family, the example for Louise to illustrate how difficult and stubborn I could be. She never understood that it might have something to do with my fear of stuttering.

"What on earth made you think of that?"

"I have no idea."

I manage a half smile. I have a tiny soft spot for the story, even though the joke is at my expense. Most of Louise's jokes were at other people's expense—especially at Lenny's, who was always such a good sport about things like that—but since there were so few funny stories in our family, I learned to tolerate it. It almost felt like a story from someone else's family.

"'Jack and Jill,'" Lydia says, first imitating Louise, then imitating me:

"No Jack and Jill."

I smile, then look down.

"Went up the hill." Lydia waits for me to answer. When I don't, she again says what I used to say:

"No went up the hill."

I laugh a little.

"To fetch—?"

Here Lydia leans over and gives me a little nudge. "Come on," she pleads. "Say it!"

I shake my head.

She tries again. "To fetch—?"

I sigh. "No to fetch."

And that's where the joke ends: at *no to fetch*, the ultimate act of refusal, of noncompliance. Not much of a joke, now that I think about it.

"Why wouldn't you say it with Louise? Was it because of the stuttering or was it something else? I've wanted to ask you that for as long as I can remember."

It seems obvious. "I was being withholding. I didn't want to give her what she wanted because I felt like she never gave me what I wanted."

Our hot chocolates arrive, and we stir our cups with the tiny spoons waiting on the saucers.

"What did you want?"

"The same thing as you, probably. More attention. More love." I take a sip of cocoa and think how it tastes almost exactly like the packets of Swiss Miss we used to make after school. "Of course she loved me. And us. I know that. But it never really felt like she did. It never felt like the love she had for Eleanor."

"Why was that? Why was it so much easier for her to love Eleanor than us?"

"Shame? I don't think you can give birth to a child with disabilities and not feel like it's your fault somehow, even though it's not. It's no one's fault."

"Maybe it was guilt," Lydia says.

"For what?" She shrugs but doesn't answer. "Whatever it was made her give everything she had to Eleanor." I think of the rhyme that I wouldn't say in a different light now: Louise pushing us all up a hill and me refusing to help because it wasn't my hill to climb. "It was wrong to have expected more from her," I say. "I see that now, after all these years. It was unfair. She was doing her absolute best in a horrible situation. Neither of us are parents. We can't possibly understand what it was like for her. For them. And how, in the midst of all that grief, she managed to transform mourning into advocacy. Louise really was amazing in so many ways." I'm sorry, and sad, suddenly, knowing I never told her that.

"I think that's why I didn't want kids," Lydia says. "I didn't want to fail them. And I would have. I know I would have. I'm too selfish."

"I didn't want kids because I was afraid of the genetics. And because I'm selfish, too. I can't help it. That's how I'm wired. How we're both wired. Like we grew up hungry and can't share our food with anyone." I think of Tom, probably dating again. Maybe he'll meet someone and have a baby, like he always wanted. Someone normal, who's there when she's there. He's still young enough. There's still time for him.

"Maybe it was meant to be this way after all," Lydia says. "Us two. Maybe it's always been us two. Though sometimes I wonder what it would have been like if we had been three."

———

You remember the vacuum cleaner marks, wide and dark, on the wall-to-wall carpet in the living room. Gold broadloom. Floor-to-ceiling drapes along the windows that faced the street. Little sconces on either side of the mirror above the fireplace. Danish modern side tables and lamps; the low-slung nubby couch and two matching wood-framed armchairs. The room always feels empty. You only really use it for Louise's meetings and on holidays when Uncle Murray comes over.

There's a piano—a chestnut-brown French provincial baby grand. Its two front feet and the one in the back are carved into what always looked like toes on animal paws. You love to dust the piano—a soft white cloth in one hand, a can of lemon Pledge in the other, you kneel around the bottoms of the coffee tables and side tables, dusting all the legs above where they meet the carpet, and then wipe down their tops, too. And then you crawl over to the piano and dust all of the paw feet and the curve of its body.

Sometimes, when the house is quiet, which it often is after Eleanor goes to Fernald, you lie under the piano on the vacuum marks.

You look up at all the strings and wooden joints, then eventually curl up, using the little dust cloth as a pillow. It's the perfect place to be. There but not there.

One time, in the late afternoon—Lenny is still at work and Lydia is upstairs drawing—Louise wanders into the living room. You can see her stockinged feet on the rug from your secret vantage point, but she can't see you. When she sits down on the bench and lifts the cover, you know her fingers are resting on the keys, lightly, barely touching them, for seconds before her playing starts. Like she's getting her bearings. Or deciding if she feels like playing. She doesn't feel like doing much of anything lately except sleeping during the day and staring out the window when she's awake. Part of you thinks she might close the cover and walk away. You can totally see that happening.

How many times have you sat beside her on the bench, to her right, when she plays, in thin cotton pajamas with your bare feet dangling and your hair wet from a bath before bed, or in a flannel nightgown and slippers on the occasional snow day when you get to stay home from school? Louise had trained to be a concert pianist—an unlikely profession for a girl from a poor family living on the top floor of a triple-decker house in one of Boston's old Jewish neighborhoods. But she had talent, and she'd worked her way through two years of the New England Conservatory as a scholarship student. Had things been different—had Eleanor been born healthy—Louise would have finished college and pursued a performing career or become a music teacher once you were old enough to be in school. But before getting her degree, Louise met Lenny, and shortly after that, they married and had Lydia, then Eleanor, then you. Louise stopped playing seriously then, though sometimes she'd sit down and play, from memory, one of the pieces she'd studied. Not often, because Eleanor didn't like it. Of all the things Louise had intuited about her likes and dislikes, her sounds and movements, she was never able to figure out why the piano playing bothered her so much.

But this day, with Eleanor gone, she plays. First Chopin—a waltz, and a nocturne—then Rachmaninoff. Her foot pumps the pedal with each measure, and you scoot a few inches back, sitting up now, with your elbows on your knees and your chin in your hands. It seems like some kind of magic, how she can make such incredible sounds come out of the piano, her fingers flying over the keys, her hand occasionally flipping the page of the sheet music in front of her.

As always, you're caught between wanting to be seen and wanting to stay hidden. The dual impulse pulls at you, both options problematic in their own way. You run through the pros and cons of coming out or staying hidden before making a move. Will she be mad if she finds you there, doing nothing, when you should be doing something useful, finishing your homework or cleaning your room? Or will she be happy if you crawl out and sit next to her on the bench to witness and admire her skill? Sometimes remaining unseen seems like the safest option. You don't want to make her pay attention to you if she doesn't want to.

Her feet move from the bench to the curvy side of the piano. Then they stop. You hold your breath, wondering if you should come out—come clean—already, but before you decide what to do, Louise is bending down. Now she's peering at you under the piano. Is she smiling? You stare at her, panicked, unable to speak or breathe.

"I thought I smelled the lemon Pledge," she says.

"Sorry," you manage, without stuttering.

"For what?"

Unlike Lydia, you have no idea what you're apologizing for—no long explanation for whatever it is you think you did wrong. As she crouches there, her black skinny pants hugging her ankles, her long gray cardigan grazing the carpet, you think she might crawl under the piano, too. And if she does? What will you do together? Louise doesn't play or even engage unless there's a purpose—to teach you something new, like a new game Eleanor can play or at least follow along with, or when she helps you with your math or spelling. She isn't one for small talk or jokes or levity unless she's with Eleanor— that's when the words and the warmth and the love flow most freely. When she is most fluid in her body and in her mind. When she is most herself.

But now Eleanor is gone, and it's the two of you in the quiet of the afternoon. You wonder if you should say something. Ask her if she misses Eleanor. Because you do.

"For hiding?" you finally answer. You realize you're still holding the can of Pledge.

"Sometimes I hide, too," she says.

You start to move over, to make room for her underneath the piano so you can hide together, but when you look up you see her knees and her feet as she's walking away.

———

Lost Doll Waiting to Be Found
Someone lost a doll
near the playground on Vassal Lane.
I rescued it and put it
on a bench
the closest one to where we found it.
My thinking was: whoever dropped it
might walk by later in a panic
looking to see if it was still there

wherever it had slipped out of their hands
or fallen out of a bag or purse
or hoping that someone rescued it
and put it where it could be found
like I had.
That's what I would have done—
that's what I always did when my son
would drop a stuffed animal or toy train or favorite blanket—
I would retrace our steps
and find whatever we'd lost on the ground
dirty and wet usually but safe.
Intact.
Nothing a good laundering or wiping couldn't fix.
But on my morning walk
I saw that the doll is still there
still waiting
to be found.
Doesn't anyone miss her?

Gideon

It's blustery on Sunday when I take my afternoon walk, under bare trees, the branches creaking in the wind. The leaves, all of them fallen now, though most of them still not raked, fill the gutters of the streets and cover the sidewalks. The smell reminds me of childhood—how Lenny would rake two huge piles at the end of October or early November, one on the front lawn and one in the backyard, for Lydia and me to jump in. It feels so long ago that I can't fathom the distance from there to here.

I kick my way through the leaves on the cobblestone sidewalk as I turn the corner onto my street, the way Lydia did on that bright late September day a few months back when Sonia and Stan moved in. At the time I'd found it annoying, but today I'm wistful when I think of her feet and legs rustling through the orange and red leaves on the way back inside. My memory has already transformed that time into a honeymoon period, all hazy and blurry and soft and golden, though of course it was really none of those things. She was annoying even then. But we were getting along, avoiding, for the most part, any and all conversational minefields—Louise, Lenny,

Eleanor, Fernald—even though we still weren't close. We still weren't talking about the past, about the future, or even about the present—about our divorces, our jobs, about why she wasn't moving on and advancing in her new life and why I was stuck in my Small World world. How did I not wonder about this?

I wonder about it now. And about my staggering and inexplicable lack of curiosity about something so obviously odd and unexplained. I'd missed the fact that Erin is gay. Didn't she and Lydia both joke about how dense I was for not catching on, about how many clues I hadn't picked up on along the way? And then, of course, I missed the fact that Lydia had been sneaking upstairs for classes for over a month. How is that possible? What a failure of opportunity on my part, to be closer, to try to understand who she is now and why she's here. All that time squandered when I should have been paying more attention. When I should have been more alert and engaged and aware of what was going on around me. What else have I missed? What else have I not seen that's been happening in plain sight?

AS SOON AS I GET HOME, WHEN I SIT DOWN TO MAKE THOSE CHANGES to the Maine photos that Erin noticed, I see this email from our new client:

> This might seem like a strange question, but are you any relation
> to someone named Louise Mellishman?
> —Gideon Bloom

How does he know Louise? She worked with many families over the years, but that was such a long time ago.

Yes—she was my mother.

A few seconds pass:

I'm Alan Bloom's son.

My mouth drops open as I type:

Camp Fantastic Alan??

An unknown local number buzzes across my phone and I answer it.

"I knew it. When I saw your name, I knew you had to be related to Louise. I mean, how many Mellishmans are there in the world?"

I'm so shocked I can barely speak. "Not enough."

"I'm Gideon, by the way."

"I'm Joyce."

"Hi, Joyce. What are the chances that our paths would cross like this?" He laughs in disbelief. "It's kismet."

"Definitely," I finally manage to say.

"You probably don't remember this, but we came to Louise's funeral. It was a while ago, and there were a lot of people there. I went with my father."

I don't remember meeting him, though I do vaguely recall seeing Alan there—older, but still bearded and with the same warmth in his face. Most of the other people from Fernald that I would have recognized were long gone, but still it was crowded with families who had been young when Louise was crusading for disability rights, first locally and then nationally. I remember being touched that someone from so deep in Louise's past—in our past—would take the time to show up for her after so many years.

"Alan is a very special person," I say, my voice cracking. "We—my sister Lydia and I—spent a week with our other sister, Eleanor, at his camp."

"He told me about that. I was too young that summer, but I came the following year."

"We were supposed to come back that summer, too, as junior counselors, but it didn't work out."

There's a pause as we process the timeline, the missed connection so long ago. "How's your sister doing? Is she still in California?"

"Funny you should ask," I say, then tell him that Lydia's been living with me in Cambridge for almost a year. "But I think she's finally moving out soon, to get a place of her own."

"I'm in Cambridge, too."

"No way," I say. There's another pause, but this time it's a short one.

"Listen, I know we're supposed to meet tomorrow, but do you think there's any way we could meet today? This feels like it can't wait."

I look at the Maine photos on my monitor—the stupid rope and the pool gate—and think of how I need to fix them as quickly as possible so I can rid myself of the residual shame of being caught in the act of unauthorized photoshopping. "Why don't you come by in an hour. Bring your materials over and I'll go through everything tonight and get a jump on things. Lydia should be home soon, too. She'd kill me if she missed you."

WHEN I OPEN THE DOOR AND SEE GIDEON STANDING IN THE VESTI-bule, I feel like I'm looking at Alan all those years ago at Camp Fantastic—at least, what I remember Alan looking like: the same dark eyes, intense but kind; the same barrel chest; not quite the same beard but handsomely unshaven. He's wearing one of those knit floppy beanie hats and a flannel shirt under a jacket, which makes him look like a hipster version of his father at this age, and he's holding a big plastic box with a snap-top lid. The archivist in me hopes that lid is airtight and has been all these years.

"This is so weird," I say, waving him into the apartment. "If you were wearing a Steppenwolf T-shirt, I'd think it was Alan himself standing here." My memory of him from that day is as clear as a photograph.

He puts the box down, unzips his jacket, then unbuttons his flannel shirt to reveal that very same old T-shirt. "When I said I was coming to see you, he told me to wear it. He remembers you. And he saves everything." He picks up the box again. "His memory goes in and out—sometimes its super sharp, sometimes not so much. His oldest memories are often the clearest."

"I'll never forget how he pointed out a ketchup stain on that T-shirt instead of sounding out the letters." I tell him how Lydia had dyslexia and I had a stutter, but he didn't make us read the word. "He wasn't like anyone we'd ever met. He let us be ourselves. And he included us in everything that week."

"Louise was one of a kind, too. She meant a lot to him. He admired her so much for the work she did." He reaches into one of his jacket pockets. "There's also this." It's a black-and-white snapshot of Lydia and me and Alan crouching down around Eleanor's wheelchair by the pool.

"I remember that day," I say, almost in a whisper. "It was the first time we felt comfortable around Eleanor. Like we were truly connected. He was the only one who had ever referred to the three of us together. He called us the Mellishman Sisters."

He follows me into the living room and puts the box down on the floor next to the coffee table. I take his coat—a bright yellow lightweight nylon parka with lots of snaps and zippers and pockets that looks like something a serious hiker might wear—which makes me nervous—and lay it over the arm of a nearby chair.

When we sit down on the couch, he tells me that he found EverMore online, that he'd been meaning to preserve his family's photos for ages, but now, given the circumstances, this accelerated schedule they're on because of Alan's rapidly declining health—he's hoping to put everything into a form that can be looked at easily, on an iPad, in bed. "There are a lot of people and places my father wants to revisit before he goes," he says, his eyes filling again. "I thought we'd have more time, but we don't."

"We can take care of that," I say softly. "It's what we do." I clear space on the coffee table and put the box on top of it. When I remove the lid, the familiar scents of age and time, of basements and attics, dust and mildew, hits me. Every family's memories are different, but they all smell the same.

"Everything's in there. Photos from my father's side, my mother's side, my brother, Asher, who my father started the camp for, before he died. All that. And then there's a decade's worth of Camp Fantastic pictures—Alan was an amateur photographer back then. I'm sure there are pictures of Louise, and there might be a few more of you and Lydia and Eleanor. But I haven't gone through everything. I'm not really sure what's in there."

I'm about to offer him a drink, or some hummus to stab at with celery or carrot sticks, when he looks up at the ceiling. The noise has started. Footsteps—heavy ones—are advancing across the ceiling.

He points. "What is that?"

"It's a long story."

He puts an arm across the couch cushion and crosses his legs. "Tell me. I like long stories."

So I do. I tell him about Lydia moving back from California finally after so long and how we were doing pretty well, living together, even though it was occasionally weird and sometimes very weird, but how everything changed when the new people moved in upstairs. "By which I mean, everything changed when the noise started." I don't bother to tell him the part about Lydia's betrayal.

He stands up. He's tall—six feet at least, I think—and he tilts his head so that his ear is a tiny bit closer to the ceiling. As if that will help him diagnose the sound. But he can't. He looks at me, stumped.

"It's a couple," I say. "She teaches yoga, among other things, in a real studio—that they built—right above our heads. Classes and private lessons and wellness consulting and medical-medium readings. One-stop shopping for the spiritual seeker."

"Doesn't it drive you crazy? Because it would drive me crazy." He follows the movement to the other side of the living room, then back again to our side. "It's so irregular and unpredictable. So uneven. I would have a very hard time with this. Not knowing what kind of noise and where it's going to come from next would make me very anxious. I'm anxious right now just talking about it!"

I'm so relieved to hear him say that, I'm almost in tears. We both look at the ceiling again. There's laughing, walking, some kind of jumping. "I thought I was being a whiner."

"You're not being a whiner." He sits down and looks at me intently, as if it's very important I understand that point. "Noise makes your heart race, your blood pressure rise; it affects your ability to think and focus. You work at home part of the time, right? Most of the time?"

"I do. And it's really hard for me to concentrate now." There I go again, being unprofessionally frank about my working-from-home problems. "Not that it will affect your project. What I mean is, in the *past* it may have been a little challenging."

"A *little* challenging? I can barely focus on what you're saying, there's so much activity going on up there!" Now there's thumping. He covers his mouth with his hand in shock. "This is insane!"

"They all just unrolled their mats and got down on the floor."

"There's a whole field of study on noise epidemiology. In fact, the woman who studies it is right here at Harvard. Noise is a serious public health issue, especially in urban areas."

Noise epidemiology. I practically swoon at the validation. "How do you know so much about this?"

"I used to be a social worker—lots of bad-neighbor issues to deal with."

When I ask him what he does now, he tells me he's a therapist. When I ask him what kind, he says: "Couples."

I laugh. "I'm divorced! So is Lydia!"

He laughs, too. "I've never even been married!" He looks up at the ceiling again, and then over at the box. "Listen, I've already taken up enough of your evening. We can do the rest of this during normal business hours, whatever those are now."

"The real reason you're leaving is that you can't take the noise anymore."

He rubs his temples under the beanie. "Seriously! I'm getting a headache!"

He stands, then I stand, then I hand him his jacket and walk him to the door. "I'll get a start on the box tonight, and we'll go from there." And then, right before I put my hand on the doorknob, the door opens. It's Lydia. She stares at both of us, like she's interrupted something intimate and private, even though in all the months she's lived here, neither of us has had anything that even remotely resembled a date.

"You're not going to believe this, Lydia, but do you remember Alan from Camp Fantastic? This is his son. Gideon."

She sucks her teeth. "Wow. I did not have Alan's son showing up at our apartment on my bingo card for how this year would end."

Gideon looks at me. I make hostage eyes at him. "EverMore is going to do a legacy project for him. For Alan. Isn't that an amazing coincidence?"

She takes her jacket off and hangs it on the coat tree, then glances at Gideon. "How is the old dude?"

I stare at her.

"Not that great," he says. "He's quite ill, almost at the end of the road."

"That's a bummer."

"Uhm, Lydia?"

She glares at me. "What?"

Gideon smiles politely, but he's clearly confused by her behavior. "You know what's weird?" he says, trying again. "I remembered on the way over here that I saw you in California, not long after you moved there. My father and I ran into you and Louise at some little fish shack in Malibu. We were out there looking at colleges for me. Isn't that wild? What a small world."

"More kismet," I say.

Lydia shoves her hands in the front pockets of her baggy chinos. "I don't remember that."

"Well, it was a long time ago," he concedes.

"Well, I definitely don't remember it. Maybe you have me confused with someone else. Hundreds of families went to your camp, am I right? And how old were you then—twelve?"

"No, I was seventeen. And I don't think I'm confused. Not about this. About seeing someone we knew, like Louise."

"Well, I do. I think you're confused."

She kicks off her clogs and walks straight through the living room into the kitchen. I turn and watch her until she's out of sight.

After he steps out into the vestibule and I apologize before shutting the door behind him, I march back into the living room and stand there. "You are so fucking rude," I call out to Lydia. "You really are." Now that she's finally going to move out, I don't have to be polite. I can say whatever I want to, however I want to. Who cares if she doesn't like it? It doesn't matter anymore.

"What are you talking about?" she says, coming out of the kitchen with a container of stabby hummus.

"Just now! You were incredibly rude—hostile, even—when he mentioned running into you in California. You shut him down for no reason."

"There *was* a reason: *It didn't happen.*" She turns back toward the kitchen. "If being honest is rude, then, well, as usual, I'm sorry, Joyce."

"Maybe it happened and you forgot."

"Why do you believe him and not me?"

"Because he seems like he knows what he's talking about."

"And I don't?"

I cross my arms across my chest. "No, actually, you don't."

She puts the hummus down. "You trust the son of some guy we knew for a week almost forty years ago more than me."

"Pretty much."

"So I'm a liar, Joyce? Is that it?"

"I'm not saying you're a liar, even though you *do* lie." I look up at the ceiling for emphasis. "I'm saying that maybe you forgot and for some reason you're too stubborn to admit it."

"Fine. I forgot," she says, before going into her room and slamming the door. "I forgot something that never even happened."

Grendel's Den

I wake up in the morning with a Lydia hangover. I half expect to find a Sorry Note slipped under my door, but when I get out of bed there's nothing there. No explanation for her awful behavior the night before with Gideon. Brushing my teeth and putting my pants on, I decide that she owes me an apology. A real one. One she should deliver in person, to my face, using actual spoken words. I've never seen her be so aggressively rude—not even those first few times she was around Erin. I don't know what happened, but something triggered her to behave like an attack dog.

If I think I'm going to get an in-person apology when I go into the kitchen to make coffee, I'm wrong about that, too. She turns her back to me while we both wait for the machine to finish brewing, then reaches into the cabinet for a mug without getting one for me. Such a child. The second the coffee is ready, she grabs the pot and pours herself a cup, then shoves the carafe back into the machine and heads straight for her room without a word. Normally she gives me a sense of her schedule and what the shape of her day looks like—conference calls for work, a deadline to meet, an exercise or meditation class—but not today. Today there's nothing.

I take my coffee to my desk and check both my email accounts— work and personal—and all my social media accounts, then scroll quickly through Small World. So many possible posts awaiting transformation into poems—free items offered for giveaway; tem- porary pop-up Christmas tree store stands; shovelers looking for upcoming winter work and neighbors looking to line up regular shovelers who do a good job and shovel down to the pavement and brick sidewalks before rushing on to the next house because other- wise what's the point—but there's no time. Alan's box, which I was too tired to make a dent in last night, awaits.

The first folder I find inside it is sepia photos of Old-Country Jews in the New Country: dark-haired, dark-eyed, anxious immi- grants regarding the camera, the person behind it, and probably every single other thing in life, with intense distrust. My people. They could be Louise's and Lenny's parents and grandparents. The same gene pool.

Next, I lift out several photo albums, the kind with padded covers and those awful inserts where you peel back a sheet of thin plastic, put your photos down on the sticky page, then smooth the staticky plastic back over the photos, trying not to leave creases or air bubbles on top of the pictures. Which is impossible. The aging pages crinkle as I flip through them—pictures from the '60s, '70s, and '80s. According to the captions, they're mostly of Alan and his wife, Gideon's mother, both very young and good-looking, in New York City; in Washington, DC; and on Cape Cod. A few pages later: Alan and his wife ecstatic with their newborn—*Baby Asher!*— leaving the hospital, then swaddled after his first bath in the kitchen sink. Now with toddler Asher, who very clearly appears to have Down syndrome, at the beach, in a high chair, asleep in a crib. And then: a few pictures of Fernald: the sign; the grounds; Asher in a wheelchair now, whatever condition he has considerably more physically debilitating, bundled up in a hat and gloves and scarf, with his parents behind him, each gripping a handle to push. Then the last of them, a series—*Asher at Camp Fantastic*—in his chair near the pool; in Alan's arms, under the giant white pines, the two of them looking up at the sky.

The next few albums are almost all Gideon pictures, taken years later, according to the captions, though in many of the same poses and places as Asher's album: *First bath in the kitchen sink*; *At the beach!*; *The view from the high chair*; *Under the pines at Camp Fantastic*. But where Asher's album ends sometime after dinosaurs and trains but before T-ball, Gideon's albums follow a full arc, from birth to adulthood: there's preschool and kindergarten and elementary school, Little League and bikes and soccer, playing drums and guitar with Alan, hiking and skiing, getting bar mitzvahed. There's long hair. Short hair. Baseball caps. Cowboy hats. Friends. Cars. High school graduation. College graduation. There's no Asher in any of the Gideon pictures and no Gideon in the Asher pictures. I wonder if Gideon was too young to know Asher, if he lived at Fernald for most of his life before he died. Kind of the inverse of Eleanor, who lived with us most of her life but died after being at Fernald for less than a year.

On top of the next layer of material is a thick accordion folder labeled CAMP FANTASTIC. As expected, there are lots of black-and-white and color snapshots from its ten years of operation—from the beginning, when Alan took over a small existing summer camp in the Berkshires, to its final days a decade later. There are the small wooden buildings and cabins, the bunks, the office, the pool. And the tall pine trees towering over everything. Nothing in the file appears to be in any particular order, date-wise, but I can tell by the clothes and the hair when I'm getting closer to the summer we were there. As Gideon promised, there are a few more pictures of Lydia and me: with Eleanor, without Eleanor, with Louise and Eleanor, and the four of us—Louise, Eleanor, Lydia, and me—inside, outside, waving goodbye from the car. I put these aside, on top of a stack of books on my desk, to scan copies later for myself.

Flipping through the rest of the accordion folder, I find more photos of Louise. Without us. Another summer. Are we there? Is this Camp Fantastic? Or somewhere else? I look on the back of one of the pictures of Louise, in a long Indian-print skirt and her hair in a braid, leaning against a tree. *Walden Pond, 1977.* Why does Alan have pictures of her at Walden Pond? *Race Point, Provincetown, 1978. Harvard Square, 1979.* Eleanor is dead by then. The photos of Louise change with each passing year—her hair gets longer, then shorter, then longer again; darker then flecked with gray; her eyes flat, then wide and full of life. She's smiling at the camera. At who's behind the camera.

At Alan.

I stand up and start digging through the box, then dump everything out onto my desk. Family photos get mixed in with Camp Fantastic photos and newspaper articles and clippings as I search. But search for what? I don't know what I'm looking for—I only know that I'll know when I find it. Whatever "it" is. And that's what happens. I feel it first—a thick manila envelope, marked LOUISE. I pinch the rusted clasp, then look inside: letters. Letters from Louise to Alan? Do I want to read them? No. Knowing she wrote them is more than enough to know for now.

There's a picture inside the envelope, outside all the letters. I slip my hand in to fish it out. A faded color snapshot of Louise sitting at a bar in a batik-print tank top, smoking a cigarette, a glass of white wine in front of her. Her arms are tan, and her teeth are white. She's smiling. I don't remember her smiling like that at home. Next to her, a waitress, with an apron around her waist, her hair in a loose bun, looks on, not smiling. I squint at the waitress to bring her into focus: Is that Lydia? On the back of the photo: *Grendel's Den, July 1984.*

I struggle to piece this picture, and the bigger picture, together: I am in high school then. Lydia is working at Grendel's one of the summers she's home from college. Eleanor has been gone for seven years already. And Lenny? He's gone from the house, but not entirely from our lives yet. Are they even divorced then? Does it matter?

I turn the manila envelope over to make everything in it fall out. Letters, stamped, addressed in Louise's perfect cursive, to Alan in Cambridge: a law firm. Is that what his real job was when he wasn't running the summer camp? Letters addressed to him at Camp Fantastic. There are more pictures, photos that Alan must have wanted to keep with the letters. *World's End, 1979. Louise, Lydia, and Gideon.*

I don't understand. I yell for Lydia to come out of her room and when she does, I stand in front of her, holding the picture up like a sign.

"Where was I?" The words come out in a low growl. An animal sound. "How come I wasn't there?"

She sucks her teeth. "You were away. At stutter day camp. I think. I don't remember."

I stare at the photo again, then at her. "Louise and Alan were involved? In a *relationship*? All those years?" She doesn't say no. Which means yes. "Why didn't you tell me? How could you not tell me?"

"How could I possibly tell you? It would have crushed you." When I shake my head slowly, like she's a stranger, she pleads, "I was trying to protect you."

I sit down on the couch. "Did Lenny know? Is that what made him fall apart?"

She sits down across from me, closes her eyes, then sighs. A lifetime of secrecy and omission is finally leaving her body. "Once or twice, maybe more, she took me with her somewhere—on an errand, on a walk, to the beach—and we'd run into Alan. Like it was an accident. Like it was such a small world. I never saw them do anything except talk. It just seemed like they were friends—really really close friends who had to see each other and who were desperate to talk to each other. I assumed it was their disability work. I guess they thought no one would suspect they were involved if I was there. Who would want a witness to an affair? When Lenny found out, it stopped for a while, but then it started again."

"Like when they came to Grendel's?"

"How do you know about that?"

I point to the box. "There's a picture." I stare at her. "Is that what happened with Gideon when he and Alan ran into you and Louise?"

"She was out there on business. Advocacy business. Some rally or march or meeting or vote. She never traveled for fun, or just to see me. We made a plan to meet for dinner afterward—the two of us—Brad was working. And that's when Alan and Gideon showed up at the restaurant. Coincidentally, out of the blue." She makes air quotes with the fingers of both hands. "Which of course it wasn't. They'd planned it. To give them cover."

"But why? Hadn't Lenny moved out by then?"

"Because Alan was still married. Because Lenny was so broken—first about Eleanor, then about the affair. The practice was gone, and he had moved in with Uncle Murray, trying to teach here and there, but losing every job he got. Because she wanted him to think that's all it was—a brief affair—that she'd turned to Alan in her grief after Eleanor died, not that it was an ongoing relationship. Because she blamed him for the decision to send Eleanor to Fernald. Because when Eleanor moved and when she died, the part of Louise we knew, and the part of herself that she knew, died, too."

I sit quietly, my mind racing. It's not the fact of the affair that bothers me as much as it is *the secret* of it. Of having been tricked, excluded from the truth, while Lydia knew and was included in it. As hard as it must have been for her to carry that knowledge as a child, and all through our adult years, I can't help but feel left out. Have I always suspected there was a secret like this? Is that why, as Lydia accused me that afternoon with the turkeys, I don't trust anyone? Why I haven't ever completely and fully trusted her?

I ask her, then, if that's everything. If there's anything else she hasn't told me.

"No," she says. "That's everything. I swear."

———

Why Can't He Be on the Same Tree
There's a turkey
sitting on the fence
between two houses
off Brattle Street.
I'm not certain
but I think it's a male turkey
who's on the fence
while there are a bunch of female turkeys
up in a tree.
Did they tell him he can't join them?
Did he say or do something offensive
after which they made it clear

that he was not welcome
to sit with them?
I just don't understand
or think it's fair
that he's alone
while they're all together
so close by.
He must feel sad
being excluded
like that.

———

You don't remember a time before your stutter, when your words come freely, when speaking doesn't instantly make you nervous, afraid that you won't be able to push your words out from around a stubborn tongue. Were you always this way? Were you born like this? One day, one of Eleanor's aides, a young woman with a long braid and a crocheted vest with a big red flower on it who is finishing up a speech pathology degree at Boston University, asks Louise about your stutter, then she asks you: *Does your breath catch in your chest and stop? Does your brain go blank? Does your throat tighten and seize, making the air get stuck somewhere between your lungs and your teeth?* Maybe? Sort of? You're not sure. When she doesn't write anything you've said down in her school notebook, you wonder if you answered all the questions wrong. All you know is that as far back as you can see yourself—at three or four years old, in pajamas, and little girly dresses, and snow pants and hooded jackets, at school slumping down in your seat in kindergarten and first grade so you won't get called on to read the letters on the wall out loud or repeat a line of a nursery rhyme—you try not to use many words when you talk. The fewer you say, the less chance you have of starting a stumble and fall that you won't be able to recover from.

Then, one day, your stutter gets worse. Much worse. You know what day this is, what happens on this day. You're seven. It's a bright morning, in spring, sharp yellow light coming through the kitchen windows, green trees behind it. Louise has put two large suitcases, the old-fashioned kind, with handles, in the hallway by the front door. You know what's inside the suitcases because you saw her packing them last night before you went to bed. They're full of Eleanor's things: tops, pants, bibs, hair ties and ribbons, sweaters, jackets, pajamas and robes, and all kinds of socks and shoes and slippers, and a few stuffed elephants. And diapers. She's not sure if she needs to bring her own or if Fernald will provide them, so she packs them anyway. *Better safe than sorry.*

Lenny is in the living room with an unopened newspaper in his lap, staring into space. You think he's taken a pill already, the kind that helps him when he's nervous, he told you once when you catch him popping one into his mouth and swallowing it without water, but you're not positive. He's waiting—we're all waiting— for Louise.

You and Lydia are at the table finishing your cereal—Apple Jacks for Lydia and Alpha-Bits for you—when Louise finally appears. She clears your bowls and brings you crayons and coloring books even though you're almost too old for them, and an Etch-a-Sketch for Lydia. Then she goes back down the hallway past the den to Eleanor's room.

You know that Eleanor is leaving today—that she is moving to Fernald because it's kind of a hospital, and Eleanor needs to be around doctors and nurses now that her seizures are getting worse. Lenny had been trying and failing to convince Louise for a while that the doctors were right, that Eleanor needed more care than they could give her at home, but Louise wouldn't hear of it. Then Eleanor had such a bad seizure that they had to call an ambulance. That's when everything changes.

She almost died, Lenny says.

No, she didn't.

Louise. I don't want her to leave, either, but it's for the best. For everyone. Eleanor. The girls. The two of us. It's too much now. It's not safe for her here anymore. We have no choice now.

There is always a choice.

At some point while you're coloring, you hear a strange sound, like an animal howling and trying to be quiet, but you don't have any pets and none of the neighbor's dogs are outside. You put your crayon down. Lydia didn't make the sound, and you don't think Lenny did, either. You hear it again. It's coming from Eleanor's room, off the den. You slide out of the L-shaped bench and tell Lydia you'll be right back, but she barely looks up from her Etch-a-Sketch.

Something makes you tiptoe past the den. The same thing makes you stop a few steps short of Eleanor's room. You know you're meant to linger out of sight, that there's something you're meant to learn.

Mommy loves you. There is another sound, like the one you heard from the kitchen—a gasp, a struggle for breath, as if she's been punched and all the air is being forced out of her lungs against her will. *Mommy doesn't want you to leave.*

You can hear Louise trying to contain her sobs, then you hear her pull out a few tissues from the Kleenex box and blow her nose.

Mommy will visit you as much as she can. The words come out in a whisper, but they're just loud enough for you to hear.

Eleanor is gurgling and fussing in her chair the way she does when she's excited or upset or uncomfortable or hungry or has to pee—only Louise completely understands the tiny differences in her vocalizations and movements; only she can correctly decipher the pitch and tone of her sounds like an actual language. *Eleanor is tired. Eleanor needs to be changed. Eleanor is overwhelmed because the music is too loud.* Louise is always interpreting Eleanor and explaining her to you, directing the action of your family. She is always clearing a path for her to get what she needs. It seems like magic, how connected she is to Eleanor, as if she can read her mind.

But today you feel like you've seen and heard something you shouldn't have. Like a secret has been revealed that should have remained unknown. *Louise loves Eleanor the most.* More than you, more than Lydia, more than Lenny. That's what you think you've learned. And what you're seeing now when you peek into the room: Louise kneeling down in front of Eleanor's chair, resting her head on the soft stuffed elephant in Eleanor's lap, Eleanor patting her hair with her hands. Louise isn't making any noise, but you know she's crying because her whole body is shaking. Later you'll understand what you saw that day: your mother, cracking open and breaking apart, every piece of scaffolding inside her body and spirit collapsing until there was nothing left to hold her up.

You back away from the door, tiptoe to the kitchen, then sit down at the table again to color, like nothing happened, but when Lydia asks you where you were, you don't answer. You can't answer. Your mouth opens, but no words come out. You try again, but you only make sounds. They're stuck in your throat, then choppy, then skippy. It's like something inside you broke, too, and little shards and pieces of words and thoughts and feelings are all that can come out.

In an hour, everything will change even more. Louise will tell Lenny to take the suitcases out to the car; then, when he comes back, she will tell him to wheel Eleanor out to the driveway. She will stand at the kitchen sink, stare out at the yard, at the forsythias and rhododendron and azaleas all in bloom, as if the beauty of the spring garden is a cruel joke instead of a balm, and, for the first and last time, light a cigarette inside the house. She will inhale and exhale sharply, three times, the way she always does when she's stressed, then extinguish the cigarette under the faucet and throw the wet butt into the trash can in the cabinet under the sink. She will not turn around to watch Eleanor's final moments at home before she leaves the house.

It's suddenly quiet, quieter than it normally is, quieter than you think it's ever been. Louise will turn to you, close her eyes, and smooth her hands first over her hair, then over her cheeks, then over her skirt. When she opens her eyes, she will look at you and Lydia like you're strangers. You are. So is she. She is changed. She is gone.

YOU THINK YOU REMEMBER THE DRIVE OVER TO FERNALD, LOUISE'S stoic silence in the front seat instead of the usual forced positivity, how you park in the circular driveway in front of the admitting building while you wait for someone to come out. Do you really remember that or is it a family story, told and retold, embellished with some film clips from Lenny's home movies of future visits to Fernald—the grounds that look like a college campus, the green-and-black linoleum floors of the lobby of the building that Eleanor will live in? A doctor in a white coat eventually comes out, along with two nurses in white dresses—both have little white caps bobby-pinned to their hair—and an orderly, also dressed in white. It looks like a movie, or one of those TV shows about hospitals and doctors you watch every week in the den.

Once the orderly removes Eleanor's bags from the back of the station wagon and opens her chair, he goes to get her from the back seat. But Lenny puts his hand up. *I'll do that.* His voice is firm. He gets out of the car, opens the passenger-side door, bends halfway into the back seat, and unfastens Eleanor's restraints to lift her out. She's much smaller than a child her age is supposed to be—she's smaller than you, even though she's two years older than you. It's one of those things that you don't understand but never ask about because Louise doesn't like that kind of question, the kind she thinks makes Eleanor seem like an alien creature, defined by her physicality, reduced to the details of her disability. But now you think maybe she didn't like those kinds of questions because they made her sad, and she didn't want to have to answer them. When Lenny puts Eleanor into her waiting wheelchair, he pushes her past the orderly, then stops to wait for Louise and you and Lydia to get out of the car, too.

You all go into the lobby, but after Louise and Lenny talk to the people at the front desk, when it's time to bring Eleanor up to the dormitory, the big room where she'll sleep—you find out that you can't go too: *No children/siblings allowed upstairs.* The doctor and nurses and the orderly go into the elevator and hold the doors open for Louise and Eleanor. You wait for them to wave, but the door closes too quickly. Suddenly they're gone. You feel your lip quiver, and your eyes blur with tears. You look at Lenny and then at Lydia. Weren't you going to get a chance to say goodbye and give her a nose kiss?

When you start to cry, Lydia puts her arm around you—for the first time ever, and maybe the only time ever—and sits next to you while you wait for Lenny to come back from the elevator. When he does, his eyes are red, and he holds out his hands, one for each of you to take. Then he walks you outside to the front of the building, to the far side of the parking circle. He turns, looks up to the second floor, and points: there's a big picture window. You can see nurses moving around in their white dresses and caps. Even though you're almost too old for it, Lenny picks you up so you can get a better view.

There they are, he says.

Louise is standing in the window, holding Eleanor. They're looking down at you and Lydia and Lenny in the parking circle.

Eleanor's arm is moving back and forth, back and forth, like she's tired or excited or upset or overwhelmed. But then you realize there's a stuffed elephant in her hand.

She's waving, Lydia says, astonished, looking at Lenny and you, and then up at the window again. *She's waving at us.*

YOU HAVE NO MEMORY OF WHAT HAPPENS AFTERWARD, WHEN YOU get home. Would you have been upset to pass Eleanor's empty bedroom—her bed with rails attached that make it look like a crib instead of a big-girl bed? Would you have gone in and looked around, taking in its sudden quiet and emptiness, it's unnatural stillness? Would you have looked at all her things—the shelf of books Louise read to her; the dolls and stuffed elephants left behind, in repose against the bed rails? Would you have taken one of those dolls or stuffed elephants to your room—like a souvenir, and so they wouldn't be lonely in her room now that she was gone?

Did you eat when you got home? Did Louise make breakfast for dinner, the way she often did when she was tired? French toast and bacon? Pancakes? Scrambled eggs and English muffins? Did you sit down together at the table and talk about what happened that day? Probably not. You probably sat down at the table, the four of you now instead of five, and eaten whatever Louise had made in silence, before all going to bed. You don't think you talked that night, or ever, about what happened that day.

IT DIDN'T OCCUR TO YOU TO ASK TO MOVE INTO ELEANOR'S NOW-unused room. But it occurred to Lydia, because a few nights later she tells you that she did. It's only you two in your bedroom and when you ask Lydia if she thinks Louise will come in to tuck you in, she shakes her head. "She's mad at me," she says. Then she tells you to put your pajamas on and brush your teeth.

When you come back from the bathroom, she's holding one of Eleanor's stuffed elephants in her lap like a baby the way Eleanor used to do. You think she took yours—the one you took from Eleanor's room—but yours is next to your pillow, right where you left it, which means Lydia took one, too.

"I asked her if I could have Eleanor's room now, and she said no."

Her words instantly sting. "You don't want to share with me anymore?"

"Everyone else my age has their own room." She recites a list of friends from school, none of whom share with a younger sibling. "And Eleanor doesn't need it anymore. But she said that it's still her room and it will always be her room. Even if she doesn't live here anymore. Even if she never lives here again."

You sit down on your bed, shocked at how much everything has changed and is continuing to change. Lydia isn't moving into Eleanor's room, but she wants to. It crushes you. Not only because it feels like a rejection, but because you're afraid to be alone. What would you do without Lydia to keep you company?

"It's not fair," she says. Lydia is almost eleven, and nothing ever seems fair. She gets under the covers with her elephant, and you get under your covers with your elephant, and suddenly it's dark and quiet and you're very tired.

At some point, Lydia must shut the light off, pull the little gold chain on the circus lamp on the nightstand between you the way Louise usually does, and give the animals a little push so that the music starts and the little piece of wood they're mounted on starts to rotate. Maybe you ask each other if you have any problems; probably you don't. How could either of you form what had recently happened into a single question?

The Reading

I go up the stairs and stand in front of Sonia and Stan's door. I'm a few minutes early for the reading Lydia arranged for the two of us, the one I finally agreed to yesterday, after the Alan secret was revealed; the one she said she'd meet me at after her walk. It seemed time, already, to give in, to concede. Lydia will be moving out soon, once she finds a place, and while her keeping Louise's secret all these years at first felt like a massive betrayal, I realized it wasn't. She was caught in the middle. She was only trying to do what any good older sister would do in that position: she was trying to protect me. Now she wants to hear what Sonia has to say. She wants someone to help us figure out what it all means; someone who can help put us back together.

I take my shoes off, then look down at my socks: by some miracle, neither one has a hole in the toe. I notice the smell of incense and the sound of sitar music seeping out after I knock. Though they're expecting me, Stan blinks when he opens the door and sees me there. I don't blame him. Since our ill-fated tea date, and then our time in the vestibule together on Halloween, we've somehow managed to keep from running into each other—in the neighborhood, on the street, or coming in or out of the house. It occurs to me that not only have I been avoiding them—they've been avoiding me.

I point down at my feet and wiggle my toes. "Look. I took my shoes off."

He smiles and waves me in. "Sonia's finishing up with someone," he whispers. "She'll be done any minute."

I put my shoes on the tray and we stare at each other, awkwardly, until he points me to his little office. The door is closed. When he opens it, purple light fills the hallway.

Now I'm the one blinking. I step inside, look around. Grow lights. Both of his desk surfaces, and a big round table in the middle of the room, are covered with plants. Pot plants. The sound of water dripping and circulating and trickling through plastic tubing surrounds me. I think I hear the whir of a motor. I do: it's a humidifier.

"Craft cannabis," he says. "Artisanal weed. I grow with soil and hydroponics." He starts pointing excitedly to the elaborate hydration system he's presumably designed himself, then at the desktop shelving units crowded with evenly spaced bright green plastic pots.

"Oh my God. It's another business," I say, but I'm surprised this time to feel more amused than enraged. It's so absurd now, it's funny.

"Not really. It's a supplemental business—a complementary business—to Sonia's. We work together."

"Doing what?"

"Helping people. Sonia works with their bodies. I provide medical-grade marijuana and edibles and tinctures for people dealing with chronic disease or pain."

We both hear the front door open and close. "They're gone," he says, waving me back out into the hallway. I follow behind him into the kitchen, where Sonia has put the kettle on for tea.

"Joyce is here, babe," he says.

"I can see that, babe," Sonia says, as she directs us both to the couch.

"Shouldn't we wait for Lydia?" I say, sitting down.

"She's not coming."

I look from her to Stan. Even he seems surprised by the news.

"She was just here, in fact. But she couldn't stay." Sonia clears her throat. "She didn't feel able to stay."

"What does that mean?"

"She thought it would be easier not to be here when we talked."

"But I thought that was the point—that she wanted to do the reading together." I look over at the studio. "And I assumed we'd be in there, and that it would only be with Sonia." I turn back to Stan. "No offense." I think back to what she said when Sonia came downstairs to apologize about Erin. "Lydia said she wanted to do this so we could learn things about each other and change our relationship. For the better."

"I think that what she wants you to learn about her, she's too afraid to tell you herself."

My stomach drops. I realize now how wholly unprepared I am for this moment, for this conversation, for the answer to a question I don't even know I need to ask until this very minute:

"Something's wrong with Lydia, isn't there." I swallow. "Is there?"

"Yes," Sonia says, leaning forward. "There is something wrong with Lydia."

I close my eyes, take a deep breath, then open my eyes again. I look at both of them—the two people I disliked instantly and have loathed intensely from afar the past few months. Now my fate is in their hands. Our fate. Mine and Lydia's. "You can tell me. I'm ready." But that's a lie. I'm not ready. I'll never be ready.

"Lydia has MS."

I blink, then slump back on the couch. I'm underwater, sinking down into the dark murk of an ocean that has no bottom.

"She was afraid to tell you. She didn't want you to worry. And up until recently—not long after we moved in—she didn't even know what was wrong. All she knew was that something wasn't right."

I'm trying to breathe normally through my shock and terror. The months of her living with me flash behind my eyes like one of those old film strips we used to watch in school—one scene advancing after the other after the other: the clumsiness, the dropping things, the little trips and falls in the apartment that she would blame on computer cords or her clogs or rug corners that didn't lie perfectly flat.

"I should have known." The words come out so quietly I'm not sure I've said them or only thought them. "How could I not have known?"

"I sensed something that first time you came for tea. That's why I encouraged her to come up and work with me. Which she wanted to do from the minute she saw our setup, as you know. Her interest in it was a source of tension between you two that she didn't know how to resolve. So she kept her visits a secret."

"I thought she was triangulating with you to annoy me, to make me jealous."

She nods. "Her work up here was definitely helping. And Stan's cannabis was helping, too."

Again I'm blindsided. "If she's been smoking in the apartment, I never smelled it."

"Occasionally she comes up here to smoke," Stan says. "But mostly she uses the oils and tinctures and gummies for anxiety and joint pain."

Sonia leans forward to look me in the eyes. "This must be hard for you, Joyce. A shock."

It is. I'm trying to take it in but my thoughts—my words—are all scattered, in pieces. I point to my head, and then my mouth. "Nothing is connecting," I say. "I don't understand how I could have been so stupid. So blind. So in denial about what was right there in front of me."

"She was in denial, too. She didn't want to know. When we moved in, she thought it was meant to be. She could come up, talk about her symptoms; we could help her with movement and give her excellent medical-grade weed products for whatever discomfort she was having, until she was finally ready to see a doctor. Until she was ready to know. She found someone great at Mass General, and the good news—and there is good news here, Joyce, believe it or not—is that it's a mild case so far. Slow progression. People can live long, productive lives with MS, so there's no reason to panic."

I take a deep breath, the first one since I've been upstairs. I feel like I'm floating up to the surface, to reality, slowly, kicking my feet to get there, not because I want to, but because I have to.

"The other good news is that it's not genetic or hereditary with families, if that's a concern of yours, which would be understandable."

I blush, full of shame. "She told you."

Sonia tilts her head and smiles. "Joyce. It was obvious after a while. Your vibe was not a relationship vibe. It was a sister vibe. Both of you pushing each other's buttons. Picking at each other. While also loving each other. I know. I have a sister. Plus, Douglas mentioned it to me after seeing her here in class."

My eyes tear up. "I'm sorry. We shouldn't have lied to you. Lydia thought it would be fun for us to have a private joke. A secret. Something we could share." As opposed to all the other secrets that she couldn't share with me.

Sonia hands me a tissue. I wipe my eyes and blow my nose, then ask her what I should do, how I can help.

"Stress is the worst thing for her, so anything you can do to lower the temperature of whatever issues you're having would be great. Especially until she finds a job, which is what she's gearing up to do next."

"But she has a job."

"Lydia lost her job a few months after she moved here—when her symptoms first started to flare and she was having trouble adjusting."

"So that's why she stayed so long. I thought she was taking her time, getting her bearings, trying to figure out what to do next after her divorce."

"She was. But she's also been afraid. Afraid of what will happen to her. And, given your family history, afraid of someday becoming a burden. To you."

———

It's the morning of Eleanor's funeral. Louise wears a black dress with a black jacket and her black hat with the netting is on the counter near the stove. She wipes the kitchen counter and fills the dishwasher with cups and plates that had food on them no one ate. Lenny sits at the kitchen table in a white shirt and a black tie with a black yarmulke on his head, holding a cup of coffee. They are talking about you and Lydia.

They should go. They're her sisters, Lenny says.

Louise shakes her head. *They're children. You don't bring children to funerals.*

So you don't go. And you don't go to school. That means someone stays with you, watches you while they're gone: first to the funeral home, and then to the cemetery. But you don't remember who: Is it a babysitter? A neighbor? A friend? Do you busy yourselves in your room—you reading, Lydia drawing? Does someone make you lunch—grilled cheese or tuna-fish sandwiches on Sunbeam toast—while Louise and Lenny watch a tiny pine box lowered into the ground? Do they come home and talk to you? Do you eat supper together? Do they say good night? Or do you and Lydia, yet again, put yourselves to bed?

It isn't until months later, on a bright warm day in late September, which Louise calls *Indian summer*, that you drive to the cemetery to visit Eleanor. You and Lydia sit in the back seat of the big Buick, side by side but far apart on the black vinyl seat until Lydia pulls the armrest down between you so you can put your arms up and touch elbows.

You're thinking about Indian summer and wondering what it means, but Louise and Lenny have their sunglasses on, and no one is talking so you don't ask and just look out the window, trying not to get carsick, which sometimes happens. When you arrive at the cemetery and get out of the car, Louise takes your hand and Lenny takes Lydia's hand and you walk on the gravel road to the grass where all the headstones are. Louise bends down and pulls a handful of weeds out from around Eleanor's. Lenny stands next to her in front of the grave and they say one prayer, then another prayer, and when they're finished, Louise takes a tissue out of her purse and wipes her eyes.

She bends down again, and her hands disappear in the grass. This time when she stands up her hands are full of little white pebbles. She puts two on top of Eleanor's headstone, then she gives one to Lydia and one to you.

So she knows we were here.

Lydia walks up to the gravestone and puts her pebble next to the two Louise put there, then you do the same. Lydia and Lenny are already on the gravel road near the car when Louise takes your hand again. When you walk through the grass onto the road, she tells you that now you'll all go out for ice cream.

———

I Followed a Sunset
At dusk I went for a walk,
and followed a sunset
by myself.
I like walking alone,
thinking my own thoughts,
not feeling pressured to talk
or respond to someone else who is talking
or ask questions
every five seconds.
I like going with a friend once in a while,
but mostly I like being on my own.
The joy of solitude
can get lost
in the banality of chit-chat.

I walked along the Charles as the sky
turned orange, then pink, then purple.
The stars came out and
people and bikes
followed the path
by the river
where the trees were reflected in the water.
It was a magical scene.

I wanted to take a picture of the beauty
unfolding around me
and reached into my pocket for my phone
only to realize: I'd left it at home.
I was so disappointed
knowing I would miss the chance to share this
sunset on Instagram.

I tried to shake it off
but could not let go of the sudden sadness
that I had no one to share
this spectacular moment with:
my husband died years ago;
I've been a widow half my life;
no children.
Only friends who walk with me
most days and evenings
except this one
when I felt the foolish need
to be alone.

Signs

I'm as relieved to know all of Lydia's secrets as she seems for me to know them. Now that she doesn't have to hide her health situation—or the fact that she hasn't been working—or the fact that Louise and Alan were involved—we're in another world, a very different world. A truthful world. It will take me a while to get used to it all, to absorb everything I haven't known, especially the truth about Louise and Alan and Lenny. As far as we've come this year, we still don't really do thoughts and feelings, and Lydia still doesn't enjoy being grilled. After a few questions that I ask and she answers, we leave it at that. There will be time for more details about tests and medications and treatments; there will be time to understand the shape and possible trajectory of her condition; there will be time to peel back the layers of our family's past with understanding and compassion. There will be time this time. We will get there.

I tell Lydia that she doesn't have to leave—that I don't want her to leave. It's unlikely that she'd be able to find as great an apartment as ours—on the first floor, with no steps, that meets her (exceedingly high) design standards. Even if she did, she'd never find one with the help she needs right upstairs. Sonia and Stan, the thorns in my side up until today, are now my partners in keeping Lydia healthy and mobile and cannabis-supplied, and maybe even gainfully employed: they both need new websites and e-commerce options. Their businesses are booming.

In fact, if anyone moves, it will be me. Not only because the noise upstairs still bothers me—even with the new sound-absorbing flooring Sonia and Stan put down in the yoga studio that doesn't actually do much—but because it's time that I find a new place to live the way Douglas once did. One that doesn't remind me of the bleak period after my divorce. To see what's out there, I post a question on Small World—for the first time—asking whether any neighbors know of a great apartment, a two-bedroom rental, not far from here. I want to be nearby for whatever might come next for Lydia, but I also want to be someplace new for whatever might come next for me. I'm hopeful about our future, Lydia's and mine, now that I better understand our past.

A week before Christmas, Erin and Sammy invite us to a party—not at their apartment, but at a nearby friend's. The evite says the dress code is *holiday semiformal*, whatever that means, and when Lydia balks at the idea of having to put on party clothes, I tell her to pretend we're dressing up for Halloween. That works. Gone are our usual sweaters and puffy jackets and ponytail scrunchies: she puts us in velvet and silk and leather and does our hair and makeup, though she has me apply the lipstick and eyeliner because I have the steadier hand. When we leave the apartment, I feel like I'm going out with Lady Gaga. I tell her that if there was a RISD award for the best holiday-party costume, she would definitely win it. She agrees.

We walk the few blocks toward Harvard Square, to an old brick building that faces the Cambridge Common—where, the statues say, George Washington took command of the Continental Army—and ride the elevator to the tenth floor. What I think will be a Christmas party with carol-singing and a dumb Yankee Swap—the kinds of events I've included in countless EverMore family legacy projects—turns out to be a surprise wedding: Erin and Sammy's. It's perfect. But not as perfect as Erin's slideshow. In the dark, holding my drink, I watch them both watch the story of their relationship unfold and marvel yet again at how pictures really do tell our stories—our family stories, and our love stories—maybe even more than words. The music soars—Chaka Khan's "I Feel for You"—and everyone dissolves. For once, I'm not the only one who's a mess, though I'm still the one who practically has to be carried home from crying so much.

Hanukkah falls late, close to Christmas, and Lydia and I make a big deal of it—in our own way. We buy frozen potato pancakes at Trader Joe's and prepared brisket from Whole Foods, because who has time to cook, and we find a big old silver menorah at a neighborhood antique store that looks like one our grandparents would have lit and feared might burn down the whole house, and even the whole shtetl. The night before the first night, Lydia gives me an early present: a replica of Lenny's Hanukkah banner that she made herself by looking at old pictures of the original and availing herself, thanks to Erin, of the professional scanners and color printers at the EverMore office. She holds the chair while I tape each oaktag dreidel to the molding in the living room.

The next night, after we light the first candle, we exchange gifts. She gives me a collage where the center image is the photo Gideon gave me of the three of us—the Mellishman Sisters—at Camp Fantastic. I give her an envelope—inside of which is a new lease, with her name on it, too, which Douglas dropped off, along with the usual holiday chocolates and wine, his braid tucked up inside a

Christmas elf hat. The only thing Lydia and I skip is the matching-pajama-photo ritual. There's always next year.

As promised, Erin gets me a promotion and a raise. Both are tiny, almost token advancements, but it's the thought that counts. Especially given my rogue photoshopping behavior, and the fact that I didn't finish Alan's legacy project before receiving a text from Gideon telling me that he had died in his sleep. Knowing he's gone now, too—that they're all gone—Alan, Louise, and Lenny—feels like the end of their story. Maybe that means it's the beginning of our stories now. I'll digitize all the photos I saved from Louise's house, and then Gideon and I will finish the slideshow in time for Alan's memorial service in the spring. I'll keep the box of his photographs under my desk until then, but I won't read the letters. I don't think I'll ever read them.

IT'S EARLY IN THE DAY OF THE WINTER SOLSTICE, LATE MORNING, when Gideon texts. He has the overwhelming urge to drive out to the Berkshires, to the grounds of Camp Fantastic, or where Camp Fantastic used to be before it closed in the early 1980s and the land was donated to a nature conservancy a decade later. To feel his father's presence. He asks if I will come with him, then stay a day or two at his family's cabin, before driving back for New Year's. He says he would really like to spend some time together.

In the car, on the way west, we talk about Alan and Louise—how he thought I'd known about their relationship—and about Asher and Eleanor—how we both grew up in the long shadows of our parents' grief for siblings we barely knew. After a while, we stop talking, looking out instead at all the evergreens whizzing by and at the sky and at the sun, which is already starting to drop. Off the highway, when we're on the smaller, quieter curving roads that bring us back to where Camp Fantastic once was, we see the first of the big red hearts, painted on a wood slatted pallet, leaning against a tree. There are others, propped up against telephone poles, and giant stones, and the steps of people's front porches.

The signs have been everywhere this year. On the routes Lydia and I had driven to the beach on the North Shore and on the South Shore; the whole length of Cape Cod, all the way past Truro to Provincetown; out to farms stands in Concord for corn and strawberries and apples. We didn't know at first what they meant, who'd painted them, why they were unsigned. Only later did we learn from newspaper articles and social media that they were expressions of love and support for immigrants, and refugees, people who among us are the most visibly different and therefore the most vulnerable. The signs were proof that people want to make an unsafe world safe for everyone. The helpers were out there. The helpers are always out there.

"The signs are a sign," Gideon says. But he doesn't say of what.

We take the turnoff for the old camp and drive what's left of the rutted road to where the cabins and office and pool used to be. Out of the car, surrounded by woods, it feels like sacred ground, even if it doesn't look like it anymore. The air is cold, the clouds are violet and orange bruises, but when we look up at the sky, there is still light—the last of the day's pale yellow rays coming through the curtain of impossibly tall trees.

It's then that Gideon tells me that his brother's name means *happy and blessed* and that his own name means *woodsman*—that his father chose that instead of Joshua (*savior*), or Jacob (*supplanter*), or Barnabas (*son of consolation*) to avoid any reference to Asher's too-short life. *He wanted me to be free of the past so I could be open to the future.*

So Alan named him after the white pines at Camp Fantastic. The tall, tall trees that had watched over Asher, and Eleanor, and everyone who had ever come here. The trees that framed a small beautiful world where joy transcended grief, and where the sounds of children, once alive, now gone, can still be heard.

Acknowledgments

I would be nowhere without you: Ann Leary, Julie Klam, Alice Hoffman, Lynn Bikofsky, Lori Galvin, Jen Trynin, Ben Dealy, Lady, Erin Braddock, Debbie Cameron, and Mona Awad.

Deepest gratitude also to Brendan Dealy, Paul Fedorko, Julie Grau, Ivan Held, Laura Rossi, Hilary Ilick, Sue Miller, Joan Wickersham, Lauren LeBlanc, and Jason Loviglio, whose brilliant and hilarious "listserv poetry" posts on Facebook inspired the Nextdoor-style poetry posts in *Small World*. And to the Adamians, who modeled inclusion with love and humor with their Eleanor and showed me what a family full of joy could look like.

I'm so lucky to have such a skilled and excellent editor, Helen Atsma—smart, sensitive, funny, and kind—and to get to work with the incredible publishing team at Ecco for the second time around: Miriam Parker, Sonya Cheuse, Sara Birmingham, Meghan Deans, Allison Saltzman, TJ Calhoun, Jin Soo Chun, Rachel Sargent, Janet R. Rosenberg, Jonathan Burnham, and all the sales, marketing, and library marketing people who work so hard to get books into readers' hands. To say I love the jacket art by the astonishingly talented painter Jessica Brilli is an understatement. I'm so grateful for her perfect work, and to Ecco for commissioning it.

Everyone should have a client-agent relationship like the one I have with Stephanie Rostan at Levine Greenberg Rostan. Besides the excellent publishing strategy and gossip, she lets me be as grim and as dark in these grim, dark times as I need to be. Huge thanks to Courtney Paganelli, Melissa Rowland, Miek Coccia, Mike Nardullo, and Cristela Henriquez at LGR Literary for always working so hard on my behalf.

My parents, Bernie and Bernice, suffered the loss of their first daughter, my oldest sister, Sheryl, when she was only seven years old. She was born with osteopetrosis, a rare and fatal bone disease, and lived at the Walter E. Fernald State School from about the age of three until she died there. Despite their grief, or maybe because of it, they continued to support and fundraise for Fernald long after she was gone, which kept all the remarkable Fernald League families we'd grown up with in our lives for decades.

Through the magic of Twitter, I connected with the extraordinarily compassionate advocate and scholar Alex Green. His deep knowledge of disability rights and the history of institutions like Fernald helped me better understand a place and a time that I had only vague memories of. He connected me first to Bob Coleman, whose youngest brother, Joseph, had, incredibly, lived in the same building at Fernald, at almost exactly the same time, as Sheryl had, and then to the novelist Caroline Leavitt, who had volunteered at Fernald during high school. I'm grateful to both of them for sharing their memories with me. Steve Brown at WBUR opened doors at the Massachusetts State Archives and continues to encourage me to track down Sheryl's medical records. Someday I will.

When I told my sister Linda that I was going to write a novel about two sisters who move in together as adults and finally come to terms with how the death of their other sister shaped their family, and them—fictionalized, of course!—she said: *I trust you.* Could there be a better gift than that? It's just the two of us now. In a way, like survivors of a small, quiet wreck, it's always just been the two of us.